MOTHERS OF FATE

A NOVEL

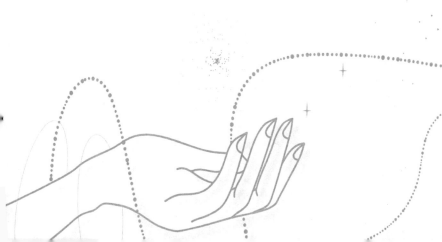

MOTHERS OF FATE

A NOVEL

LYNNE HUGO

Blank Slate Press | Harrisonville, MO 64701

Blank Slate Press
Harrisonville, MO 64701

Publisher's Note: This book is a work of the imagination. Names, characters, places and incidents either are products of the author's imagination or are used fictitiously. While some of the characters and incidents portrayed here can be found in historical or contemporary accounts, they have been altered and rearranged by the author to suit the strict purposes of storytelling. The book should be read solely as a work of fiction.

For information, contact:
Blank Slate Press
www.amphoraepublishing.com
Blank Slate Press is an imprint of
Amphorae Publishing Group, LLC
www.amphoraepublishing.com

Manufactured in the United States of America
Cover Design by Kristina Blank Makansi
Illustration: Shutterstock
Set in Adobe Caslon Pro, Ametis, Gravesend Pro

Library of Congress Control Number: 2024945989
ISBN: 9781943075911

Also by Lynne Hugo

PRAISE FOR LYNNE HUGO'S WORK

"Choice, destiny, or force? Wrapped around the threads connecting the mothers, fathers, husbands, and wives caught in a decades-secret and fraught adoption are the ingredients for disaster—or deliverance—for all. Lynne Hugo, a writer of immense talent and rare insight, dips her sharp yet sympathetic pen in a well of revelation as she brings each character to life. I cared and worried about all of them, despite their transgressions, rooting for them to find their path. Pages whipped by in my need to discover their fates. *Mothers of Fate* places self-determination on the stand. —Randy Susan Meyers, international bestselling author

"With her usual engaging prose, Lynne Hugo unspools a tender tale of parenthood in all its many faces as her characters struggle to live with the outcome of their past decisions. Those past choices color the present in bold strokes, raising the stakes to keep the pages turning. Hugo's compassion for her characters—and her readers— shines through." —Diane Chamberlain, New York Times bestselling author of *The Last House on the Street*

"Lynne Hugo's brilliantly prismatic story is about choice verses destiny, forgiveness versus acceptance, all told through the lens of a heartbreaking adult adoptee, his adoptive parents, his birth mother who is now desperate to contact her son, and the attorney she hires who is part of a Lesbian couple with an adopted bi-racial child. Secrets emerge, relationships fracture, but out of the wreckage, Hugo has built a moving, extraordinary story of hope. I loved it." —Caroline Leavitt, *New York Times* bestselling author of *Pictures of You* and *Days of Wonder*

"*The Language of Kin* takes something we all possess—our ability to communicate with others—and has us examine that gift with new eyes. Hugo's words are beautiful, but this riveting story shows us how words can often fail, and forces us to see the many others ways we communicate, sometimes even unintentionally. This novel is an emotional read full of page-turning highs and cathartic sorrows. I fell in love with this complicated, compelling cast, both human and otherwise." —Katrina Kittle, author of *Morning In This Broken World*

"A timeless and emersive story exploring the complexities of human engagement and the lengths we will go for those we love." —Donna Everhart, USA Today bestselling author of *The Education of Dixie Dupree*

"Filled with empathy for all and a plot that will keep you flipping pages as fast as you can." —Audrey Schulman, Author of Philip K Dick award-winning *Theory of Bastards*

"Brilliant, fascinating and deeply moving...gracefully written, this is a book that astonishes, even as it shows the way to cross divides...Full of science, love and drama, I couldn't love this book more if I tried." —Caroline Leavitt, *New York Times* bestselling author of *With Or Without You*

"Hugo takes a compelling look at the ethical issues and connections between humans and our fellow animals. *The Language of Kin* offers a well-researched, unbiased perspective into this multifaceted issue through a well-written, captivating story," —Samantha Russak, Ph.D., Primatologist

Hugo's writing might remind some readers of Annie Proulx, although her ear for dialog is closer to Larry McMurtry's …Hugo offers convincing three-dimensional characters with convincing psychic wounds." —Ben Steelman, *Wilmington (NC) Star News*

"The kind of novel one longs to read…beautifully written, full of crooked fates, terrible loss and hard-won second chances." —Laura Harrington, bestselling author of *Alice Bliss*

"I lost hours of sleep as I raced to finish this extraordinary novel." —Randy Susan Meyers, bestselling author of *Waisted*

"Sparkling prose, wry humor, relevant themes abound." —Donna Everhart, *USA Today* bestselling author of *The Saints of Swallow Hill*

"Hugo's latest is a sweet, sad, funny, meditation on the nature of aging and grief…This is a novel that would fit right in on the shelf next to novels like A Man Called Ove and similar books that balance humor and heartbreak." —*Booklist*

"A widower takes up her late husband's mission to get revenge on the man who killed their grandson in the gripping latest from Hugo." —*Publishers Weekly*

"A winning and wonderful novel, with a unique and distinctive storyline, there is a little bit of magic for everyone within the pages of this book." —*The New York Journal of Books*

"Hugo writes about loss and redemption in a way that makes you laugh out loud one minutes and tear up the next." —Diane Chamberlain, *New York Times* bestselling author

"A richly told tale that explores the human/animal connection and the journey to get past tragedy... a tender hymn of hope and rebirth that stays with you long after the last page." —Kim Michele Richardson, *New York Times* bestselling author of *The Book Woman of Troublesome Creek*

"Full of intrigue and heart, as gritty as the inside of a clamshell and tender as a beach sunset." —Jenna Blum, *New York Times* & internationally bestselling author of *Those Who Save Us*

"A profound and heartfelt book...Hugo is a tender and wise guide to the realities of aging, and Hannah, her chocolate Labrador retriever, who brings love and life to residents of a Midwest nursing home, is a true charmer. Where The Trail Grows Faint charts the territory with a rare spirit of hope."
—Floyd Skloot, author of *In the Shadow of Memory*

TABLE OF CONTENTS

For Alan, again and always, with gratitude and love.

Who loves the rain
And loves his home
And looks on life with quiet eyes
Him will I follow through the storm
And before his fire keep me warm.

—author unknown

It is the stars, the stars above us govern our condition.

—William Shakespeare

More stars in the north are seen not to set,
while in the south certain stars are no longer seen to rise.

—Nicolaus Copernicus

PROLOGUE

Mercy Hospital, Pittsburgh, 1983

I didn't lose everything. I am still Deana, and I still know what was true. We ate. A flask passed between us. A good presence was there that I took as blessing. The locusts' songs. I don't know if he heard them, but I did and said nothing. I believed they did not matter. Winter would not matter.

(All true. The sky had been an inverted black stoneware bowl with a white chip moon. They'd laid in a field on the stadium blanket kept in the trunk of his car, white-splotched with the crust of liquid stars that had fallen through May, June, July, August.)

My ragged breath through his name as I cried *Tony*, like yes or love or mine. I heard myself.

And the yes there was no need to speak, the yes I chose to speak, a promise.

(Over his shoulder, above her, the brim of eternity. Their bodies, silver chalices, were full in the small light.)

Tomorrow, tomorrow, we each said. I heard him.

I

DESTINY

1

PITTSBURGH, 2013

"It usually works best if you tell me what you want." Monica leaned over her desk and smiled at the new client, trying to put her at ease. She was in the habit of staying behind it, a personal safety thing with her, particularly with men, but that was hardly an issue with Deana Wilkes, a woman at least twenty years older and so disabled as to make her lurch with a metal crutch, the forearm kind that Monica associated with polio victims. She considered moving them both to the conference table, but her laptop sat open there, and the briefs she'd been reading before court were hastily raked together like a messy pile of leaves. Deana had been early for the appointment. Besides, it would be awkward now.

"May I ask a personal question first?"

Monica tilted her chin. She didn't like it when a client started down that path. "That depends on how personal it is," she said, keeping her tone airy.

"Do you have children?"

Slight nod, no invitation in it. "A daughter." Then her eyebrows went up, just enough.

"Okay. Sorry." A long hesitation then that Monica waited out. "I've never talked about this to anyone. I don't know how. I wish I could take it all back," Deana said. "I'd rewind to the first yes I ever said to Tony Hamilton. Before anything was inevitable." Deana's gaze went to her hands, clenching one another in her lap, and Monica looked at them too. They were veined, knuckles prominent.

Finally, Deana looked up as if expecting a question. Monica didn't ask any, but nodded, and as Monica had learned was likely to happen, the client went on. Some people ended up talking to their lawyer with about the same level of reserve as they did their psychologist, if they had one. And if they didn't, the lawyer ended up serving the purpose, in Monica's experience. That it wasn't necessarily a good thing was also her experience; once they'd told her, what they really wanted was a fix for their minds and hearts. No lawyer could do that.

But the times she hadn't heard the whole story had come back to bite her, and it took time and patience upfront. She needed clients badly; she had time, way too much of it. But patience, patience for these tangled human dramas like vines that put out shoots taking root here, there, and seemed to have no clear beginning, and even no end? She was working on that kind of patience.

She'd thought she was going to be a corporate attorney, but that door had been hard-slammed behind her. Now she'd opened a door of her own. Alone. General practice was a rough go. She picked up domestic relations cases, guardian ad litem work for the court, small suits here and there. It was enough, barely, but she was in control, which was what mattered.

"He was my boss," Deana said. Her hair was mainly a pale dingy gray, wavy, blunt cut with nothing to soften it. No makeup to ease the sooty smudges beneath her eyes or perhaps darken what were once good eyebrows, now too faded to bring attention up to nice hazel eyes and away from the deep parentheses around her mouth. A short nose with a bit of a bulb at the end.

Deana continued speaking as Monica catalogued these details. "Tony had an office with a window, and a big wood desk, something like yours, in fact, and a phone with a whole row of buttons. I had a cubicle, a typewriter, and an intercom. We worked at an insurance company, which turned out to be ironic. His eyes and brows and hair were dark brown, but his skin was fair, and his nose was thin and elegant." She drew her own nose out lightly with a thumb and forefinger to illustrate greater length than hers.

"Handsome. Not like a movie star, because his teeth weren't so straight." Deana smiled then and Monica noticed that Deana's teeth were even and fairly white. "Anyway, he was thirty-five, nice, fairly handsome. Maybe I flirted. I did flirt, my fault—but then things were different in nineteen eighty-three. You wouldn't know this, but thirty years ago we all flirted back and forth at work, but it was jokey and harmless, never likely to make it from anyone's desk even to the water-cooler. Oh, there were a couple of high-ups." She stopped, seeming to study the gold titles imprinted on the spines of Pennsylvania law tomes jammed in the bookcase next to the window, then finally went on with a shoulder shrug. "A couple big bosses made their secretaries' lives a living hell, pawing them."

Monica thought she hadn't moved and kept her face neutral, realized she must not have when Deana went on because she said, "Oh, they were different," in an almost apologetic tone. "I'm talking about the regular men. With them it was all just fun and none of us worried. Not about that, I mean. We worried some about losing our jobs because of the recession. Some of the small regional sales offices had been closed, but it hadn't really hit us at headquarters yet. I was flattered when Tony found reasons to stop by my cubicle. He was one of the good ones and I figured it didn't hurt that my boss liked me. I mean, he was my boss and all." Deana stopped again and looked at her hands, clasped in her lap.

Yes, Monica thought. Damn. I know about wanting the boss to like you. No, needing the boss to like you. Thinking he's okay. Aloud she said, "I understand. Is this about what you need legal help with?"

"Yes, in a way. See, I never knew if it was an accident the night he was in the elevator at the same time I was leaving the office. I wanted it not to be, so see? I can't pretend innocence. I'd been raised to be something of a prude, and maybe I resented missing out on what everyone else was enjoying. I blame myself." She stopped talking abruptly, then, and looked to the side. "This is a nice office."

"Thank you. It's my favorite color, that pale peach on the walls. I painted it myself." There, Monica thought. That gives her a second to gather herself. Maybe she'll get where I know she's going.

"It's a nice friendly color. Goes well with the wood, too."

Monica suppressed a sigh, and tried again, keeping her voice gentle. "I'm glad you like it. So—did he...did something happen in the elevator?"

"Not then. When we got out, he looked at his watch and said, 'Are you busy? There are some openings coming up that would be a promotion, protect you from the layoffs likely in the fall. Would you like to grab a drink and talk about it?' That's the yes I'd rewind, no matter what I wanted.

There was no bribe to it, though. I didn't take it that way. He might as well have said, 'Gosh it's been a long day. Feel like getting a drink?' I liked him, and I knew he thought I *was* pretty. Back then, I could tell those things. Well, back then I was pretty. Only twenty-nine, none of this sooty gray hair, which I've about decided to color. It was dark blonde, long," as she spoke, she gestured to show where her hair had fallen to her upper arms, "and I didn't iron it straight like other girls with curly hair did. I didn't look twenty-nine either; not with my hair swinging loose, and the freckles I hated. The only good thing about getting older is how they've faded. They'll probably come back soon as age spots. Are you even forty yet?"

"Not yet. Not quite, I should say."

"How old is your daughter? Is that her picture?"

"Yes. Thirteen months." Monica smiled at a silver-framed picture of a baby in the arms of a woman who at first glance appeared smitten. A second glance, though, would add bedraggled. That woman wore glasses, and untucked hair straggled over one lens.

"That's not you—"

Monica laughed. "No. Could we get back to—"

"What's her name? Your baby."

"Celeste."

"That's so pretty. Like stars or...heavenly?...celestial, right? Thirteen months. She a handful?"

Monica looked at the picture, unable not to grin while she answered. "She is for sure. She was ten months when that was taken. It's all over when they're walking." She had to get this back to the client, do it now and keep it there and extract what Deana wanted. Still smiling Monica shook her head and looked back at Deana. "But let's not run up your bill unnecessarily. You're here about you," she said. "What is it you need legal help with?"

"Um...I was telling you, back then I was slender with a good chest, like my mother, and knew how to make myself up. I'd started to wear miniskirts. Couldn't wear 'em now, that's for sure, not with the scars. Didn't have this bad leg. Didn't need a crutch. Anyway, Tony and I walked to a bar, The King of Clubs it was called, about two blocks from the office building. It's gone now. It was a beautiful April evening, and the air felt, you know?—really soft, and there was a sunset—and, anyway, I wished we could stay outside, but I didn't know him well enough to say that. When we went through the door, my eyes didn't want to adjust.

"It was dark and smoky from businessmen already there. Tony put his hand on my waist to guide me to a booth. It was the first time he'd touched me and the rest of the evening I could feel his hand there. But...I'd said I couldn't see. When we sat down, Tony took off his jacket, loosened his tie, and ordered a Manhattan. I had a whiskey sour. The candle wasn't lit, and Tony used his lighter on it. You know, everyone smoked then. That night Tony drank two Manhattans."

Deana shook her head. "No, actually, he had three," she said, correcting herself. "I had two whiskey sours. I was hungry, and I ate the orange slices and the cherries. When Tony saw me do that, he ordered us club sandwiches without even asking. He was thoughtful like that. Anyway, I think it was just an ice breaker, but Tony talked about the openings there might be at the office for a couple of minutes and then—Rick Springfield was singing Love Somebody and later I thought that had been an omen— the conversation veered off."

"To what?" Monica said, although she was sure she already knew the essence of the details to come. They made her sick. She wondered if the smart thing to do would be to spare herself, refuse the case, but if she could bear up, maybe another woman could find her own strength. And who was she kidding? She was in no position to turn away business.

"What did it veer off to?" she repeated when Deana hesitated, then to be ethical, she added, "I want to make sure you know that I bill by the hour, and I don't want you to run up the charge unnecessarily. I probably don't need all these details. You can cut to the chase, and if I need to know more I'll ask."

"I'm sorry. I've never told anyone this, and I...need to. It's hard for me. I'll pay overtime or whatever. The conversation veered of...right...to what men and women talk about when they're flirting for real and pretending they're not. Silly stuff, like were you good at algebra or English in high school. It was all in our eyes, in how I flipped my hair back, and how he was being funny and wanting me to have a good time. Haven't you ever had a man do that, and you knew?"

Monica hesitated, and then said, almost too quietly, "It wasn't your fault."

"But I—"

"Women always blame ourselves...themselves."

"Does this all sound worn-out, make you tired, like you think you know what's going to happen?"

"Yes."

"You do. And you don't. Not at all. I promise—you just don't."

2

1983

"Daddy! Can we go out and throw the ball with you? Daddy? Daddy! Look what I made!" Two rockets launched toward him as Tony came in the door. The force of his sons hitting him one exactly a second after the other knocked him back a step.

"Late again," Kathleen said in a light tone as she picked up the smaller boy. It was her eyebrows that made the observation a complaint. "I had to go ahead and feed them."

"Boys, Daddy hasn't had dinner yet," she said, gathering the children toward her. "We'll get you two ready for bed while he eats. Maybe tomorrow if Daddy gets home on time."

"No, that's okay. I want to play with them," Tony said and whisked his lips in the area of her cheek without eye contact. He put his briefcase down and walked toward the stairs taking off his jacket and removing his tie. "Come on, boys. You guys come upstairs with me while I get out of my suit. What do you want to play?"

A cacophony followed him up the stairs. "Pass the ball! Me on your shoulders, the lion game! No, play trains first, that's the best one." Tony tried to shake off Kathleen's irritation to concentrate on the boys. "Okay, okay. Too chilly for outside now, I think, so let's start with the sponge ball. Keep the ruckus down or Mommy will worry we're breaking the house again." Kathleen said he cheated the children of time with him when he worked late, and when he wasn't home until after they were in bed. Well, he could see her point about it all. He knew she wanted to say she wasn't getting her time either, but it was easy to talk about the children and better for him if she left it that way.

He tried to focus. "Hey, buddy, let your brother have a turn. Nice shot! Hey, you've been practicing..." As long as he kept moving and kept talking it seemed to be enough for the moment. Except there wasn't a person in his life he wasn't shortchanging. He needed more time to think. If he could just dry the clamminess of his body and stop his heart from pounding like galloping hoofs in his head—so loud—and stop the waves of shameful fear. His father would call him a little girl if he ever said he was afraid.

"Whoa, there! Okay, up you go." Sturdy legs dangled from around his neck to just below his armpits. "Grrrr.... ahhh...the lion is prowling. Gonna get Jason." Christopher clutched Tony's head and mimicked his father's growling while his brother screeched and scrambled from his room to his brother's.

All he had to do now was growl and follow Chris' prodding (*there, Daddy! by the closet*), while his arms made clawing motions. The boys did the rest.

When the children were finally in bed and asleep, after they'd taffy-stretched the process with their entreaties for another drink of water, the covers to be fixed, one more kiss, one more *please, please, I need...*which Tony stayed and indulged after Kathleen said *no more* and went downstairs, Tony finally made his way to the kitchen.

The room was papered in a cheery daisy pattern and had light green curtains that matched the color of the daisy leaves. Kathleen's decorating, like the rest of the house. She had good taste. Expensive, but good. Even Tony's mother said so.

"I saved you a plate," Kathleen said, her voice coming over the running water. She was loading the dishwasher, almond colored like the other appliances. It had taken them two years to get a new stove, refrigerator and dishwasher, all the same modern color that Kathleen said was best, but it looked really good now, and the last one would be paid off in seventeen months.

She turned off the faucet and turned around. "It's in the oven. Sit down and I'll get it for you. You know, it's not good for them to get away with manipulating you like that. *That* was ridiculous. You actually fell for 'my foot itches like a real hyena' and *helped him scratch it*?" after you agreed to search his bed for *hyena feathers*?

Her voice bubbled with laughter, but it didn't feel bad to him, just like it was funny, the way parents find things their children come up with hysterical and she was including him. He felt like he was someplace new, his feet suddenly heavy and confused about where to go. And then she got a foil-covered plate out of the oven and pointed him to the table. Putting meatloaf and mashed potatoes and succotash in front of him, Kathleen put her hand on his shoulder and said, "You know, if you feel guilty about not spending enough time with the boys, try coming home. You know, they're starting to get your number." Then she laughed again, and what surprised him most was that he laughed with her, and it was hearty, about their boys, but about the two of them too, and he said, "Damn. You might just be right. They're too smart. I think I'd better make some changes."

He resolved that he would. He definitely would. He felt better. The horses didn't gallop around his chest that night, and his body wasn't sweaty.

The next night he didn't have a drink with Deana. Deana was fine about it, even said he needed to be with his boys. He didn't say anything about Kathleen to her.

The next day, the secretary to one of the Vice Presidents was sick and Deana was called on to sub for her all day. She was taking notes in his office when it was time to leave and Tony went on home, seeing it as a gift. He and Kathleen took the boys to the Dairy Queen for ice cream after supper, and there was still enough time to play ball in the yard for a while. At bedtime he didn't let them play out the itching foot dramas, but he did fold them in his arms and eyes closed, held his breath, so great was their fragility, their need and his own. It extended to Kathleen, that fierce tenderness for the four of them, and when they went to bed, his wanting her was genuine.

"I've been thinking it's time for us to make a little girl," Kathleen said. "I can't go on being completely outnumbered around here. How 'bout it?"

He didn't lie to her when he said, "I'd love a little girl."
Neither did he lie to Deana.

He took her out to lunch the day after next. In their
office, it wasn't common for men to take women out to
lunch unless it was a group, but it wasn't that big a deal,
and Tony made a show of bringing four manila files with
him. He kept the conversation light.

"Yep, the big guy actually stormed into my office, not
his own secretary's—who was apparently making him
coffee at the time--demanding I find his stapler."

"Well did you?"

"I stole one from Jenny's desk when she was in the
bathroom. He couldn't tell the difference. I doubt he
knows how to use it anyway."

Her laughter was warm and full, and he had such a
good time. With Deana he felt like the self he'd lost along
the way, unafraid, at ease in his own skin. No stampeding
horses in his chest, which he took as a sign. He hadn't
sought her, asked for her, willed her. He'd never made
a decision to open himself to her, but finding himself
open, couldn't make a decision to close. He couldn't say
she pursued him; it wasn't true. Yes, he could protect her
from the layoffs that were coming, recommend her for a
better position, but he hadn't done anything yet, and she'd
never once asked. With Deana he could be in a realm of
something magical that had just happened, and he could
take it and love it and love her, too. He was not a bad man.

As the recession deepened and there was more
pressure on him, it was easy to show Kathleen a few of
the memos he received, and the quarterly report. It got
simpler to explain why he stayed at the office so late so

often: cutbacks in staff, more responsibility on him. He devoted himself to the boys and Kathleen most of every weekend and resolved to go home early at least one night a week, maybe two. He told himself *quality not quantity counts*. He missed Deana when he was away from her; they'd found a place to be together. The strength of his passion and need for her gave him joy, comfort, and terror.

3

2013

Monica couldn't discern whether it was rue or bitterness in Deana's voice, although she spoke as if her meaning was obvious when she went on. "Some days I believe my memory. Other days I think it was only a quicker end. A more ruinous one, to be sure. But I tell myself it *would* have ended. You know. Fatigue, cold, winter," she said. "Winter?" Monica asked. "I'm sorry, I'm not following here."

"We had one spring, one summer. See, there was an open field, nothing around it, maybe three or four miles from the company, out between Whitewater Road and the river. There's an office complex there now, it's all built up, but back in the early eighties, it was just field.

"In Tony's and my year, no late frost came to ruin spring, the way it so often does. You know how spring in Pennsylvania can be spotty and disappointing, but in our year, it was like the land was all fragrance and color. After work, Tony and I would duck out separately, trying to be discreet.

"That's the old, tired beginning that tricks you into thinking you know exactly what's going to happen, Monica. He'd pick me up in his Buick down the block, a half-hour later, after he picked up sandwiches and chips. He always got me two dill pickles. We'd park on the side, well off Whitewater Road, and walk deep onto the field toward the riverbank where there were rocks and more trees. It only took us ten minutes to get there, but I wish I could tell you how lush the grass was, the sun low in the sky," Deana gestured as if measuring where the sun would be in the horizon. "How far from the world we were. We'd eat the sandwiches. Drink the beer or bourbon from Tony's flask while sitting on the red plaid blanket he kept in the trunk of his car. I don't mean to make it sound like it was every night. It was every night that mattered.

"It was peaceful. We never saw another human being. I couldn't find our spot now if I wanted to, which I shouldn't, but sometimes I do. Pathetic. It's maybe a mile south of the new bridge over the river. Well, I still call it new, but it's been there, what? Twelve years? Six lanes over the river that still either runs too high or shrinks way down, but, you know, it always moves on and disappears, like we did. There's an underwater dam now, too, You know, like the way Tony and I had all this passion that we hid." Deana shook her head.

"Of course, it doesn't stop anything, only slows it awhile. It reminds me of us." She put her hands into a cup shape. "But I dream I'm there again in that field sometimes, that I'm *running* on damp grass. Running along parallel to the river in that field with my life, only I'd be careful this time not to spill it." Hands dropped back into her lap, almost thudding them there, like a defeat. "Am I rambling?"

Monica gentled her voice, the way she did with Celeste to avert tears, comfort, and direct her at the same time. "Sort of. Can you tell me how *you* spilled your life?" Deana shook her head and put it down, looking at her hands in her lap. If Monica hadn't stuck herself behind the desk, she would have touched the other woman, patted her good leg or taken her hand.

"He was your boss. He had power over you. That changes everything," Monica said quietly. She wanted Deana to hear what she herself never had. But she'd never told anyone, either. "How did you spill your life?" she repeated when Deana still hadn't said anything.

Deana looked startled. "Oh. I *was* rambling. But, I'm afraid it was my fault. I shouldn't have…this is so hard to talk about, even backing into telling it. I'm sorry." Deana stopped and looked out the window then. It was behind Monica, who knew that all Deana saw was part of a brownstone across the street through the boughs of an old city maple. The tree was just starting to bud out, reddish now instead of the green they would become.

She could tell that Deana wanted to give way to tears and was fighting them back. Good. Easier to keep her own down. She swallowed, feeling slightly sick to her stomach. She resisted checking the time; it was her last appointment of the day and the other three cases she'd picked up lately would scarcely cover rent. Her wild hope of getting home a little early was gone, but basic income came before getting home early or on time. She waited for Deana to go on, and she did.

"Those twilights in the field, on his red plaid blanket..." Deana shrugged, "and April just turned to June then August."

Monica slid a box of tissues across her desk. "Help yourself if you need any. Can I get you some water?"

"Yes. Please."

"Hang on, I've got some bottles in the fridge. I'm going to make a quick call home. Be right back."

"I'm sorry, I don't want to hold you up. I'm taking too much of your time." A hasty swipe at her eyes with the tissue she pulled from the box even as she hunched forward to pick up her crutch.

Monica waved her back down, shaking her head. "It's fine—you haven't told me yet what you need legal help with. I have to know that." She closed the office door.

It wasn't fine at all. Nothing about it was fine. Monica leaned against the door she'd closed against Deana and breathed. *Breathe*, she told herself. *Breathe. Whatever she wants, you have to help her. He was her boss. It wasn't her fault.* Then she made her call home to say she was running late.

"So anyway, the accident," Deana continued when Monica came back with two bottles of water. "One night out there in the field...oh god, see, we were making love. There was an accident." She raised her long skirt slightly and pointed down at her leg and special shoe, braced in metal, as if Monica might have missed it and her crutch. "It one of those freak things, horrendous. I sensed—maybe I heard the engine, too? anyway something big was coming at us. At the time, I couldn't even tell it was a car. There were no lights, nothing, and only like a second before a big jolt, and it was on top of us. I screamed, but from pain instead of warning. Tony never made a sound. Not a sound. All the screams were mine, and I didn't stop. I couldn't make my body move. There was another big jolt and another. I reached down to where the pain was. Bones jutting out, blood all over me. I felt for Tony in the dark, and I couldn't help it, my hand jerked back when it reached what I couldn't see: something thick and wet, jagged. I screamed, and I tried to make my hand go there again but it wouldn't, and I screamed from my own pain. And then suddenly there were lights and I saw that his head was crushed and, maybe it was a while, I don't remember, my screams mixed with sirens and I blacked out again.

"My parents were at the hospital when I woke up. I remember asking for Tony. 'The man you were with is dead,' my mother said. She wore her blue cardigan sweater over a yellow blouse, but everything else—her face and eyes and hair and even teeth looked like shades of ashy gray. Maybe it was the light, but I know I saw revulsion when she said, 'You were naked!'

I remember how I cried and neither of them tried to comfort me. Their faces were saying, 'How could you?' and 'Why didn't we know about this man?' and 'Look at the mess you're in now!' My hip crushed, leg in traction, a white sheet draped over me, an IV taped on me. Something beeping. Oxygen tubes in my nose. A curtain was drawn between me and somebody else in the same room, and Mom and Dad were standing farther away from me than they needed to. Farther away than I needed them to, except that my father put his hand on my other foot, I mean the one that wasn't on the leg in traction. Only for a few seconds, then he took it away.

'I have to see him.' I said. I was using the sheet to cry into because there weren't any tissues. 'I love him.' And then my mother said, 'That's not going to be possible. His wife is making arrangements. Her name is Kathleen.' Maybe her voice was kinder than I remember it."

"Oh lord." Monica was quiet a minute. "Had you known he was married?"

"Of course I knew. Married with kids. And I knew it wasn't right. But it *felt* right. Doesn't that sound ridiculous now, so cheap, like such an excuse? We were crazy in love. It seemed like there was nothing we could do about it. And it still does."

"You said that if you could, you wouldn't say the first yes."

"You have a point. Do you know how I got my name?"

Monica shook her head. "How? "

"My mother named me Deana after Dean Martin because she wanted me to have his easy-going personality. My point is that I felt like some force drove my fate, and I was along for the ride. A wild, beautiful, amazing ride. I believed there was a plan for my life. That was what I thought brought Tony and me together. Then he died. The destiny thing is either still true, or it never was, and the damage didn't have to happen. It was pointless. What do you think?"

"Pfft, my mother probably picked Monica for me because it meant control freak." At least I try, Monica thought. I fight.

"I can see that. Your office is incredibly neat, even your desk." She gestured with her chin and a slight rueful smile, as she pushed gray hair back from her face. She'd been pretty, Monica could see that. Now, she looked like her face and clothes were clean but of no importance to her.

"Fate isn't what you're here to talk about, is it? There must be something you want to *do*, something you need legal help with? You said this happened in the early eighties, so...?"

"You're right. There is more to it. A lot. I just want you to understand. I want to do this right."

4

Twilight was gathering in the office faster than beyond the one window. Monica didn't get up to turn on a light.

"I found out from my mother," Deana said. "I think the surgeon told her while I was in the recovery room. No privacy laws back then. I guess I really should look at it from my mother's point of view. She assumed I knew I was pregnant and hidden it, same way I'd hidden Tony. One more thing for her to be hurt and furious over."

"You didn't know?"

"No. I really didn't. The doctor had ordered blood work before surgery. He came in and said something about how I would need proximal femur reconstructive surgery and that I'd be under anesthesia quite a while and was already on morphine. I remember him saying, 'I'm so sorry. You're going to require a good deal of pain control medication, then there'll be rehab. You may lose the baby, I just need you to be prepared. We can use a lead shield with x-rays after this, but there's the trauma, and we don't know how these medications may affect the fetus, but we know that they definitely can. Think about it.' It was like he was speaking in code, but I got his meaning. He said, 'You don't need to decide anything without thinking about it.' But he was nice, and it seemed like he felt sorry. I sort of remember a southern accent, but that can't be right."

"Your parents must have been shocked. But more to the point, you must have been shocked yourself. Pregnancy can really throw everything into chaos." She had to be careful what she said.

"They were very disapproving. You don't realize how good your generation has it. How much easier it is for women to decide now without having to make up a bunch of hooey. The seventies were supposed to liberate my generation, but a lot of us had one foot on the dock of our upbringing. I was raised by a mother stuck in the nineteen fifties, fixated on my being a lady. My parents were conventional. Middle class. I have no idea if my mother ever liked her life. If she did, her eyes didn't show it. But she still wanted her life for me. Expected it, at least. I think they only sent me to the community college because they thought it would help me marry better.

"I did try it my parents' way. I was an only child, you know, and my mother was pretty controlling. Anyway, Tony was the just second man I'd been with. The first time out, I'd been a twenty-two-year-old virgin, with a twenty-one-year-old college boyfriend, and we fumbled around trying to figure out the sex thing together. I liked Randy, and we pretended we were in love to make it okay that we were having sex, but I never wanted to spend my life with him even when we got engaged. Even when we got married. A lacy church wedding complete with bridesmaids in buttercup yellow. All that time, it was like I was still waiting for something. Going through the motions, waiting." Deana shrugged. "No idea what I was waiting for."

"Mmmm," Monica nodded understanding, not knowing if she did but not wanting to slow Deana more.

"Randy did me the favor of having a transparent affair, and we were divorced in three years. After that, I didn't have a clue exactly what I wanted. Something else, though. Something alive. My mother didn't approve of the mini-skirts and hoop earrings, or that I grew my hair long. Both my parents thought I wore too much make-up. In their eyes I was becoming loose and trashy. Maybe I was. Anyway, imagine what perfect confirmation of their worst fears they had in that hospital room. No wonder they looked like a judge and jury there at the foot of the bed. They were ashamed."

Monica rolled her eyes to let Deana know she understood that concept for sure.

"Yeah," Deana said. "So, anyway, my mother's lips were tight. She was so grim and determined when she said, 'This can be taken care of. If you need money, we'll find it for you.' I was lying in traction, drugged up, had just found out that Tony was dead and I was pregnant...well, can you imagine? I couldn't get out a coherent word. A nurse finally asked them to leave. So much emotion wasn't good for me, she said. Too much crying. Once they left, I remember how she wet a cloth and washed my face with warm water. She asked if I was okay and I told her I'd never be okay again. She told me yes, I would, it just didn't seem like it, and she was so sorry. She had red hair, and her name was Carla. I'll never forget her.

"What happened then?" Monica asked. She turned on her desk light, now aware of the gloom in the room, the darkness creeping in. She'd be terribly late getting home, and it would probably start trouble. It *would* start trouble. But this was income, which her family needed. And, Deana felt delicate to her, like she was somehow made fragile by the telling. Monica still didn't know what she wanted, either. She avoided the clock and kept eye contact with Deana.

"It was bizarre," Deana said, shaking her head. "My mother thought abortion was wrong, but that flew away like a scared bird. She worked on me for days. I was going to be disabled, she said. If the baby's father was alive, he'd not exactly have been available to marry me anyway. What would I tell the child about him and exactly how he'd died? How could I pass on such a legacy of shame? Did I really want the rest of my own life to be shaped by the poor judgment I'd shown in this situation? Who was going to take care of the baby? Did I realize that something could be wrong with the baby? How was I going to pay for it? And what would happen if I lost my job? Did I think she and Dad could support me and the baby? She said I had to grow up and think for once.

I was the one who'd always thought a woman has the right to control her own body. I still believe it. In the end, that's what I did. Controlled my own body."

"So you had the abortion." Monica said, careful to keep her face and voice neutral. Not to reveal relief that she agreed with Deana fully about something.

"No. I didn't."

5

PITTSBURGH, 1983

Joyce loved keeping house. She always had, even back when Deana was a baby. Polishing furniture, vacuuming, making sinks and faucets shine gave her a sense of order and peace. Grocery shopping, too, always from a careful list. She'd memorized where everything was at the IGA and over the years she'd made friends with Butch. "Butch The Butcher," he called himself to be funny, making it all one word, and she could get exactly what she wanted, custom-trimmed. The ladies she played bridge with thought she was over the moon crazy. "You waxed the kitchen floor again? You just did it last month, didn't you?" said Lois, demonstrating her ability to raise just one eyebrow.

"I'd kill for a maid," her friend Mary Lou said, peering over her bridge hand. "Golly, did you hear that Nanette has one now, comes twice a week. Her husband got a big promotion. Kindly don't look around too closely. At least I got this room cleaned," she said, using her head to indicate the formal living room in which the card table was set up. "And it's all right for you to use the guest bathroom, but don't wander further." She laughed gaily. "We should forget this rotating business and always meet at your house, Joyce."

"Maids are nice, I'm sure, but I just like to do it myself, so I know it's done right. If you keep it up, you can have everything done by noon and still have plenty of time to do what you want. Obviously. For heaven's sake, look where I am right now. And I've got dinner for George and me ready to pop in the oven as soon as I get home."

"Well, you're just interested in housework, I guess. I'm like Mary Lou. Can't stand it. But I'll work in my flower beds 'till I crash," Lois said, wrinkling her nose. Her hair was naturally curly, and she left it un-styled, which looked like open laughter to Joyce, who wouldn't have considered leaving hers just loose to wander like that. She and the two others had theirs teased and sprayed. The four of them around the table were in their fifties, with varying amounts of droop in their faces, spread around their middles, and gray in their hair. But no one was old, to be sure, and they called themselves "the girls." Joyce thought she was the second youngest looking of the group. Lois had more of a knack for fashion and the legs and nerve for short skirts, not that the look wasn't a bit slutty.

Housework was an old conversation, a safe one, and Joyce had led them to the topic so she wouldn't have to think up something diverting to say, or keep suspiciously quiet, or outright lie while she dealt the next hand if the topic went to the usual: their children, and sooner or later one of them would ask her how Deana was. She and George had been arguing during the last episode of

Dynasty, or she could have used that. If only there were friends to talk this over with, but it was too shameful. They'd spent years sharing their children's big successes (an A in Algebra I, and from that dreaded Mrs. Johnson, you know her reputation!) and fake failures (Henry scored ten points last night, but he'd been so hoping for at least twelve). If she told them, they'd always think of it when they were around her. They'd know she'd failed after all. Being mothers was who they were, even though all their children were gone now, at least to college and most of them already married. What else except being mothers had they done? What else about them counted?

It was a feeling Joyce couldn't shake, that everything she'd thought had been right about her life had been wrong all along. She'd raised Deana to have morals. She and George had even taken her to Sunday School because it seemed the right thing to do. George had never been much for church, and Joyce couldn't bring herself to really believe a lot of what she was supposed to, but they'd been determined to be good parents.

Sunday mornings, they dutifully dragged themselves to the First Methodist Church on River Road, Deana between them in the pew until the minister finished the children's sermon and dismissed them to their Sunday School classes. Joyce had watched her daughter leave the sanctuary chattering with the other children, boys in miniature suits and girls in sash-tied dresses, lace-topped white socks, and patent-leather shoes, and taking comfort that she was doing everything right, even if George was itching to skip out on the rest of the service to go out and have a smoke, and she was doing a grocery list in her head instead of listening. Having Deana there had seemed like an insurance policy at the time.

It wasn't like she and George didn't live out what was preached in the church anyway. They were faithful, and they were good people. They taught Deana right from wrong. Joyce had, for sure. Be honest, don't cheat, don't hurt other people. How many times had Deana heard variations of the Golden Rule?

"Have I wasted my entire life?" she mused to George. She rubbed her eyes, pressing against them and then above them. The aspirin was wearing off. "Would you turn that light off, please," she said, pointing to the offender. "It's too bright. The other one's enough."

"It's not enough to read by," he said, mild irritation edging his voice, although he complied. The newspaper rustled as he switched it to one hand to turn off the light closest to him. "A headache again? Why don't you just go to bed? I'll do the dishes for you."

They were in the living room with cups of instant coffee, George across from her, on the overstuffed couch with *The River Review* spread on his lap. "Yes, a headache," she said, "And I don't want to go to bed, and I don't want to fight with you either. I just want us to figure this out. What to do I mean. She's refusing an abortion, and it'll be too late pretty soon."

George sighed. "What the hell do you want me to do? I'm not her mother. You think she's going to listen to me?"

"So, she's either a slut or thicker than a five-dollar malt, and I'm responsible?" Joyce's hand shook as she set her cup hard in the saucer and the coffee sloshed over. She mopped it quickly with a napkin. The room had been redone just a year and a half ago, the new carpet a beautiful country blue. She'd be furious with herself if she spotted it.

"Don't have a cow. That's not what I said," George looked up over his paper. "What I mean is I don't have any more to say about it than you do. She listens more to you than to me. All we can do is help her out."

"If we help her, she might think she can keep the baby. We have to hold back, let her see she has to do something." Joyce was quiet a moment, then nodded her head. "That's it, George. Deana has to make the hard decision now. She can't lollygag around maybe thinking we're going to help her raise an illegitimate baby. One that belongs to some dead but very married man who was her boss."

"Well you're right about one thing. She'd better not rely on us for money. I don't want you worrying, but admin announced there could be a merger coming. Feds have been in. Goddamn recession."

"Oh no. Why didn't you tell me? It won't be you, though. You've been loyal to them for twenty-three years."

"Yeah. Tom Ryder sent a memo day before yesterday. No point in freaking out, you're right, probably won't be me. Still, it's good Deana's going to be able to go back to work. When she gets out of rehab."

"Should we get you a new suit, do you think? I mean so you look...like someone they need to keep? One of those power suits?"

"If I have to buy a new suit to keep my job after twenty-three years, it's pretty sorry state of affairs," George said, bitter, running his right hand over the top of his head. "I'm gonna be a chrome dome soon anyway. No suit's gonna make me look young. Or like I have a degree."

"You never needed a degree to be in banking before. Adoption's the right thing to do since she wouldn't have an abortion. That's what Carol says, too."

George shrugged. "Thought you wanted this kept quiet. Sounds like everyone east of the Mississippi knows now. Look. I don't know about Deana. She's hard-headed. She'll do what she's gonna do. Like the Feds. If they say we've gotta merge, then we've gotta merge. It's a question of solvency. A bunch of S and L's have gone under. You know real estate's tanked, but I've got seniority, I oughta be fine. Let's not worry about either one. Nothing's up to us."

"Carol's my cousin. It's different if I talk to a close family member, and get a clue, George, she lives what? Five hundred miles away? Anyway, I'm trying to get Deana to make a good decision for once. I have to do what I can. So do you. We can't be wishy washy spineless and leave things up to chance." The mauve and blue paisley print of the wallpaper had started to dance in front of Joyce's eyes. She closed them. "I'm going to bed," she said. "My headache's bad. I'm sorry for everything. And I think you should buy a new suit."

6

2013

"Were you able to carry the baby to term? With your injuries?" Monica asked, being careful about what she conveyed in her tone, unsure of what terrible fragility she might be digging toward, how breakable Deana might be even here, even now.

"Yes. Not easily, but not because anything was wrong with that part of me. It was my left hip, that side of my pelvis, and, you know, the femur that had been crushed. An orthopod was called in that night to save my leg. Prosthetics were nothing like they are now, so I guess it was for the best. There was an OB, too, I was told. They didn't know if I'd lose the baby, but I didn't, so I was really lucky, even with the morphine and the codeine and other stuff they gave me. Or maybe that's not what could have made me lose it, I don't remember now." Deana tilted her head and looked into the distance as if searching for a memory picture.

In a moment, she shook her head, and went on. "I'll tell you one thing, rehab was a bitch. I suspect the doctor thought my mother was right about an abortion, but he just said, "We don't know the effect of serious trauma and these drugs." Of course, I wouldn't hear of the idea. It was Tony's baby, all I had and would ever have of him. I was committed, you know? I'm sure the doctor also thought it would have made rehab so much easier. I mean, really, think about it. Learning to walk again with a center of gravity constantly changing. I'd been in a wheelchair for months." Deana closed her eyes briefly.

"Hmm. Am I remembering that right? Was it that long? Maybe not. Some details are fuzzy and some, oh my God, some I can give you like a scene in a movie I've memorized. I was transferred from the hospital to a rehab facility—fancy name for a nursing home if you ask me—before I could go to my own apartment and manage by myself. There were merciless days and weeks when it was just a fog of pain and tears. Days and weeks that I didn't want to live.

"I was showing. The therapy hurt. My parents were angry. There were visits from people at work, but I felt like they came to nourish the gossip mill, which I knew had to be in high gear. I made up an out-of-town boyfriend and fed that whole story in, but I wouldn't have believed it myself, so what can I say? Why hadn't I ever mentioned him before? And afterwards, I felt dirty and disloyal. I cried a lot."

"Well, you were grieving." Monica leaned back and gave a small head shake. "And I imagine you were angry. Maybe you still are? I know I would be." She reminded herself again to be careful what she said. But damn this made her mad—not at Deana, for Deana. "I haven't heard anything actionable yet, so I'm not sure why you need an attorn—"

"Heartbroken, yes. Not angry, not then. However it all started, you have to understand this. I loved Tony. When I felt life, quickening the doctor called it, the finality of Tony's stillness was complete. His death seemed my fault. It all was my fault. Something would be wrong with the baby. Cosmic punishment. I was afraid to love it. And yet I did."

"Not your fau—"

But Deana interrupted, brushing her off with a headshake and wrist gesture. "The little old ladies and old men at the rehab clucked over me. I mean the ones up and around on walkers and in wheelchairs, the ones with their minds and not many visitors, ones who thought a pregnant woman there was the loveliest gift, as though they might, after all, get to skip winter's terrors and know another spring after all. They were so hungry for hope. The surroundings were cheerful enough, but in an utterly fake way, as if the patients were all in second grade.

"I remember early October. Instead of taking people outside, no matter how blue the sky, or how bright the leaves, a staff member would write on a chalkboard in the dining room. 'The weather is sunny. The season is autumn. The leaves are turning pretty colors.'" Deana stuck air quotes around the words and her tone turned sarcastic.

"Now wouldn't you think anyone who could read that could look out the window? And the patients in wheelchairs, why couldn't they be outside in the courtyard breathing in that warm sunshine instead of parked in the hallways? Honestly, colored cutouts of cutesy pumpkins on those walls, just like in an elementary school! Everything once or twice removed from the world. It was enough to scare anyone who thought seriously about anything—like what's being kept from me? There is nothing true here. I think it was because something new and real and good was happening to my body, something they could see, that they glommed onto me. I promised I'd come back to visit them with the baby. It's one of the things I feel worst about.

"You didn't visit?" Monica felt badly as soon as she said it, the judgmental surprise in her voice, but Deana didn't seem to pick up on it.

"They believed in me. I let them down." Deana pulled a couple more tissues from the box on Monica's desk. "I'd go back now and ask them to forgive me, but it's too late. They're dead, the ones I knew." Head down, she wiped her eyes. "I'm sorry." She whispered it. Then she looked at her wrist and seemed startled that she wasn't wearing a watch. "What time is it anyway? It's getting so dark. You must need to get home. I'm sorry."

"It's okay," Monica said, even though it wasn't and wouldn't be when she got home. "I don't know what you need from me yet. Can you just tell me that?"

7

CHARLEVOIX, MICHIGAN, 1983

Jennie said she couldn't do it anymore after the fifth time. It was expensive, and sometimes she told herself that was a reason. But it wasn't. Brian was an orthodontist who had a way with both kids and parents, a reputation for kindness, and the practice he'd taken over was long-established; patients in treatment had made a comfortable transition to him four years ago, and he'd attracted new ones since then.

As a kindergarten teacher, Jennie didn't make nearly as much as her husband, but it had helped pay off their school debts, and they'd bought a pristine colonial home in a Charlevoix neighborhood of young families. It was white with dark green shutters, and the previous family had built a tree house in a big sturdy maple in the back yard. (Brian laughed about it: they'd bought the damn property for the tree house, he said.) Jennie and Brian had savings, they had insurance, they even had a retirement plan.

No, it wasn't the expense. It was the foolishness and humiliation of hoping again, of sitting in an infertility specialist's waiting room, everyone knowing why they were there. The cheery blonde receptionist probably pictured what Brian had done, when he handed her the small container, with its time of collection label filled in. It didn't help that she wore scrubs and a name tag that said Nancy. It didn't help that the few other couples who might or might not be in the waiting room at any given appointment were there for the same reason.

Jennie had been pregnant for four months once when she was twenty-five, after a year of trying. After surgery that removed one fallopian tube along with the fetus the doctor said wasn't viable, wasn't a baby, or even really the beginning of one, they hadn't panicked. She hadn't panicked. Whatever disappointment Brian felt, he kept to himself. "Nothing is your fault," he said, so many times, that she became convinced that she was to blame. His Scandinavian face, blonde eyebrows smooth as waves, light sea eyes, seemed to sculpt itself into an impassiveness she'd not known in him before. (The baby would have been blonde for sure; her own hair hadn't darkened much since childhood.) They waited four of the six months the obstetrician instructed and started trying again. By the time another fourteen months had passed, each time she got her period she'd cried, then counted the days until she might be fertile again. Every month she analyzed everything that could affect baby making—who was on top, had they let enough sperm build up, had she gotten up too soon after lovemaking? What had started with easy confidence had diminished to hope.

The less natural hope Jennie felt, the more she did to manufacture it. Nothing that Brian didn't endorse, but sometimes it was difficult to discern when he was trying to soothe her and when he wanted something himself. She began taking her basal body temperature every day.

After a year of that, they went to Dr. Bostrum. Testing. Brian's count was fine, and his boys were great swimmers. Maybe Jennie wasn't ovulating every month. Sometimes her temperature chart said she ovulated on the eighth day, sometimes on the eighteenth. "Makes me suspicious," Doctor Bostrum said, bushy gray eyebrows gathered. "Let's try some Clomid." Another thirteen months, the drug and the temperature charts and a pillow under Jennie's hips.

"We don't want to let this go on," Dr. Bostrum said, when he referred them on to another infertility specialist. In one way it was a relief to sit in a different waiting room, one with different carefully neutral magazines (*Good Housekeeping, Better Homes and Gardens, Time, Sports Illustrated*). But, it was also a measure of how much further they were from having a baby.

This specialist had Jennie call the office every morning to report the temperature she had to take every morning before she moved from their bed. When the number signaled that she would ovulate in the next twelve to twenty-four hours, the doctor would call back—now! Brian ejaculated into a specimen collector and they'd rush to the office where portly Doctor Harcourt would put the semen up Jennie's vagina, suctioned to her cervix in a rubber cup. Cramps doubled her over afterward.

Then each month, the waiting began again. Silently, Jennie would beg her body to do what other women's

LYNNE HUGO

bodies did, secretly vigilant for the smallest early signs. *Am I nauseous? I'm definitely tired.*

No, it wasn't the expense. It was life mocking her, punishing her, emptying her out again every time when it should have wanted to fill her.

"I'm not giving up or anything," she said to Brian on a Friday night. She'd gotten her period the day before, which he knew, but not that she'd left work when the first deep pink spots appeared, or that she'd called in sick today. Too many tears, too unbearable to see the other teachers, two of whom were pregnant. "But I need some time off from Harcourt's office."

They sat in their family room, an irony she didn't mention, and she'd made them each a martini. The olive in her stemmed glass, oval as a green egg, felt like an insult when she studied it to avoid meeting Brian's eyes. Because she'd pictured their baby crawling on the sculptured green carpet and because the room was deep with flowered-cushioned comfort, ready for delight, it hurt to be there. It hurt to be anywhere there were reminders of longing and failure, which was everywhere. "I feel like I'm going crazy and I need to get myself together," she said.

He was quiet for perhaps a second too long, studying her face. "Okay," he said, sliding closer on the sofa and taking her hand. "We'll just let it alone for now." She had no idea what he felt and didn't think she could stand to know.

"Thanks," Jennie said. "How about it we go out for dinner tonight? Just to get out of this house."

42

8

PITTSBURGH 2013

The streetlights came on outside Monica's office window as Deana continued. "Right, I'm getting to the point, I promise. I was finally released from rehab in late November. After saying they weren't going to, my parents did have the family for Thanksgiving, including me. I think they'd fought about it. Maybe my father won. Maybe I'm just wishing. Anyway, I'd learned to walk again, or maybe I should say lurch, with a hand crutch. Even less graceful than I am now, although, as you saw when I came in, I'm not exactly a ballerina, am I? A physical therapist came to my house four times a week to work with me, but then my disability ran out, and I had to go back to work when I was just short of six months pregnant. I'd used up all my disability leave, sick time and vacation time. Can you see where I'm heading here?"

"No time off to have the baby?"

"Bingo."

"Oh god."

"Oh god is right. I wondered if there was a God. I still do."

"Who was helping you?"

"I don't think anybody was, but I want to be fair. I remember it as a time of crushing loneliness. People at work had figured it out. Tony was someone they missed, the victim of a tragedy. Since I'd survived, I must have been the cause, a cheat and a liar to boot. Maybe I made up a lot of that in my head. Maybe they just didn't know what to say to me. But I felt like a pariah, and my dad lost his job, so he went on unemployment then. That was because of the savings and loan crisis—the one where he'd worked went belly up.

"It didn't have anything to do with me, but it felt all rolled together in time, you know? It felt like I'd brought trouble on them, like spreading a contagious disease. My mother found a job half-time in a dress shop, while he left coffee cup rings on the furniture, reading the smallest print in the employment section of the daily paper to see if he'd overlooked anything he could apply for. They were floundering, ashamed and scared for themselves now almost as much as for me. They didn't want me thinking they could take care of me or the baby, so they pulled back. They'd have me to dinner maybe once a week. Was that a help? I guess so. I think they tried in their way."

"Friends?" Monica asked.

"You know how you alienate people when you don't take their advice. My best friend didn't think I should have the baby. And before that, I'd lied to her. About Tony, I mean. I'd been protecting him, but she saw it as a failure of trust, and then she didn't trust me anymore, and it was never the same. What could I say? I had chosen him.

"When I was about seven months, my mother started up again. She wanted me to give the baby up for adoption. Mom had talked about me—lovely, huh?—to some cousin of hers in South Carolina that I don't even know. That cousin had helpfully told Mom that there was a second cousin on her husband's side way out on the upper peninsula of Michigan, and she'd heard he and his wife desperately wanted a child, but it hadn't happened, some medical problem. He was a dentist, and she would quit her job as a teacher to stay home with the baby. It would be happy, safe, loving, plenty of money, two stable, healthy parents—Mom figured they had everything to offer that I didn't."

"And you said?"

"I said no way. I felt the baby moving. I'd loved Tony, and I wanted the baby." She shrugged, "I was scared to death, so I'm sure part of it was stubbornness. I felt like my parents—or Mom as proxy for my old world, maybe—was blackmailing me. Sort of 'Give up your baby and maybe we'll take you back.' Everything felt wrong. Push me, I always push back. Not my best trait."

"I guess we get our strength however we get it. It seems like it worked?" Monica said.

"An interesting theory and probably true. Funny, because my mother used to say have some spine. Guess that backfired on her. Anyway, it worked until the other shoe dropped. And it wasn't a shoe. More like a boot. A steel-toed boot. Remember that promotion that Tony had mentioned the first night we ever went out?"

"Uh huh." Monica muttered. "He was your boss. Your boss."

"Nothing came of that before the accident." Deana said. "Then I was out so long on disability, and the circumstances of the accident wouldn't have exactly helped me move up in the company either. When I was able to work, I applied for an account manager position that Tony talked about at the beginning. I didn't get it. I'd only been back a couple of months when the pink slips started to be passed out at headquarters. I was eight months pregnant when I got mine, in April. Like a year after I'd strutted out on my own and said Yes to Tony, 'Yes I can, yes I will,' life shouted another 'oh no you won't!' at me."

9

CHARLEVOIX, MICHIGAN, LATE 1983

"This isn't something we have to just take lying down," Brian said, pulling his head up to look his wife in the eyes, although the bedroom was nearly dark. The light from the hallway was just enough.

"So to speak," she said, infusing her voice with irony and a hint of bitterness. "I guess that means we should get up now?"

"Far out. Gorgeous and a sense of humor. That's my girl." He shifted more of his weight off her, one elbow and hand a tripod to prop his head now, but the other playing with one of her breasts. "I say we tell my mother to pass the word back through these seventeen channels of people we don't know—and she doesn't either, not really—but we tell her to say yes. Just a simple yes. It's totally legal, all handled by our attorney and the birth mother's, she never knows any identities and neither do we. But we know there's good health, mentally and physically. Smart people. That's enough, isn't it? No endless waiting lists, either."

"But you said it's only a maybe."

"Well, she can't sign the papers until forty-eight hours after it's born. Or I thought that's what my cousin said but remember she's two or three times removed from the source. And the source isn't even directly connected to the...uh...person having the baby, if I get it right. Our lawyer has to give us the legalities straight."

"You've already decided, haven't you?" she said. "Your parents won't approve."

It was a complete reversal of their old process on the baby issue, she once so transparent and in charge, and he so masked, doing whatever she wanted. Jennie's recognition of the switch was sudden; when had it had happened?

"They'll come around. It's not like they don't want to be grandparents," he said.

"They say if it's God's will, I'll get pregnant, Brian. Your mother believes that."

"I know what she believes." Brian shook his head. "Who's to say this isn't God's will? If there is such a thing. I think we make our own fate." He didn't ask what she believed.

They both knew he wasn't one to relinquish control, not the man he'd become anyway. Like an elm branch, the way it can abruptly depart from the direction of the limb, Brian was a transformed adult from a small-town altar boy in southern Minnesota, who'd been so much his parents' son.

Ingrid and Will would never change, though, still rooted as deeply as ever in tiny Syversen; fourth generation Norwegians who'd met in high school and married in the First American Lutheran Church of Our Savior. Ingrid was a deaconess now that women were allowed to be. The church was dominant in the village—white, tall-spired at the head of Main Street's neatly tended shops, and its tilt toward pietism shaped community thinking. God's will explained disasters—when, say, the river flooded in mid-spring every fourth or fifth year—and rising to acceptance was the model. And Brian, as if his life was already decided on God's shrug, had once expected he'd spend his life there or in one of the nearby prairie towns after he went over to Marshall or Mankato for college. Somewhere close and inexpensive, which was what his parents said.

At the beginning of Brian's senior year in Syversen High School, a new, young guidance counselor encouraged him to expand his horizons beyond the small town life planned for him. Why not try a major university, she'd suggested and mentioned that he might challenge himself, apply to a pre-dental program to try on the career Brian had set his sights on since his aptitude for science had emerged in high school. He'd been cheered on in that thinking about expanding his horizons—to his parents' annoyance—by his maternal uncle, younger and more glamorous and more materialistic than they, a dentist who'd already had the money and inclination to buy himself a red mustang.

"Why not give it a shot and apply to the University of Michigan? I know that going away is radical around here," the counselor said to Brian, "and Ann Arbor would be really different. But Michigan is awesome. They teach you how to think and expect you to do it." She seemed like she knew a lot about the wider world and had fallen in love with it.

Without saying anything negative about Syversen, particularly around his parents, she'd put a new lens in front of Brian's eyes, entrancing him. Her hair was as light as his family's; had it not been, he doubted his parents would have listened when they came in for his conferences. Although when she talked to them, it wasn't about learning to think independently or creatively, or "getting a look at the other side," but about scholarships, education, and career.

"Once they look at Brian's ACT score and grades, they'll be interested. And if he doesn't get in, or doesn't get enough financial aid, well no harm done. He has plenty of local fallback options." She added, "But an undergraduate degree from Michigan would set him up in the best possible way for their dental school."

Ingrid and Will had hesitated, but when Brian received the scholarship to the University of Michigan, they finally gave their approval. Michigan, after all, was one of the best schools of dentistry in the country.

The guidance counselor had been right about a lot of things. Brian had gone to Ann Arbor and after a floundering freshman year of culture shock, he'd never seriously looked back. Acceptance was not considered critical thinking at the University. It was all about being proactive, questioning authority, independent thinking. As it had turned out, Brian was very good at it.

But as he and Jennie had done everything to conceive, he'd been radically different from the man he'd become. Seeing her readiness to blame herself, he had purposely reverted—externally—to the passivity of his boyhood model, regardless of how it chafed; he hardly recognized himself, but what scared him was the way he hardly recognized Jennie.

She was a Michigan graduate, too, after all, but now it seemed she'd lost her reasoning capability. The tears, always the tears, a creek that ran almost daily over stony determination. Lovemaking strictly by a schedule, and the schedule had nothing to do with him, only with what a temperature chart said. He'd made sure he never pushed for different procedures or tests, never showed any sign of discouragement or impatience. Didn't ask the hard questions of their doctor in front of Jennie.

When Jennie said she wanted to stop, he'd taken it as her stepping down from the role of Fertility Director, too. In his own way and without advertising, Brian took over. He did his own research, called the specialist to hear the difficult odds after so many attempts.

The truth was even before they lay in bed together in the gathering dark, he'd already told his cousin to pass along a yes. Yes, they would be interested in a confidential private adoption of a Caucasian newborn expected in a couple of weeks, if it was fully legal. It would be understood that their identities would not be available to the birth parents, nor would he and Jennie have access to potentially identifying information regarding them. All either side would have would be relevant health information. It was all Brian wanted: a healthy baby, and his wife back.

Now Brian smoothed Jennie's hair back, off her forehead, and traced her hairline, where the squarish shape of her face was revealed. The only illumination was from the glowing numerals of the bedside clock and the dim indirect remainder that rose to the white-curtained window from the porch light a story below.

"Yeah, honey," he said softly. "I have decided that we should take the next step. I'm passing back the word that we're interested and giving them the name and phone number of our attorney."

"You flake," she laughed, as if she'd suddenly realized something. "This is ridiculous. You need to back up, buddy. You're acting like we've talked this over and made a decision and already have a lawyer and—"

"We do," Brian said. "As of this morning. He went to Michigan Law, in fact. I called the alumni association for a referral. Office is over in Petoskey."

"You…what?" Jennie raised her head, not laughing any more. "You've given up on me? On our having our own? I told you, I just want to take a break. I didn't mean quit. I haven't quit."

"It's time, honey. This is the way to go."

She sat up, agitated, getting teary. "No, I can do it. We'll go back to the clinic."

Brian studied his wife's face. She wasn't angry. He wasn't reading anger on her. Not yet. That would come next, he figured. She was at the pleading stage. She didn't want him to give up, for him to make her fail. If there was one thing Jennie couldn't stand, it was to fail.

"Just breathe, baby. We'll see. And meanwhile, let's make our baby in our minds, put the idea of him—or her—in us." He leaned over and kissed her. She might have started to say something, but then she seemed to give way, to kiss back. He kissed her more deeply then and their hands became hungry, too, and then their bodies.

This was an argument he could win. And would.

10

PITTSBURGH 2013

"So, I was out of work, and not exactly able to job hunt. A blind Director of Personnel was too much to hope for." Deana said, bitterness crimping her voice. "I had a bassinette and some disposable diapers, and a few newborn-size clothes, what I could afford. It wasn't as though people had been lining up to throw baby showers for me. How many soap operas can you watch in a day? I took books out of the library, and I kept my doctor appointments, and I waited. I knew I was in way, way over my head.

"Anyway, I'd never been to Tony's grave. Of course, I couldn't after the accident, when I was in the hospital and the rehab place. And then it was winter, when I went back to work, and it was already dark when I'd get off. You'd think maybe the weekends, but I was drained, trying to get laundry done, buy some groceries, do my physical therapy exercises, go to Mom and Dad's for my weekly dose of disapproval. And I think those were excuses, that I wasn't ready. I'd gotten a copy of the obituary from the newspaper, so I knew where he was buried. Maybe I imagined that the stone might say Beloved husband, devoted father, and I thought that whatever hadn't killed me yet didn't matter, seeing those words carved into stone would." Deana paused, considering. Then she nodded.

"Yes. What I've just told you is the truth," she said. "Everything else was an excuse. But in the last weeks, as the baby dropped, turned its head down, ready to be born, as strong as the need to stay away had been, the need to go to visit Tony became as strong, matching it, until one day the scale tipped, and I went.

"He's in a beautiful cemetery with enormous maples, and dogwoods were blooming, like palms up to the sun." Here Deana lifted both her palms up and raised them, briefly closed her eyes. Shook her head once and went on. "Bradford pear trees. Lilacs. I had to stop at the cemetery office and ask the location of his grave. I felt awkward because I was so pregnant, you know, even though I was just being paranoid, so I said, 'I'm his cousin from Tennessee.' And then I realized that was stupid, people from Tennessee have an accent. But the woman didn't seem to notice, just gave me directions, and I got in my car and whispered, 'get over yourself.'.

It was hard to find the grave. I had to park and walk in a fair way between lines of stones. Me big as a house, the ground squishy from rain the day before, my crutch not as solid as it is on pavement. And finally, there was Tony's: a big, simple gray marble stone. Son, husband, father. Beloved, devoted, the exact terrible words I'd feared. And Monica, there were round planters on both sides. Beautiful pansies, blossoms hanging over the edges, yellow, orange, blue, purple. They were just starting to get a bit leggy, shooting too far out of their greenery the way pansies do late in the spring. But none of the blooms were dead or dying. They were cared for. It was so strange. The stone itself turned me to stone, and those pansies broke me. I had to sit. I remember the ground was so damp and I didn't know how I'd get up. I don't think I would have cried like that if it hadn't been for the pansies."

"I think I understand," Monica said quietly.

"And that's where she found me. Everything turned again on a moment in time at a particular spot on the earth. My God, it was the first time I'd gone to his grave! So was it chance? Or some kind of fate? What should I accept? What should I fight?"

"Your destiny question."

"Yes. My destiny question. Even now."

11

1983

When Kathleen had gone to the front door and seen the two policemen there, she'd thought there was most likely a neighborhood problem. The area swarmed with kids, and they all played outside until it was just a breath less than fully dark, which Kathleen thought wasn't safe. Her boys were much more closely supervised, never out without her right there, and in their baths before twilight. But they were upstairs, sound asleep, when the doorbell sounded. Tony was working late, and she'd just gotten off the phone with her mother. Her world felt bound like a blanket.

It wasn't until one of them introduced himself as the Chief of Police and asked if they could come inside that an edge frayed. Then, when the Chief asked if they could all sit down, and he spoke, it unraveled entirely.

"Hit in a field by the river? No, he's at work. It's not Tony, he's at work," she denied, her voice squeaking.

The Chief, Charlie Fritz, told Kathleen that a 1980 green Taurus registered to Anthony John Hamilton was parked behind trees at the edge, and that his wallet was on his body. They didn't mention the woman he'd been with: who had the stomach for that when the widow had begun to hyperventilate without that information? Enough is enough. She'd know the details all too soon. The patrolman with the Chief asked for the number of a relative he could call to come be with her. Kathleen was not intelligible, and the Chief dispatched him to see if a woman neighbor was available, one who might know if relatives lived nearby.

No one had wanted Kathleen to see the body, but she had the right and insisted on it. Summoned by the neighbor, Kathleen's parents tried to step in and make the positive identification for her. When she refused to let them, Martha and Bob had gone in with her, along with a doctor, a nurse, and the hospital chaplain.

Martha and Bob couldn't anticipate the next hammer blow—as if the body hadn't been unbearable, crushed and crushing, even with sheets judiciously placed. Kathleen had moved them. Martha, gray curls in sweaty disarray, had made an involuntary moan, and Bob had tried to guide her to the door, but she'd been determined to stay with her daughter and did, keeping an arm around Kathleen's waist and breaking her fall when her knees buckled.

Once back in the grief room the hospital provided, Kathleen had insisted on knowing exactly what had happened; the driver was in jail, now, wasn't he? Why not? Slowly, painfully, with the hospital chaplain present, the Chief, who hadn't even been home yet that night, told Kathleen the circumstances of the accident.

Kathleen's father, Bob, was a Korean war Marine vet who'd stayed in the Reserves right through mandatory retirement. He'd cleaned up snafus by Marines under his command. He could spot a fucked up job without having to put his glasses on. Bob listened—and watched—as the Chief talked to his daughter. He noticed how the Chief kept decent eye contact when he told Kathleen that Tony and his "female companion" had been engaged in illicit activity on a blanket in the field near the river, but when he tacked on "…at the time the officer was dispatched to the scene," he'd looked away. Bob sensed what the Chief was doing because he, too, knew how to make a skunk smell like perfume. He'd done that himself in his day. Marines who'd stayed out of the brig, even got their promotions, knew he'd had their backs even though the Colonel had reamed them a new one himself.

Now Bob let Martha think he was going to the men's room and put in a call to his friend Gregster from the pay phone in the hall. Gregster's son was a crackerjack lawyer. "Something's rotten and it ain't in Denmark," he said to his friend. "Chief of Police is lying about something. Don't know what. Need someone who can poke around and find out. Can your boy help or get me somebody who will?"

He hiked his pants after he hung up, wet his lips, ran his hands over his thick gray hair, composing himself for what was to come. He had to take his handkerchief out of his pocket to clean up his eyes. He straightened his posture and tucked his chin in before stepping back to his daughter. At least there was something he could fight, and he knew how to do that. One thing he'd learned in war:

you couldn't stop damage from happening. Sometimes it was your own men gone wrong. You couldn't stop that, but you could damn sure make them pay.

12

2013

"I don't know where Kathleen had left her car, but it wasn't over on the little lane near mine. I'd have heard it, caught a sideways glimpse of someone walking my way, and pulled myself together if I'd known anyone was around," Deana paused, looking at Monica as if to check if this made sense. When Monica nodded, she went on.

"As it was, she came up behind me, and I was completely unprepared. When I heard a voice, I startled and tried to force back the sob that was already on the way out, and that made me cough. I was fumbling around with tissue, just a complete mess."

Deana shrugged and put her palm in the air. "And, I was on the ground, remember. The only way I could get up was to crawl to the headstone and use both it and my crutch for support. It was humiliating. I felt her standing there while I floundered."

"Wait. Tell me who Kathleen is? Not…" Monica's brows tented, incredulous.

"Good guess. Tony's wife. When I finally got to my feet, I saw she was carrying two big pots of new summer flowers. One in each arm, like they were toddlers. Gorgeous blue lobelia trailing over the edges, asparagus fern, all shades of dark and light pink and maroon impatiens."

Monica didn't want to hear horticultural details. "She spoke to you?"

Deana nodded. "It wasn't like I could escape. My crutch had slipped—oh it was all so awkward, her looming there while I struggled to pick it up. It felt like she was glad to see how hard it was."

Monica leaned forward again. "What did she say?"

"Pfft," the sound came with a dismissive gesture. "Exactly what you'd expect. After I finally got my crutch and could have left. And her voice was hard and cold as any stone in that cemetery. 'What are you doing here?' I was terrified and embarrassed, like I'd suddenly been caught, which, in a way, I had. Ashamed. Right then, I understood some of what my parents felt.

'I apologize, I'll leave,' I told her. Which I was trying to do, right then. But she said, 'Do you know who I am?' And I couldn't meet her eyes. I finally managed, 'You're Kathleen, aren't you?' I couldn't bring myself to say Tony's wife. So, of course, she said, 'That's right. I'm Kathleen, Tony's wife.' Then I followed her eyes and realized I was still using his headstone to balance myself, one hand on the top of it. I got my hand off it then, oh God, Monica, like it was erupting molten lava."

"When my hand was off, I stood for just a second or two trying to decide if I should tell her I was sorry, so sorry. Should I try to explain myself? Or should I just quietly go without saying anything? I saw her stare at my belly and then back up at me. There was huge silent emptiness between us and when she finally spoke then, it became charged. 'So you're Deana. Did you know Tony and I were trying to have another baby when he died?'

"I just said 'No, I didn't know that.' And then Kathleen looked at my belly again and her eyes turned into pools, with the pupils like stones under that glittery surface. 'Did you know I've talked to your mother?'

I said, 'I didn't know that either. I'm very sorry if she's bothered you. I'll try to get her to stop.'

'I was afraid she might not…pass along the message, but she assured me she had. I didn't want to see or talk to you myself, but now here you are, big as life and twice as real.'

I couldn't wrap my mind around that. 'You called her?' I asked Kathleen.

"'A couple of months ago' is what Kathleen told me then. I thought she sounded so satisfied with herself when she said it, but maybe I imagined that."

Monica was leaning on one elbow, focused on Deana's face. Letting the client run with her story instead of pushing her to get to the point, but she wanted to hear it as much as she didn't, and she was so late getting home now that, doubtless, the fire was already burning.

Deana continued. "Kathleen must have seen my bewilderment and realized I really didn't know, because then she used the back of her hand to swipe at her eyes and told me that her lawyer had met my mother in the hospital, when all the first investigations of the accident were going on. They'd heard—from my mother, of all people—that I was pregnant. I'm sure Mom was pretty worked up and not using spectacular judgment.

"Kathleen said she'd been paralyzed for the first few months. It had been all she could do to take care of their boys, but apparently, the police had to work with her lawyer. Or something. My mother and father wanted my name kept quiet, very difficult, but somewhat easier than Tony's name, since I wasn't dead. It was a mess, just a mess. When Kathleen called my mother in January, it was to tell her that she wanted me to give the baby up for adoption. It was the right thing to do for Tony's legitimate children. They had enough to deal with, according to Kathleen.

"I remember I gave a bitter little snort that I regret and told her not to worry, her message was being delivered just without her calling card, and that my mother had been pressuring me to give the baby up. The hand that had been on Tony's grave was resting on my belly. I was so defensive, but so sad, and I felt so in the wrong. There was Kathleen with new flowers for her husband's grave and her hurt and loyalty to her children, and there I was, trespassing, with the aftermath of what we'd done so huge and unmistakable. The baby moved, an elbow or a knee or a foot stretching out in slow motion, and I hoped she didn't see.

"'So, will you?' she said. Up until that moment the answer had been no. Monica, I wanted that baby. I had never seen having it, keeping it, as something more that would hurt her. More damage. I answered by telling her I hadn't decided and right then it wasn't a lie.

"Then Kathleen said, 'I know you're out of work. You have nobody to support you, there aren't any jobs out there.

What kind of life can you give the baby? Doesn't the baby deserve two parents? And how are you going to even take care of yourself? Wouldn't you like to go back to school or something?' Monica, she did everything but point to my leg and my crutch. She wanted me to remember she'd seen me scrabbling.

"Of course, I was defensive, and I said, 'What are you talking about?' But then, I started to get wobbly on my feet. A little lightheaded. 'I've got to go now,' I said. 'I need to get off my feet. I'm sorry.' I was just proving her point, which made me all the more upset.

"Kathleen put down the pots of flowers she'd been holding. While she did, I realized: she looked strong, much stronger than I was, with a good body. Thick, dark straight hair, sculpted eyebrows, blue eyes with black lashes. White, straight teeth. She was really pretty and something about that bothered me, as if my mind suddenly said, You idiot. Tony was never serious about you. He had her, they had children and a home, they were trying to have another baby. She was the Madonna, you were the whore, or whatever made him stray that you'll never know, but it never was what you thought. It was not destiny.

"'I'll help you to your car,' she said. Well, you can imagine just how comfortable that was for me, but what was I going to do? It felt like my field of vision was narrowing, and the ground moving, rising. 'You look pale, take my arm,' I heard from some faraway place and suddenly I was leaning against Tony's wife. The dizziness passed, and I shifted more weight to my crutch and took tentative steps with Kathleen—Kathleen, of all people—supporting me.

"We got to my car and she helped me in. Then she asked if she could talk to me. I wanted to say no, but I dropped my head into my hands and whispered okay. She went around and got in the passenger side. I don't think I've ever felt so trapped in my life. It wasn't like I could even drive away if I couldn't take anymore.

"'I know there's a couple that really wants the baby,' Kathleen said. "Good people, stable, well-off, two parents who'd be totally devoted." My mother had told her. I realized they must have talked recently, and my hoping that my parents were going to support me was pure fantasy. They were allied with Kathleen. Then, Kathleen played her ace. It was a card she either hadn't given my mother yet, or my mother had been holding back to play at the end. 'Look,' she said. 'You're not going to get rehired at Midland Mutual whether the economy turns around or not. I can guarantee you that. My husband was your boss. He'd been with them for twelve years. He was married with children. Who do you think they're standing behind? They could have kept you on, right? Okay, so, unemployment benefits run out. Then, if you can even find another job, with almost nine percent of the population out of work, daycare costs a fortune. You've got to think about clothes, formula, diapers, maybe a few toys. Have you really thought this through?'

"Monica, you know I thought I had, but it was as if Kathleen put a pair of glasses on my face and the whole world looked different—including Tony. I couldn't conjure up the man I'd adored. All I could see was his widow. I don't know if she was working me or completely sincere. She fished her purse for her wallet and pulled out pictures of two little boys. My God, they looked like him. 'These are Tony's children,' she said. 'You can't do this to them. It would be best for everyone, including the baby. And you could go back to school, remake your life. I have plenty of life insurance from Tony. He always took care of us. Everything will be arranged privately through my attorney to take care of your expenses. He can handle the adoption too. Or the parents may want their own lawyer. You can start over, a new life.'

"How would I know..." The minute I started to formulate the question, it was a done deal.

"Kathleen said, 'You can have it upfront.'

"I remember crying and saying she wanted me to sell my baby, and she said, 'No, not at all. It would be selling your baby if I was the one taking it. Tony would never want that for his wife or his sons. He'd want what was best for us. But as it happens, this is best for you and it, too.' She gestured at my belly as if it were a bomb."

13

1984

"Is this for real?" Jennie whispered. "Daniel. Is this happening? Oh. Do you think we should let people call him Danny or insist on Daniel? I like Daniel. Seven pounds one ounce. And healthy, right? Didn't what's his name—our lawyer—say anything at all about what he looks like?"

"Ron Pedersen. Remember? He got a call from the lawyer there. It's not like he's seen the baby. All he told me was seven pounds one ounce, nineteen inches, and physically normal—like ten fingers, ten toes, one head— and healthy based on the Apgar scores. And then the thing about do we want him circumcised and how the mother—I mean, not that she's going to be his mother, well, anyway, how she said that it should be up to us. I didn't know we had to decide about that, but I knew it would be weird for him to look different from me, and I thought, well, hell, that's a decision for his father to make anyway.

"One minute I'm up to my elbows in Andrew Allen's mouth cementing bands, and then Shannon's saying 'Excuse me, Doctor, there's a call you need to take,' and I'm making parental decisions. I wish we could have been together."

Brian sounded jubilant telling Jennie all this, then nuzzled his wife and kissed her neck. They'd gone to bed late thanks to a suddenly long to-do list, but now neither could settle down. "I guess we won't have too uninterrupted many nights like this for a while. Our lives are about to change forever."

Both were quiet then, absorbing that idea. A tree branch scratched another on the roof. "You've got to put child guards in all the plugs. And safety latches on the cabinet doors," Jennie said into the silence."

"God, you're right. Maybe I can do it tomorrow morning before we leave."

"That would be good. There'll be that home visit, right? Before it's finalized. Everything has to be done."

"Yeah, but I think that would be closer to the six months thing. Ron will tell us."

"Still, everything has to be done ahead. We want it all safe anyway."

"For sure."

They were quiet again. Jennie felt Brian reach for her hand, and they each lay on their backs clutching hands, thinking.

"I wonder what she's feeling," Jennie said into the cool dark air. She'd spent the afternoon in frantic nesting mode. She and Brian hadn't had time to talk until now. He'd gotten the call and called her. It was that simple.

A friend was putting together a shower for next Saturday afternoon, but the list she found of what newborns needed was daunting. Bottles, diapers, rubber pants, sheets, towels, undershirts, sleepers, blankets. How many receiving blankets did she really need? Who knew these things? She wished she hadn't refused to ready the nursery when Brian had first told her that he'd said yes to the private adoption and engaged the lawyer to represent them. She'd been too upset by his giving up, although it was really her fault; she'd been the one to stop the infertility treatments. But, she'd only said she wanted a break, not to give up.

Well, it was her own fault either way she looked at it. Still, even though Brian had said the birth mother was in the last six weeks if the due date was right, Jennie hadn't gotten ready. Nothing seemed real until today when the phone call came. Suddenly it was real, and she hadn't even gotten to feel like part of the club of expectant mothers. She should have spent the month, at least, telling people and buying things for her baby instead of running out in a rush to buy a crib and bumper pads, changing table, even a lamp and rocking chair for the nursery. Not only that, here she was, tonight, lying in the dark. And what should Jennie call her anyway, the woman lying in a hospital in some other state who'd had a baby boy this morning? The baby's mother? Was she still his mother, though? If she was his mother, when would Jennie become his mother? Jennie really didn't like the idea of her son having two mothers. She wanted a simple, exclusive claim on his heart.

"I wonder if she's sad or relieved. It must be so hard." If she is sad, how can I be happy at someone else's expense?

Jennie thought but didn't voice it. Brian was tired of her doubts. She knew that. She was grateful that the lights were out, and she didn't have to smooth out her face, only her voice.

"Most likely relieved, but don't think about that," Brian said. "She's not you. She had a choice. Just like we had a choice. Anyway, this baby is ours. We've loved him, made him with everything but our bodies, but even that, we know that part too," Brian said. Jennie felt him tighten his hand on her breast, draw her body to him with a leg.

"Do you feel like this is what was meant to be all along? I've always felt that way about you, that you and I were meant for each other." This was something she could say and mean.

"If you like it that way, honey, that works for me. You work for me. Always have, always will."

"I feel like I'm exploding," Jennie said, her body meeting his and now her arms gathering him in a fierce embrace. She had to do this, had to be ready. Her husband deserved it.

"Ready for tomorrow?"

"I think so…. No, I mean I am. Yes.

14

1984

"The doctor said, 'Looks like a healthy baby boy,' and asked me if I wanted to hold him. I did." Deana used the back of her hand to wipe her nose now, embarrassed that she had to.

"I kissed him and told him how much I loved him and that he was going to have a good life with another mother, and he'd have a father. That it was really important for a boy to have a father. I asked him to forgive me, and then they took my baby and I never saw him again. I signed where they told me to sign. The worst day of my life. God be my judge." Deana shook her head. "I'm sure He is, actually."

"Do you need more water?" Monica got up and turned on another light, the one in the corner, and moved the desk lamp toward her to leave Deana in shadow. It did spare her eyes, which she kept closing. Her face was swollen and bleary now. Deana had said her mother used to tell her she mustn't cry, that she looked like one of the dying peonies out in the garden when she did.

"No, thanks, but I think I've run you out of tissue, and it's so late."

"No charge for those. Had you seen Kathleen again?" Monica was trying to be sensitive yet move to the point. She wanted Deana to stop talking about the baby she'd had and lost. Too hard to hear, just too hard, her own tension like a scent in the room Deana picked up.

"No. But she made good. Or her lawyer did. Here's the thing. It wasn't life insurance money. Or not necessarily. See, there was a settlement that she got after the baby was born. While I was applying to schools, I saw it in the paper. She had a settlement for wrongful death. An undisclosed amount. It must have been huge."

"Could you tell me about the accident?"

"What does it matter now? I could have sued. I should have sued. There was just so much shame and embarrassment, and my parents wanted my name out of it. Well, there you go, out of it is the operative phrase for that whole period. I was so out of it. Pain, grief. Grief, pain. I just agreed. You see now how many yeses I would unsay if I could? But I couldn't. Fate is a trap you can't change, I don't think. Except, if I'd never..." Deana gave a small head shake, eyes closed as she did. Then she went on.

"Anyway, it was a police cruiser that hit us. He was driving across the field in the dark with his lights off. He claimed he was investigating an official call, and the dispatcher backed him up, but couldn't produce a record. Everyone knew cops did that, turn their lights off and find a place to take a nap." Deana closed her eyes again, seeing it, wanting to and not. "It was like the stars were everywhere," she said. "Close and big. Tony and I'd been drinking, but we weren't drunk. We were on our blanket in the field above the levee. Naked. Making love."

15

1983

Tony had struggled for months. Tonight, he told himself, he'd do it, he'd tell Deana, even though he stuck to the usual pattern: the back way to the old access road through woods where he'd stash the car in the shadows on the edge. He and Deana would walk the quarter mile to the deserted field above the river and spread the red plaid blanket. Utterly private. It was like the end of the earth there in the place he'd found, safe from intruding eyes and ears. For at least a couple of hours one worry would be eliminated.

He reached over and patted Deana's knee, his hand moving on up her thigh, too far to suggest talking was on his mind, although they would talk. They always talked, and about things he'd not even thought about before. But not about his life away from her. He never mentioned it, thinking it would hurt her. Hadn't the word love gone from him to her? He'd felt the word as he said it first, both familiar and utterly new. Today he'd called himself a lily-livered fake, sick at how he'd wrapped Deana in his arms when she'd questioned, and he'd answered, over and over, just as clearly with a promise: yes, my love, we will have our tomorrows. He didn't know if he'd lied either, that was the damn thing.

The blanket was in the trunk along with the sandwiches—club with extra mayo for him, tuna salad with lettuce and two dill spears for her, a bag of potato chips. His full flask for the two of them. An iced tea for her because the chips made her thirsty, and she didn't like to wash food down with liquor.

When he was home it was so clear. He was a good man. Or wanted to be a good man. If he was sure of nothing else, he was certain he loved his children, and truth be told, he loved his wife, even if there were times lately he'd convinced himself he didn't. Eleven years they'd been together, fourteen if he counted dating and being engaged. She'd been too young, her father had said, and he wouldn't walk her down the aisle before she turned twenty-one.

Bob, a retired jarhead, could be a prick, but he and Tony were friends, something Tony had once thought impossible. The man had become a father to him. He knew exactly what Bob would think of his relationship with Deana. Another reason to put an end to this.

The car bounced. "Let's leave it here," Tony said to Deana now, pulling beneath a cluster of trees. "Bodaciously bad road. Anyway, the car's hidden in case aliens land.

"You've driven in farther than usual," Deana said, peering out the windshield.

"Oh, I won't need a car to do that," he chuckled. He heard himself and knew he should shut up. He gathered his resolve around him and opened his mouth but was too slow. Deana fell right into playfulness, grabbing at his crotch.

"All right, Mr. Dirty Mind."

What could he say then, when he'd started it? He shouldn't have brought her back here.

They carried the paper bag of picnic food and the blanket a good distance from the car, away from the screen of trees, where they'd be able to see the moonrise and evening star. August. Already dusk was coming earlier. At the solstice, it hadn't been fully dark until nine-thirty. They hadn't talked about fall, never mentioned what they'd do in winter.

On the blanket, the sandwiches came out and then the flask. They talked about the life spans of grass and stars, about wanting to visit the Badlands, Yosemite, Acadia. They talked about why neither of them thought much of organized religion, but he said he went to church because of his boys.

"But I think there must be a God. Or something. I don't mean anything like the creation stuff. I understand the Big Bang theory, well, sort of, and I believe in science and evolution. But the soul, I think human beings have a soul. Don't you?" Deana said.

Tony did, but he hesitated. He had an idea where this might be headed. The damn thing was her logic was going to kill him. He sighed. "Yes. I think so."

"Because we are soulmates. We were meant for each other. You know? Like fate brought us together."

He answered by pulling her against him, holding her and caressing her hair with great tenderness. There was no breeze that night. More cicada songs than last time; he thought she'd say something about what that meant but she didn't, and he hoped she wasn't aware.

What Tony felt as he stretched there with Deana lying alongside, her head on his chest, his free hand roving around and under her clothes and hearing her breath catch now and then, was not something he could articulate. He only felt it—again—as powerful, a need beyond his intentions. It was confusing, even mysterious to him that when he was home he could see and decide who and where he would be, but when he was with Deana he couldn't turn away, as if he had no more separate will than one of the planets, though he was a man who liked to think of himself as in charge. Tony imagined it was much easier for Deana. She was single. She'd just fallen in love, the way people do. That could be her singular focus, passion, reason and meaning. He understood what she felt, the soulmate idea, but she wasn't married, didn't have children, didn't have in-laws whom she respected and loved, didn't begin to know that someone's soul could be so divided. Could he possibly explain that to her?

He unbuttoned his shirt and opened his belt. Deana was undoing her blouse and he took over, his fingers too big on the tiny buttons, but it was important to him that she let him.

"I remembered the mosquito repellant," he said. "So, do I get to?"

"Yes, my love. You do."

The last two times they'd made love still as clothed as possible, having been bitten in awkward places several times. After three and a half days of rain raised the river, the mosquitoes had worsened in the moist heat. Deana had taken off her bra but put her blouse back on, and Tony kept his shirt on; both quickly dressed when they were finished and pulled the sides of the blanket over them, nestled together. Now Tony helped Deana out of her shirt and bra and sprayed her lightly with repellant.

"Cover your nipples," he said. "I don't want to poison myself." She laughed easily. "Okay, nylons and panties off. Time for your bottom…half, I mean. Roll over. Who knew that mosquito repellant was such a turn on?"

"Just remember, mister, you're next," Deana said in mock sternness. "Oh, that's cold."

"I'll warm it," Tony said, pulling her toward him, caressing. "Better?"

"Let's get you mosquito-proofed," she said. "I need you."

"Well, you have me." Tony pulled from the flask as Deana sprayed and rubbed him. She still wore her short cotton skirt, though it was bunched around her waist now; he was naked.

"Sit up and let me see you for a minute," he said. "Please, can I take that skirt off? My God, you are such a gift. Are you real?"

He lifted her breasts, admiring how the light silvered them as it did the curve of her cheeks, and when he laid her back down, the half circle of her hips, the shadows of her body when his hand parted her legs. How could he look at her and have her at the same time? How could he say what had to be said, and yet never say it?

"I do love you," Tony said. "You have to know how much I do love you." As he spoke he lifted her hips, slid the skirt down and off. It wasn't much cloth, but he felt her reluctance. She'd never let him do this. He didn't stop. He didn't think it was about the mosquitos, but he quickly sprayed around her waist. He needed her to be as vulnerable as he was, if only in this small way, though it was never his nakedness that had made him so.

He gave her the flask and she lifted her head to drink. He wet his fingers from the flask and circled each of her breasts, then mouthed them.

"Yes," she said. "Yes."

"Yes what?" he asked, confused. Her skirt was already off, her body answering his.

"Yes to what you're asking of me. But I'm asking you, too."

He was surprised that she seemed to understand what he'd felt when he hadn't wanted her to. Not really.

Tony tried to answer by covering her mouth with his. His tears embarrassed him.

She pulled back from a kiss, yeasty and fragrant from the flask.

"Tomorrow?" she said.

"Tomorrow," he said. If he hadn't, he thought he wouldn't be able to make himself go home tonight, which he was going to have to do. He had to have hope. He gathered her in a tight, fierce embrace hoping she'd mistake it for passion, one arm holding her back, the other her rear. Then, he parted her legs again with his knee, and in a moment, he was on top and inside her.

"Tomorrow."

"Yes."

16

2013

"Oh my God, Deana. My God. It was a police cruiser?" Monica said, unable to keep shock off her face or out of her voice. She leaned forward, disbelieving.

"The cop was lighting a cigarette. Never saw us. We'd been drinking, and at the moment, we were very absorbed in each other, to put it delicately. The cop panicked when he felt the thud and threw the car into reverse. That was what crushed Tony's skull. He'd rolled away from me."

"No running lights, in a field, no dispatcher record? Permanent damage affecting your ability to walk unassisted? And you got medical expenses?"

"Uh huh."

"But you'd have signed releases. And this was...you say you were hit in nineteen eighty-three? Thirty years ago? It's too late. Way too late. I'm not going to be able to do anything." No masking her outrage now.

"Yeah. I realize I messed up a long time ago. I don't want to file a suit."

"Oh. What do you want then? Does this have to do with—but you said he's dead—what do you need a lawyer for?"

"I don't have anyone to turn to. This isn't something I can do myself. It wouldn't be the right way." She shook her head once. "I looked in the yellow pages, and mediation is in your listing…and I saw, uh, mediation and domestic relations, so I thought…anyway, I wanted a woman. I don't know if it's the same thing, but I need an intermediary. I want to pay back the money Kathleen gave me, and I want to find my son. That's what I want. My son."

Monica leaned against the back of her chair and closed her eyes. Exhaled. "He's…"

"That's right. He's an adult. He's thirty. I've been more than fair. Maybe more than Kathleen deserved."

"How—"

"I used the money she paid me off with to live on and to finish college. I became a CPA. I was always good with numbers, and that let me work out of a home office—which was good because I didn't have to deal with personnel directors who might have their reasons not to hire the handicapped. I volunteer as a tutor for kids struggling with math, and I mentor a couple of disabled kids—I mean, I try to do some good. Local school stuff. But that's all beside the point." Deana paused, looked out the window, and then back at Monica.

"This might sound ridiculous, but I have a very logical mind. It bothers me that when I think back, nothing I did makes much sense. I've got to know if everything about it was wrong—you know, like there really is no meaning, no plan, no destiny-thing. Or if maybe something valuable did come of all of it—something I couldn't see then. But it wasn't what I thought at the time. Different, maybe, or bigger than I thought? Wouldn't that be something good?"

Monica stuck out her lower lip and blew. The hair above her forehead lifted slightly. She gave a slight shrug but made sure her tone was kind when she answered. "I can't say that I've ever thought about destiny." That was a lie.

Deana shook her head, unsatisfied. She looked frustrated and drained; the unflattering tan sweater she was wearing aged her, too. "But you get it, don't you?" It's taken me all these years to both support myself and save up enough to completely pay Kathleen back. You can hand her a cashier's check. And just so you know, there's no way I'm looking to my son for anything, ever. I've got my own money in a retirement account. I just want to know him, to see if maybe…. Well, you get it, don't you?"

"I get it," Monica said, telling the truth. She didn't add that if something good had come of it, accidental causes weren't ruled out. Or, that they were entirely the creation of another person's intentional intervention. Who was she to say that to Deana, though she questioned why Deana's logical mind hadn't landed there on its own. She wondered if Deana had ever been angry. Why hadn't she been angry, enough to fight back at the time, pay the cost of fighting, risk losing anyway? Monica swore at herself silently. Stupid. Of course she blames herself. Like I don't know how that feels?

Afterward, having promised only to "look into what would be involved," Monica gathered her purse and laptop to leave for home, but before she pulled on her coat, she sat down in the chair Deana had used for the past hours. Monica shook her head and then put her face down, covering it with her hands for a moment before looking back out.

"You married prick," she said, spitting the words to a conjured ghost. "Got yourself something on the side, didn't you? You thought 'oh, I'm her boss, nothing she can do. She can't afford to. Anyway, she makes a stink, I just say she's an unstable liar and get rid of her.'" Monica knew the story and this time it made her mad enough for her and Deana both. Enough is enough.

She drew on her coat one sleeve at a time, checking out her reflection in the window as she did. The coat looked old and dated—which it was—but a new one would be expensive, so she just lined the neck with a white scarf that had silver threads running through it because the metallic look was in style. Outside, it was fully dark. Well after hours now, the building would be eerily quiet. She'd not parked under a streetlight when she came to work; the good spots right in front of the building had already been taken, probably by early arriving professionals whose babies hadn't smeared oatmeal on their suit jackets.

The office wasn't in the Squirrel Hill section of Pittsburgh where she lived. She couldn't begin to swing a Squirrel Hill home mortgage plus office rent, so, though she'd hoped to, she hadn't moved the office to a better location. It was best for the baby that they'd bought the house where they did. It was diverse, tolerant, stable, with lots of professional families. Stanton Heights and other areas in the East End would have been less expensive, but Monica had heard the arguments that maybe the schools in those sections weren't quite as good. In Squirrel Hill, Celeste would grow up surrounded by the children of educated black, white and biracial parents. There were Asians and Latinos, too, if not as many. The house they'd bought even had a small yard nestled under the protective arms of old trees.

It wasn't that the office was in a dangerous area. It wasn't. Still, there was pepper spray in Monica's purse that she moved now to her coat pocket. After she locked the office, she'd have to manage the laptop and purse both by cross-body straps so her hands were free; one for her keys, one for the spray in her pocket, a finger ready on the button while she walked briskly to her car.

II
CHOICE

17

PITTSBURGH, 2013

"Maaaa!" It was a cross between a shriek and laughter as the pajamaed toddler leaned in a wild arc from Angela's arms, lunging for Monica's neck. Monica set her purse down and started to take her daughter but stopped. The toddler's face and hands were chocolate-smeared, sticky with it.

"What's she had? Ice cream? I've got to get out of these clothes," Monica said, careful not to sound annoyed. She was late after all.

Angela set the squirming little girl on the hardwood floor of the entryway where they'd met Monica. "Sorry," she said. I'll hose her off. She heard the car and went nuts. Whoa!" She held Celeste back by the shoulders which started an anguished "Maaaaa!"

"Just let me change, and I'll take her. Celeste, Mama will wipe your hands and face while Mommy goes and puts on old clothes." Grasping a small hand coming at her and fending off the baby as she took a step backward, "No, honey, please don't wipe it on my skirt. I'm happy to see you, too. We'll snuggle lots before you go to bed. Did you and Mama have a good day while Mommy was at work?" Monica called the last out as Angela pushed errant hair out of her own eyes and picked up the protesting baby, heading for the kitchen.

Monica went to their bedroom, eyed the queen bed. In pre-baby times she'd come home from the office and stretched out for twenty minutes without changing if she felt like it. Then, she'd pour a good wine, put All Things Considered on NPR while she and Angie made a simple dinner that did not include macaroni and cheese. She and Angie went out on the weekends, saw movies, danced at clubs, laughed with friends, made love often. They'd had friends over to dinner, read books together and talked about them.

Back when she and Angie were just living together, Monica used to think she was tired at the end of the day, but tired had a different meaning now, as if the language of fatigue had added an entirely new lexicon. But, love had entirely new dimensions, too. They'd made a good life, the two of them. If Angie spent more money than Monica could make, well, she mainly spent it on Celeste, didn't she? Monica remembered how her father had bickered with her mother, complaining about spending money, how she wasn't the one who had to earn it. Monica never wanted to sound like that. She just needed Angie to understand why she had to put in the hours.

Companions, lovers, partners, parents. A life she'd once believed was out of her reach, but she was surprised, gratified, grateful.

And very tired. In beat-up jeans she'd forgotten to put in the laundry on Saturday, Monica headed to the family room that would be littered with puzzle pieces and dolls and way too much plastic stuff that was terrible for the environment, but those big toddler Legos are good for developing coordination and so are riding toys, they'd read. There was no point in picking it all up before Celeste was down for the night—she and Angie agreed.

"Come here, sweetheart." Monica cooed to Celeste. The baby climbed out of Angie's lap and ran across the floor of the great room. Her footie pajamas were pink with little white hearts on them. "She's a lot more sure-footed on this carpet, isn't she? I'm glad we did it," she said to Angie, as she scooped the little one into her lap. Angie had recently bought a much larger area rug, one that covered all the hardwood except the edges. Celeste kept tripping on the other one, and slipping on the hardwood itself, and a couple of times she'd banged her head.

"How's my girl? Look, Mommy's got Goodnight Moon. Want to read it now?" She fingered the baby's sable curls. "You're so pretty. And you're my smart, smart girl."

"Ma," the baby said, sparkling. She was very awake.

"Yes, yes, yes," Monica said. "Mommy. Let's read."

"I'm glad, too," Angela said. "And I don't think it looks bad."

"It's okay. We can always switch back to the one we really like when she's older."

"Right. I'll go see if I can find something for us to eat. Shall I pour you some...?"

"Oh god, yes. As soon as I get her down. Which looks like it shouldn't take more than three or four hours. We'll call you for the night-night kisses."

Later, they had salads and cold chicken in the kitchen. Angie closed her eyes and sighed. "Not a great dinner, I know," she said. "When you're that late, I don't have the time I need to put something together. I can't cook and watch her, too."

"It's fine, I don't expect you to," Monica said. "Honestly, I don't. I'm sorry I was so late today. My four o'clock appointment was a new client. She--anyway, she's a talker, and she was upset, and it took forever. That's why I called you."

"It's a long day. I know yours is, too, but she didn't really nap today, and I'm just shot. I ended up giving her ice cream after her bath and letting her watch Barney, too, because you weren't here. She thought she hit the double lotto. Let me tell you, listening to Barney will put me in the looney bin. Our daughter has very questionable taste." She laughed a little, shook her head, and poured herself more wine from the bottle on the table. It was a lovely chardonnay, Angie's favorite, though Monica would have been fine with something more quotidian. The kitchen lights were on a rheostat and turned down. Angie had lit a candle, which either meant she wanted to talk or she didn't want to look at the mess. "More wine?"

"Sure, a little, but I can't get soused. Got to get up for work."

"You think I don't?" That edge in her voice. Monica knew it meant the day had been too long, and she too late getting home. This was how it would start.

"Ang, honey, I didn't mean it that way. I know it's hard to take care of a toddler all day."

"That baby is my life. You know that. I'm not complaining. I'm just asking you to get home on time. When you stay at work, I end up keeping her up too late, so that she can spend some time with you. She gets a second wind, as you saw, and it's harder than ever to get her down. Then her schedule is off, which means the next day is bad because she's overtired. It's not like she sleeps in, and it's not like I haven't told you this."

"You're right. She's my life, too. She, and you." Monica put her hand on Angela's and squeezed. It's…you know, billable hours. But I get what you're saying."

Angie looked at Monica as if she were going to say more, but she shook her head slightly and didn't. "You said that before." She sighed. "Okay. Thanks. I love you. Tell me about your day."

"Oh lord. You don't want to know."

"Yes, I do."

&

"You can't take the case!" Angela's mouth was an oval of disbelief in her square face, its shape accentuated by her bobbed haircut. Monica noted this in her mind and sighed. She did not want to have this conversation. Not any more conversation, really. She wanted to have another glass of wine, maybe watch the news, or if that was too depressing, an episode of a well-written drama on television. Or go to bed and read the novel she'd started weeks ago and only made it to page sixty something.

"I have to think it over," Monica parried instead of challenging with *why shouldn't I?*

"What's to think about?" Angie leaned back in the kitchen chair.

"There's a lot to it, Ang."

"Was it an open adoption?"

"No. But that was a different era, there wasn't that--"

"Well, ours wasn't open either. I wouldn't have agreed to one. Ever."

"I know that Ang." Monica sighed. "This isn't about our family. That's the point. It's about my client. It's about her. Look, she believed everything that man said to her. He told her he was leaving his wife and kids for her. She believed him. Now men don't even have to say that. It's all normalized. Oh, I suppose, they do just leave sometimes, and get themselves a trophy wife, so they feel young and virile. Until they throw her out too. We are disposable."

"But think about the fam—"

Monica got up and got the wine from the counter. "You want more?" She used the bottle to gesture to Angela's glass. "Can we not talk about this? You were already mad."

"About your being late. This is a different topic. I'm capable of keeping them separate."

"Now I'm suddenly the adversary of people who adopt? Isn't that a little crazy?" She was drained and disheartened, angry but without the energy to argue, especially against Angie's blind spot.

"Look, she thought she was meant to be with this guy. She believed in destiny. It was all she had. She's trying to find a piece of her soul again." What she didn't add, because it felt dangerous, was that they'd each told the other they felt like Celeste was meant for them. How had they meant that, if not in the same way Deana had felt it?

She poured more wine into Angie's glass and her own, corked the bottle, which had only two inches remaining, and refrigerated it. Monica picked up her glass but didn't sit back down, intending to signal that she was finished, she was taking her glass to the family room, or the bedroom, anyplace but here, anyplace but this conversation, which was over.

Angie drank the wine in her glass all at once. She stood up.

"It was her destiny? Fate? Like written in the stars? And that's somehow connected to her doing this?"

Monica sighed. "That's how she feels."

"And you can't point out that the stars have been cold and dead for like a jillion years?" Angie tented her brows, disbelieving.

"I dunno, Ang. It's not my job to argue with her beliefs." Monica smiled and shrugged, like a physical end punctuation to the conversation, hoping it would work. "Want to go watch the news?

Angie was having none of it. Monica knew why. She'd been plain dumb to have said anything about this case. No way Angie was going to let this go now.

Sure enough. Angie went right on. "That baby your client had—he has parents too. A mother, like both of us. There was a contract. It wasn't an open adoption. It's the whole point of a closed adoption."

"He's an adult now. It all happened thirty years ago," Monica came back quickly but her voice still calm, offering facts as an easy fix.

When Angie didn't back down, Monica's temper flared. "For god's sake, Ang, what's going on? Why do you think it's your place to suddenly be a grown man's protector? Isn't that... inappropriate? This isn't your job. He's not a kid in foster care, and he's not my client. His mother's my client."

"No." Shaking her head hard and fast, Angie slapped her open palm on the table in front of her. "Your client's not his mother. She's a woman who relinquished her rights to that role. He can look for that woman if he chooses. She can't. That's the way it works."

Oh, there was a whale that wasn't breaching. Angie wasn't talking about what she was really thinking: how she never had, never would look for her biological mother. Angie had the kind of memories no child should have. She'd been hungry, frightened, dirty, left alone, too hot, too cold. And finally, at three she'd been taken away when someone, maybe her mother's pimp, maybe a dealer, or maybe even a John who had children and felt guilty, someone, anyone, called the child welfare people.

There were big gaps in what Angela remembered, and what she'd ever known. She'd been put in foster care and moved four or five times, maybe more she thought, and that there might have been a lot of other kids. She remembered being scared in the dark, crying. Hungry. She remembered being given to Rose and Bill, though, because they were so nice, so happy to have her. Angie couldn't talk about them now without smiling and getting teary at the same time. She had a pink room, stuffed animals to cuddle, dolls, and a tricycle. Rose taught her how to ride it. New clothes. An older couple, Rose already had some gray in her curly hair. Bill wore thick glasses over laughing eyes, and his hairline started halfway to the back of his head.

Almost from the first day, Rose and Bill were Mom and Dad. They delighted in Angela, and Angie thrived. Later, she learned that the first time her caseworker visited after she'd been placed with them, Rose and Bill had asked to adopt her. After marrying late in their forties, they'd hoped to adopt a newborn but were over the age limit. They'd agreed to try being foster parents to an older child. Angela had been the first child placed with them. How many times, and with what shining combination of reverence had Angie told Monica, "They were over the moon for me. Every kid should have parents who feel that way about her. Like we do for our Celeste." Angie had been nearly six when the state terminated her biological mother's parental rights. Workers had been unable to locate her for two years; she'd disappeared a month after Angie had been taken away.

Rosie, Bill, and Angie had celebrated the day of her official adoption every year with cake and presents all around. Bill and Rose and Angie forever, they'd said. And then, when Angie was nineteen, Bill had a massive stroke, and it was just Rose and Angie to carry on. Ten more years Angie had Rose, then Rose was gone, too. Now Angie put flowers on both graves August sixth of every year. Love, honor and gratitude, the card read. Your daughter forever.

Angie's history was the reason she'd become a social worker and spent her working life with kids in the foster care system. Her victories were seeing those become good adoptive homes. It did happen sometimes. She was determined to give back, as she put it, a quality Monica respected. Admired. And Angela had a strong sense of justice at the same time she was all heart, most especially for her kids. Oh, she'd been easy to fall in love with. How could Monica not love someone so generous with her kindness, and yet so strong? Monica had wondered how Angie would have handled it had she been the one working at the law firm; part of her thought Angie would have done much better than Monica herself had, and it shamed her.

They'd worked and made a good life together. A family. That was what mattered. The mounting debt shouldn't matter, even though it weighed heavily on Monica. Angie wanted Celeste to have the best of everything. Didn't Monica want that, too?

Now Angie said to Monica, "I had a real mother—and father—and I will always love and honor them, not the junkie who couldn't be bothered with rehab either time she got arrested, too busy turning tricks. She'd better never show up."

"I know this, honey," Monica said. "I get it. But all situations aren't the same. You know that. My client isn't your mother, I mean your birth—" Monica started to correct herself, too late for Angela.

"Rose was my mother, and she damn sure never walked away from me. And Rose has nothing to do with this. The point is that the rights of the child are all that matters. There are ethics involved. If parental rights are terminated or relinquished, they don't exist anymore. If the adoptee is an adult and wants to, he or she can search. But if the adoptee doesn't do that, it's their right."

Well, okay. Monica would try to stick to the subject supposedly at hand: her client, a conversation she didn't want to be having. She wished she hadn't said anything. But, they'd always enjoyed talking about what had happened at work, and Monica was used to it. "Dammit, Ang. What about she wants? Aren't there some rights that just go along with being a person? She's a person. I was a person when I worked at the firm. You just don't realize how women get fucked in the workplace."

"What are you talking about?" Angie demanded, her forehead wrinkled, eyes squinting.

Monica's slippers were almost soundless in the hallway as she removed herself to the family room. She'd go to the bedroom, get into bed and turn out the light if Angie followed her. She never should have let the conversation get tangled like that. She'd been tired and careless. Angie didn't know anything about the corporate world, about men who had power over women and their jobs. The man Deana had been so in love with: how different had he been from the Spencer Darcys of the world?

18

PITTSBURGH, 1998

"There's nothing easy about working here, Monica, but I think you're the sort who could get on the partner track down the road. We could use a woman. Make us look good." Spencer Darcy had chuckled at his own little joke.

Monica hadn't had a clue about the correct response to that and worried that the pause she left before answering might hurt her chances. "I'm, um, very much hoping to work here, sir."

"You have to really want it," he said.

Spencer was tall, much taller than she, and he'd come from behind his desk while she was still sitting. He'd looked down at her then as he leaned against the front of his desk, which was enormous, mahogany or cherry, she never could keep those woods straight. She hadn't been sure she was decoding the message correctly at the time, but she'd figured there must have been one.

"I definitely do, sir."

And she had wanted it. She was just about to come out of law school, looking to be a junior associate in her first job. It wasn't a huge firm, which she liked; it was well thought of, and it would give her a chance at litigation down the road. It had been too much to hope for, that she might land a job where getting on the partner track was mentioned as a possibility. She'd sat there, knees and ankles neat beneath her chair, in her one interview suit purchased by her mother, purse in her lap, hair in a plain bun. Don't wear it down to an interview, ladies, the women in her law school class were advised in private. The new twenty-first century wouldn't mean that old boys weren't the deciders.

"You impressed us during your internship, I'm pleased to say. Of course, continuing in the position is contingent on passing the Pennsylvania bar, but I have confidence in you. How much time do you think you'll need to study for it?"

"I can start work—well, may I have the month after I graduate to study? My lease goes through May anyway. I can't afford more time off than that. Then maybe I can take the bar during the summer?"

Mr. Darcy's throaty laugh was deep, rich as the plush light blue carpet. During her internship, when she'd done little more than case research for associates, Mr. Darcy had interviewed her before she started and greeted her in passing. Now he was acting as if he was conversant with her work. Was he? The senior partner's shoes gleamed up like mirrors. "You'll need more than that, I suspect. It's tough. But yes, that's fine. We'll start you July 1."

"Actually, graduation is May 5. Perhaps I could start the first week of June? If that works for the firm?"

He looked surprised, then smiled. "Absolutely." He'd walked around his desk and flipped pages on a desk calendar. "Let's see. How's Monday, June 6, then?"

It would leave her stranded for almost a week; but on the other hand, she'd have to move anyway. "I'll be here. Thank you, sir."

"Welcome aboard, Monica. And make it Spencer, now. You're part of the team. I'll have Sarah set you up for orientation at eight o'clock on the sixth of June."

Later she'd think she shouldn't have told him that she couldn't afford more time off. Had that cued him that she couldn't afford to quit or lose the job? Maybe he'd have figured she could have stayed with her parents for the whole summer to study like a lot of law school graduates who did nothing the summer after graduating but study for the bar exam. He'd have no way to guess that wasn't an option for her. But then, he didn't know she was gay, either, nor how her parents felt about a lesbian living in their home. Not that they didn't love her, of course. As they said.

19

2014

"I thought we should talk more before proceeding," Monica said. "I hope that's okay." For this meeting, she'd thought ahead and put a chair for herself across from the client chair in front of her desk so there was no barrier between her and Deana. Not that she'd decided how honest to be. She couldn't tell the truth, that she was being pressured to refuse the case outright.

"On principle," Angie said. Monica didn't want to remind Angie about her need for billable hours and that this case would involve a lot of them, knowing Angie would immediately take that as another complaint about her spending and derail them into a different argument about what Celeste really needed and what she didn't. To stop the argument, which was growing bitter, Monica had told Angie that she would talk with Deana about the effect on the adoptive family, about leaving it to Deana's son to seek her out if he ever chose, a kind of dodgeball that had at least temporarily mollified Angie. No need for

Angie to know the heart of how much or why she also cared about Deana.

Deana looked down and adjusted where her crutch was positioned, as if she were considering picking it up and making her way out, Monica thought. If so, it would sure make Angela happy, though the idea of Angie having influenced what case she took infuriated Monica. If Angie had her uncrossable red lines about principles, well, so did Monica, and having fought her way free from corporate law, wasn't about to yield control of her solo practice.

But Deana didn't move to get up. "I don't know what more there is to talk about. I told you way more than I had to. I told you everything because I wanted you to understand. I thought you did. I want to hire you to talk to Kathleen, return her money, and then find my son, talk to him—be the intermediary. I know you do mediation, and this is like that. I don't want to mess anyone's life up. I'm trying to do it right." By the time she finished the few sentences, Deana had tears in her eyes.

Monica sighed. "I do understand, but we need to think this through together. That's what I'd like us to do today." Is that true? Monica thought. Am I giving in? Is it all starting again? But Angie's running the show, not Darcy.

"There's the matter of the contract you signed," she said to Deana. "The ethics of it. But, and this is what I really want to talk about; have you thought about the effect on your son's mother? On his family—I mean the adoptive family?" There. She'd told Angie she'd bring this up with the client.

"Yes, I've thought about them. What is this? You think I haven't felt guilty enough? Felt bad enough about myself? Felt like a bad woman, bad daughter, a bad mother? Is that it? Do you think I don't lie in bed and list everything I've messed up? Yes, I've especially been a bad mother. All I want is a chance now."

"I don't mean to put you on the defensive. I just think we should talk about options. What about the registry? Do you even know if he wants to find you?" Monica knew that sounded critical and wished she hadn't said the word *even*. Of course, Deana felt defensive.

"I was under physical and mental duress when I signed that contract. And I've waited until my son is well into adulthood. I'm returning the money I was paid, which I don't have to do. In all of this, did anyone ever think about me?" Deana reached for the tissues on Monica's desk. Monica got up and handed the box to her, and Deana pulled two, but remained dry-eyed. "Tony didn't. Kathleen told me they were trying to have another baby. He told me he was leaving her, and we'd be together. But I don't know anymore. I know I had that baby, and he's all I have left. Maybe he was my destiny. I'm a person, Monica. I'm a person too. Wasn't I meant for something? Aren't I a person too?"

Monica got up and took the two steps to where Deana was seated. She bent slightly, and put her arms around Deana's shoulders, even though it was awkward. "Yes," she said. "Yes." Over and behind Deana's shoulder, she saw sun fanned through the blinds in the southeast window, how it drew line after line of pale winter light on her desk.

&

When Monica worked at Darcy, Anderson and Follett, Anita Hill had already long since made her splash in 1991 and been shot down by the old white boys in the Senate. That the Civil Rights Act of 1964 applied to women in the workplace, and in 1975 the term sexual harassment had come into widespread use thanks to the Working Women United, formed at Cornell University after an employee resigned because her supervisor kept touching her inappropriately hadn't made a lot of difference, not really. Maybe the big problem was the giant pushback. Maybe it was because of Phyllis Schlafly who testified in 1981 that women who were accosted had "asked for it." Seemed that if they were "virtuous" it wouldn't happen. That's what Mrs. Schlafly said.

Was that the reason none of the rulings made a lot of real-world difference? Even though in 1977, three different court cases had said yes, women can sue under the Equal Opportunity Employment Act, men must have taken that with whole shakers of salt. In 1986, the Supreme Court had to uphold that right to sue in Meritor Savings Bank v. Vinson after Mechelle Vinson sued her employer because her boss had forced her to have sex in vaults and basements upwards of fifty times. Monica guessed Mrs. Schlafly must have somehow had a magical knowledge that Mechelle, a black woman whose boss was white, was "asking for it."

Well, one thing Monica knew for sure was that she, for one of many, hadn't asked for it. Not from Spencer Darcy, that was for sure. She knew she was gay and had made the mistake of sharing the information with her parents. She'd known better than to make that mistake with the senior partner, he with the shoes like mirrors, the bleached teeth, the groomed eyebrows. His suits, shirts, ties and socks and pocket handkerchief all coordinated like he exhaled money on his minty breath.

All that was as true as the University of Pennsylvania Bachelor's degree and the University of Virginia Law School diploma on his wall, the license to practice law, all expensively framed. Everything in his office—in the entire firm that bore his name as a senior partner on the masthead—was expensive. Earned success, cases won. He was the president of the state bar association and had held national office. He knew every judge in the city. She heard he knew most of the state appellate judges, too, and around the office it was rumored that soon he'd be on the appeals court himself, and then the state supreme court. And that he wouldn't lose. Spencer Darcy didn't lose. Except maybe a wife. His profile mentioned two daughters, but not a wife. But Monica had thought he was a kind man. He'd been nice, helpful. It was that simple. Was that what had entitled him?

His hands had perfect fingernails. Not that he touched her for the first six months. Did he know when she was not only paying rent, utilities, food, but her grace period was up and her student loan payments had started, too? Did he know that she couldn't possibly afford to quit? Did he know that she didn't have any vacation time accumulated to interview for another job, that it was way too soon, that she wouldn't get another job without a reference anyway? The Senate hadn't believed Anita Hill, a distinguished law professor with an unblemished reputation. Who would believe her, a junior associate who hadn't passed the bar, who had no credentials, no experience, no connections?

20

"You don't get it, Ang. There's so much more to it than that." Monica jostled Celeste in her arms. They were at the playground, a twenty-minute walk against the late February wind, which they'd not figured into their calculations of air temperature and sunshine. It wasn't going well. Not with Celeste, who hadn't a lick of sense about what she could pick off the ground and put in her mouth, and not with Angie, who hadn't a lick of sense about when to ask her about that birth mother who wanted Monica to find her son. That was, apparently, all Angie had absorbed. "But can we just focus on Celeste now? I mean, let's just be with our daughter and keep her from eating sticks and dog shit, okay?"

The second meeting with Deana hadn't gone well, though, not that Monica had told Angie. After Monica brought up the registry, whether she'd thought about the effect on the adoptive family, Deana had been so distressed that Monica suggested they finish their discussion another time. She'd had to help Deana up from the chair; when she did, she'd put an arm around Deana's shoulders to steady her. All Monica had really accomplished was getting Deana terribly upset for nothing. And now Angie wouldn't let go, gnawing a hole in their fragile truce.

As she handed Celeste a cracker, Angie dogged the subject. "No. I have to know that she's my daughter forever, and that you're not going to be okay with it when someone shows up in thirty years and says, *oh hi, I'm her mother*. That you won't say, *that's cool, I'll help you with this*. I can't do this. I'm not built this way." And then there were tears, not usually Angie's style.

Monica put Celeste down—the baby immediately squatted and started parting the grass, doubtless looking for a pebble to put in her mouth and choke on—but she needed two hands to rummage through the diaper bag for, what else,? A baby wipe to hand Angie. There weren't any tissues.

"I don't need that." Now came the anger. "What I need is to know we're together on this." Angie swooped to pick Celeste up. "For god's sake, don't let her eat that." She pulled a clod of dirt from the little girl's hand and tossed it. "No, no, honey," Angie said to the baby in a completely different, gentle tone. "We don't eat that. Not good."

Monica tried to defuse. "What? I thought dirt had some good minerals." She gave what she thought was her warmest most supportive smile, put her hand on Angie's arm, and said, "Let's put Celeste back in the swing. I don't want her to see you upset. Maybe we can talk when she's napping."

Angela gave a weary sigh. "I am upset. And here's something only the stay-at-home mother knows, lately her naps have been for shit. She's getting more teeth. I did tell you that."

"That's why everything is going in her mouth."

Angie had been right that Celeste's naps were for shit while she was cutting these new teeth. They didn't get to talk again until after eight that night. Monica opened a bottle of expensive chardonnay and poured two glasses, too tired by then to lay a fire in the fireplace even though it was cold enough, for sure. She turned the lights down anyway and picked up enough of the toys in the family room that it looked less chaotic. She found that if she kept her eyes at chair rail level or higher, she saw hung pictures, pleated lamp shades in their comforting neutrals, and the backs of upholstered furniture. The room was downright recognizable. She dreaded this conversation, one that she'd planned not ever to have. Now she didn't see another way. Angie loved her; Monica was sure of that, so maybe Angie could recognize the woman she loved even as she'd been five years ago, in the ruin of her former life, and even to empathize. To accept. Then surely it wouldn't be a reach too far to accept Monica's taking Deana's case?

Monica took a breath, sat on the couch, and infuse her voice with warmth while looking both relaxed and serious. "Hey, honey, let's talk about this...thing," she said, patting the cushion next to her. "Come, sit by me. I don't want you to be upset. I can explain it better." She plumped a decorator pillow, one of the red ones that used to bring out the rich amber of the hardwood flooring, now covered up for Celeste. "You can put this behind your back. I know it's bothering you."

Angie came over to the couch but remained standing and didn't pick up the wine. "I don't know what there is to explain better. I know how I feel about it."

"Can I just tell you about what else is involved? This client's situation was nothing like ours in the way you're thinking of. It's that I understand what happened to her in a different way. Just hear me out."

Angie sighed. Then she sat. Monica handed her the wine, lifting the glass to her first. The side table light shone through it like a small white fire at the center.

"You know how I wasn't out when we met. You know how Mom and Dad are. Even now—"

Angie narrowed her eyes and tilted her head. "What does this have to do with them?" Her tone was an accusation that said, this is just more crap.

"Nothing, sorry. I was just getting to what it was like when I was hired at the firm."

"I'm seven years older than you are. I was around. I was supporting myself, like a big girl. I know perfectly well what it was like when you were hired at the firm. In case you've forgotten, I am also gay. This isn't about being gay. It's about the children."

Monica knew Angela's history, more open and adamant than her own by a distance, and she saw that Angela was in no mood to listen. She could even tell this discussion would go nowhere, quite possibly never would, and that she should stop. There's a time and place to pull into a rest area and think things through. Later, Monica thought that someday maybe she'd learn when to stop driving ahead full speed when it was plainly a bad idea because the vehicle was about to go over a cliff. She hadn't intended to blow up, not meant to at all. But she did, and then, in the way of spilled wine and secrets, the good carpet of their life was ruined. Every word was true, but later Monica would wish she could unsay it all.

"Dammit, it's not about the babies, Angie. And it's not about you, either. It's about the men and what they did to women and got away with. Still do, too often, way too often. Why I understand the situation my client was in and feel for her. That's what I want to tell you about. So shut up and listen for once."

21

1998

He'd done nothing but mentor her at first. Other than correct her to "Spencer" a couple of times when Monica called him Mr. Darcy, there was nothing even personal. He'd provided her with Pennsylvania state bar review material and answered questions. It was all professional; he'd twice referred her to another partner, saying "That's Henry's area of expertise," or "Better ask DeCew about that one. I recall an appellate judgment that might be relevant, and he'll know."

Even the first time he put his hand on her waist as they went through a door, Monica's radar didn't switch on. When he encouraged her to wait and take the bar in February instead of the July after she graduated, saying that he didn't see how she could possibly be ready, he was helping her; it wasn't reasonable, he said, take your time and don't risk failing. The firm gives you a year to pass the bar, so you could take it next July. We'd give you those extra few days. But you'll be fine in November. Monica heard that and thought she'd landed herself into some kindly safety blanket, even that she had a protector. She'd later think of herself as a complete idiot.

She stayed at work late many nights to use the law library and the review materials the firm bought for new associates. She noticed he too worked late a lot of nights but sometimes other associates were there as well so it signaled nothing. Every now and then Spencer would drop by her office on his way out to pick up a sandwich, and he'd come back and ask what he could bring her. She always said, "I'm fine, thanks, don't need a thing." A half hour later, he'd show up with a coffee and a turkey sandwich, or a coke and tuna on wheat, and say, like an apology, "I didn't know what you like, but at least it's something. I can't have junior associates faint from hunger. It's bad for the firm's reputation."

She'd try to thank him, try to pay for the meal, and he'd set it down, wave her off, and leave.

There was nothing to make her uneasy. Unless gratitude and a sense of being in debt were to make her uneasy, which they didn't until it was too late.

It was just all so well done, so very well done. When an inexperienced, in-debt, insecure, in-the-closet lesbian who is terrified of being seen as an ingrate and ending up unemployed, unreferenced, and unemployable has her boss move from putting his hand on her waist as he opens a door for her to squeezing her shoulder, to touching her hair, and stepping back doesn't work, she's afraid. She avoids being alone with him. He's the boss and has unfettered access. He asks her out, and she politely declines saying she has other plans, but thank you. He says he'd wanted to discuss her work and let's make it soon.

After the first and second red flags, she's careful about how she dresses, skirts always fully knee-length, to hell with the shorter styles in her closet. Thicker heel than the fashion, too. She has a good body, always has, but does nothing to flaunt it. Tames her wavy hair into a bun almost every day. Doesn't give up makeup—there's a bit of vanity in her; she's still a woman after all—but it's conservative, tasteful, just not sexy, not sexy in any way.

Monica knows what her fantasies are, knows what she thinks about. She knows she likes women. But she's never actually been with one. Just a few kisses and some fumbling around, just breasts and ass, in college with a girl who thought she might be gay and decided she wasn't, which disappointed Monica immensely. She'd tried it with guys, in high school and her first two years of college, a much bigger, different disappointment.

Then the three-year chastity belt of law school; her study group was all male. If there was another gay woman in her class, Monica didn't know it. If there was, maybe she, too, was afraid there could be consequences to coming out in the boys' club. Monica had, after all, tested the water with her own parents and found out it was inhospitable for staying afloat.

But she thought then, and thinks again every time she remembers, I knew. I knew way before Spencer that I was gay. It was all wrong for me. It wasn't violent rape, but it was against my will, and he knew that, he forced me, so it was rape. He used my vulnerability. He knew I couldn't quit, couldn't get another job without having passed the bar, without any references. He knew I was helpless. It was all so wrong.

Monica has replayed scene after scene in her head. Could she have averted Darcy's advances? Had this happened to other women? There were no women senior partners; one associate was a woman, but she was severe, buttoned-up, her straight-line mouth like the top of the T, not a bit of a come to me if you need any help aura about her. And she didn't have power with regard to a senior partner. Nor, of course, did the couple of women secretaries, obvious mothers and grandmothers who bustled out at five every weekday, pushing away from desks littered with pictures of children like so many bright flowers. Talking with them about it was unthinkable. So, what should she have done when he backed her against the wall of his private inner office, the office no one entered without clearly hearing him call "Come in." When he backed her up and said, "I just have to let you know that I think you're beautiful," and very lightly kissed her on the lips then stepped away and went right back to work, picking up the file he'd been looking for on his big mahogany desk as though nothing had happened: should she not have answered the question he asked her then about Branson v. Conrad. Should she not have breathed out a professional response about the case as though nothing had happened? Was it a test? Had she passed or failed?

And the next time, when his hand went to her breast, so briefly. What should she have done then? And when he pulled her to him, and she backed away, but he just pulled her in harder until she felt that he was hard, what should she have done? What about when he slid his hand up her straight skirt, so smoothly the skirt didn't even bunch awkwardly around her rear, she realized in retrospect. Was that a practiced move?

He went up the side of her thigh and then his hand was cupping her ass. She had her pantyhose on, yes, but he was under her skirt and pulling her against him, feeling her, moving his hand, and then he'd worked fingers between her legs from behind, lifting one of her legs just enough to slide one of his legs between hers. Each time, a little more. Each time, just a little more. A kiss, a feel, a grope, then his hardness, his tongue probing her mouth, wait until he let her go. Back to work.

How long until he unzipped his pants?

She tried to discuss "our professional relationship" with Mr. Darcy, as she called him when she raised the subject to object to his advances just once, after a case review. Early on, not after he kissed her the first time, when she was too rattled and repulsed, but after he touched her breast. His tone was even when he answered, staring her down, like a dare. "Your reputation is of concern to you, I imagine. It would be very unwise for you to pursue this line of discussion—with anyone. I can't imagine that you would give me reason not to recommend to the partners that you be retained here. Presuming you pass the bar, which I'm confident you will. I think that so far, you're doing everything you need to be doing."

She'd thought she would cope by avoidance, by creating excuses, ducking him.

It was a little over a week later that he sought her out, dropping some hard copies for a client to sign on her desk himself rather than having his administrative assistant print and deliver them to her. "I'll need you stay late," he said, his baritone smooth as good whiskey, nothing amiss, "to run over some points of Pennsylvania administrative law."

She'd not been staying late, to avoid him. That was the night his hand snaked up her skirt the first time, and he told her he wanted her to have a study session after work on Tuesday nights. The partners all mentored a new associate, he said, and that it was up to him, and a matter of pride, to make sure she passed the bar. She lied and said she had to help her parents a lot of nights, that her father was sick. He told her to work it out.

She went to a doctor, got a prescription for Valium, said she was anxious about the bar exam, and it was interfering with study. No, she didn't think it would help to talk to someone. She took it at night, so she could sleep, and half the prescribed amount during the day so she could get through. It's not like it happens every day, Monica told herself. Not even almost every day. Just after work if she couldn't fly it past him that her parents needed help again, and otherwise, if his secretary was out and the partners were in court or meetings. She tried to arrange out-of-office appointments when the office was too empty by turning herself into a regular schedule snoop hoping the court calendar worked out in her favor.

But she didn't quit. She couldn't quit, not then, not yet. It went on. She berated herself, even wrote to Anita Hill, but did not get an answer. She had to pass the bar, so she took the valium and kept working. She was frightened, disgusted, and blamed herself for ducking, avoiding, failing to avoid, for working and putting up with it, working and trying to save herself.

She saw a few women on the side, nothing serious, not much of a social life, no time for it anyway. Anyone in the field knows that a junior associate is expected to work eighty hours a week. But she had just enough dates to know that nothing like love took root or bloomed with any of them. She blamed herself.

Until two things happened. She passed the bar. And she met Angela.

Passing the bar astonished Monica. She'd been certain she failed. One of the crucial essay questions—one which should have but hadn't been covered in her preparation—was about Pennsylvania administrative law, which was an obscure specialty. She'd panicked and punted.

Tried to come up with what she knew was bullshit, but having to try, she'd spent too much time on it, and not left enough time to finish the multiple-choice questions. That was a huge mistake; there wouldn't have been a penalty for guessing on those. She'd left the computer station at the end of the second test day drained and despairing, sick at what it would be like waiting for the result, opening that email, and once she told them she'd failed, either being let go from the firm or reminded that she could take it a second time after six months. But could she possibly do that? Endure more of Spencer to try again? She couldn't do that. She couldn't. Her loans weighed like a boulder on her chest at night. She'd stay until the results came, she decided, try to make at least one payment ahead. She couldn't think past that.

Monica waited two weeks in something of a fatalistic fugue for the results of the bar exam she expected to end everything. Then, although the email wouldn't come for over six more, she was surprised out of it by the happy, bizarre accident of meeting Angie, which, at the time, Monica thought proved that maybe there was a god after all. Even a no-kidding real God that had something to do with life and meaning. And if so, She was, indeed, good and there was hope.

22

2014

"That's terrible! Terrible. He was a creep—a criminal. That shouldn't ever happen to any woman, least of all you. Angela's face had been a frisson of disbelieving horror, and Monica thought her wife understood, that she'd relent, that those were only tears of sympathy in Angie's eyes.

"Why didn't you tell me?"

"It wasn't like—" Monica started but Angie cut her off, red-faced.

"—He was forcing you all the while we were getting so close? He was forcing you and you didn't trust me enough to tell me? My god, I even met him at that one office party. You married me without telling me?"

"Ang, that's not the point." Monica heard her voice go up. She didn't want to plead, but she was. "I didn't even know you when he started up. Did you hear me? I was just out of law school, hadn't taken the bar. I was ashamed. I kept trying to figure out how it was my fault.

I didn't want you to think I was that flawed...or weak... or dirty. Which was how I felt. I didn't want you to see me that way. I wanted to see myself the way you saw me."

Angie didn't say anything. What more did she want to hear?

Now there was a mix of begging and raging in Monica's voice. "I had no parents to go to, like my client didn't. But you always did have, by the way. I had no money. I had huge debt, which I still have. I had no place to go. I had no choices. Deana had no choices when she had her baby. The choices were all taken from her. It's about helping her claim back some power in her own life."

"No. You're telling me two things. You did it to keep a job, and you hid it all from me. All the time we were dating and when we were having sex, you were letting him rape you? Do I have that right? Did you ever think I should know that? Did you ever think that maybe I could have helped?"

Angie slid further into a corner of the couch, away from her by a couple of feet more. "I don't even know who you are. How can I trust you now? Would you sell me and Celeste out for something you decide is more important? Like this case?"

"Fuck you, Ang, I was scared out of my mind that I'd lose my job and lose you, too," Monica flared. "You ever think maybe I was protecting you, protecting us? Maybe I was afraid you'd react exactly the way you are reacting. You know damn well I left as soon as I could. I had to pass the bar. I was trapped. How can you not get that?"

It felt like a country separated them, not the middle cushion. Angie's eyes were narrowed, and her mouth hard. Monica forced herself to stifle her anger.

"Good lord, Ang. I'm not sure what we're fighting about now. This isn't about Celeste. You were a little kid when—and Deana's son is an adult. I'm sorr—"

Angie wouldn't let her finish. "Two separate issues. What you did then and what you're doing now. Both are about whether I can trust you, and I've just learned I can't. Now I find out what you did to be a lawyer. What does this client need a lawyer for?"

"I told you. Mediator—so" Monica tried again, realizing that could be a potholed road. "—look it's completely different from your situation, it's not like what happened to you. When your biological mother—"

Angie got red in the face again. Monica knew she wanted to get loud, except she wouldn't risk the baby hearing.

"We are not discussing me," Angie hissed. "Or my parents, and definitely not the horrible person who skulked around my family. We are discussing that I can't trust you now." Her eyes shone, and Monica wasn't sure if they were wet or fiery.

Through the baby monitor they heard Celeste, a couple of small cries. Monica raised her eyebrows, a question. Angie shook her head. "She'll put herself back to sleep. It's the teeth. She's looking for her pacifier." A moment later, the baby was quiet again.

"Okay. But, see, this client had no choices back then, and I didn't—" Monica started another sentence, but Angie was ready.

"No, that line won't work. You said she believed it was her destiny. But destiny isn't a choice, right? Destiny is what is set out for you, out of your hands. People who believe in destiny say that something was all planned out for them, by something greater than themselves."

"I guess…"

"Well, I don't believe in destiny, that bullshit.. We're the mothers of our fates, the ones who are responsible. Whatever meaning something has, it's because we create that meaning and live up to it and are faithful to it." Angie was one of the few people Monica knew who could get furious and still argue logically. It used to amuse Monica; she'd say that Angie should have been a lawyer. It wasn't amusing now.

Monica's stop sign hand gesture went up, something she knew Angie hated. She remembered and put it back down. "Hold up. You yourself said you felt like Celeste was meant to be ours."

"I never meant that like a preordained destiny. I meant that you and had created the home and the love and the security so that when that beautiful sweet little girl turned up needing parents, and our hearts were ready, there was a fit. I never meant that it wasn't a choice. There are always choices. I had one. I became Celeste's mother. And I have a choice now." Angie stopped and was quiet. She looked at Monica, a challenge.

"What are you saying?"

"I'm saying don't do this. Can't you see how hard it's going to be for me to trust you now? I want to—but this—can't you see that your taking this case is another betrayal of everything you know is crucial to me?"

"This is about a woman I can help. I get what she feels. She was alone and ashamed—and shamed. She was damaged and she's trying to make herself whole. She's trying to make some sense of what happened to her. This case has nothing to do with you or with us," Monica objected with an adamant head shake, her mouth setting into hard lines. "Whatever you think about me or my past, you do not get to run my practice. You do not get to be in control of me. You don't get that power."

"You've lied to me for years. That was your choice to keep that from me. I'm begging you to make a choice now." That was the other thing about Angie. Black or white stubborn. So damn sure. Always sure she was right.

Monica swallowed, closed her eyes, waited. "For god's sake, Angie. I felt forced to do what I absolutely didn't want. I can't believe you're using it against me this way. That's what I was most afraid of back then, that you wouldn't understand. And now you're trying to make me do something. I can't let that happen again."

Angie didn't back down. "You sort of took my choice away, didn't you?" The anger drained from her voice then. "If I'd known, I would have chosen you." Angela's face was red, which always happened when she got emotional. "Can't you choose me now?" She paused, and her eyes filled as she thought of something else to be upset about. "Maybe you'll go back to that way someday? Straight? You did it once. How can I know?"

Monica spoke slowly, precisely, controlling frustration now. "You're not even listening to me." Angie started to interrupt, but Monica went right over her. "No, listen to me. Angie, whatever you're thinking, get it out of your mind. Yes, at first I thought he was a nice man. I thought he was one of the good ones. That's all. There are some good ones, Ang. And then it was too late, I was out of options. Do you think I'm the only woman this has happened to? Are you seriously that naïve? Or that stupid? Or just that lucky? In your little world where it's pretty much all women working in it?"

She saw Angie start to open her mouth, an argument gathering on her face, and wouldn't allow it. "No, Angie, try to remember I left as soon as I could set up my own practice. Remember? I relied on your contacts. I couldn't get a damn reference from my damn boss. Do you have any idea what that means? Even if the partners gave me a decent one, what he would say quietly would kill me for a job with another firm. All of law school would have been for nothing. Tell me the point of that. Why do you think I'm still struggling? I can't use my internship or first job as a reference."

Angie shook her head. "Well, apparently you could make it stop because you did. You are capable of making a choice."

"Right. Of course. The woman gets blamed for what the man does. If she speaks up, she's a liar. If she doesn't, well, obviously she was asking for it." Monica was hot-faced, dry-mouthed, wet-eyed. "Maybe some version of this argument is exactly what I was most afraid of."

Angie ignored that. "You know what security with Celeste means to me, and why. You even know what Rose and Bill went through with that...that horrible woman... later, after they adopted me. There's nothing I've kept from you. I don't care what happened to your Deana—

she was an adult just like you were an adult. I know what happened to me and my family. I can't handle this. I can't live with it. I thought I could trust you, but I don't know who you are anymore." She swiped at her eyes. "I'm going to check on Celeste and go to bed."

Angie set down her glass too hard on the coffee table and left the room. She hadn't finished the wine, and it sloshed onto the wood. It was cherry, expensive, a piece Angie had picked out before they had Celeste, and she was always trying to protect it, but now she didn't clean up the spill. Angie always cleaned things up. Monica watched Angie's feet as she went, in bright yellow socks patterned with green bananas. Angie loved crazy socks. The sound of her footsteps receded as she disappeared. Monica wiped up the wine and stuck the soggy napkin into Angie's glass.

Monica stayed on the sofa, legs gathered underneath her. She heard Angie in the baby's room, closed her eyes, listening to the small tender sounds of mothering, that side of Angie she especially loved. Finally, she got up and refilled her own glass for the third time since she'd started defending herself. No more, she promised. No more. No one is going to take away my power. Not again.

23

Angie felt old. Old, worn out, and beat-up, like one of Rose's rag rugs that she used to throw over the clothesline and hit with the broom to shake the dust free. Only too much of the dust was still there, and each dust mote was a vague floating memory of her life before Rose and Bill were Mom and Dad, and year after year after year wasn't enough to beat the dusty memories out of her. She might have forgotten, she wanted to forget, and she'd tried. She might have except for the woman who'd stalked her. That's what Angie had called it, once the word was in her vocabulary. The woman who'd claimed to be her mother.

It hadn't happened until sometime when she'd been in elementary school. Angie didn't remember when she'd first seen the woman sitting on the ground beyond the metal fence enclosing the playground. It was during recess. She was staring at the children, all of them, her face pressed against the wires. Angie remembered that it was sunny, and she had on her red sneakers, and Melody Buck had tripped and got her knee bloody while trying to jump double dutch. A teacher went over to talk to the woman because some of the kids were asking why she was there. Angie had been going down the slide when the woman pointed to her.

It wasn't her teacher on the playground, but another third-grade teacher. "Is that your mother?" she'd asked Angie.

"No, my mom isn't here, she's at home," Angie had said.

The teacher had gone back shaking her head and frowning as she walked toward the fence, and Angie saw her point to the road. The woman had talked back, and it looked like she got mad, and was maybe yelling at the teacher. Angie couldn't hear, but saw this, and when the woman pointed at her again, she got scared and made Melody go with her to get behind the cluster of boys who were on the jungle gym. It wasn't like there was any place to hide. The teachers had to be able to see everybody; hide and seek games weren't even allowed. They could see that the teacher got the woman to walk away, even though she kept looking back. She'd been in ratty clothes, a long skirt, untucked blue shirt, a scarf tied under her chin; that was all Angie remembered later.

"She said she was your mom?" Melody said. "That's not your mom! I know your mom." She was Angie's best friend. She had a broad face and shiny black hair that her mom put in two braids with ribbons that matched her dresses or tights, which made Angie jealous. But Melody craved Angie's red sneakers, so they were even. They had sleepovers sometimes when their moms let them.

"I know. Who was that?" Angie asked the teacher.

"I don't know who she was," Mrs. McMahon said. "I'll let the office know. Sometimes people have mental illness, you know, or they use drugs, and they think things that aren't true. Don't worry. You're safe at school." But the school had called the police and notified Rose and Bill.

After that, it had happened twice more. A police car came, and Angie got taken to the office, off the playground. Or maybe it was three more. Even now, Angie was confused because there was that other time that Rose had grabbed her in the grocery store and hustled her to the car, and wasn't it after that Bill had stayed home from work for a week? They didn't let her take the bus that year or the next. One of them took her to school and picked her up. Really, there was no proof it was her birth mother. How would she have found Angie? It made no sense.

Rose and Bill were frightened. And their fear frightened Angie. They tried to be nonchalant, but Angie felt it when they hugged her, made themselves let go, felt their eyes, how often they checked on her when she played in the yard, knew they wanted her in the back yard, not the front. And then they'd moved, too. Angie remembered being upset about changing schools and leaving her friends. Rose and Bill had said it was because Bill got a better job, but it was after the grocery store incident, which Rose said was because she'd forgotten her wallet. But hadn't somebody come up to them in the cereal aisle? Rose said that person just wanted money.

After several years, it seemed the fear faded, but that it had been put there was unforgivable. That was the frightened dust that time would never beat out of her.

24

Long after she knew the baby was settled and Angela had gone to bed, Monica still sat, her legs growing numb, which she ignored. She'd pulled the fringed white afghan her grandmother knit the year before she died—though her eyes were bad then, the handwork was still perfect in the wedding ring pattern she'd chosen, hopeful on her granddaughter's behalf—from where it was folded over the upholstered arm of the couch and covered her lap.

"This will be for your marriage bed, sweetheart," she'd said, stroking Monica's hair. And Monica had, indeed, put it on the bed she shared with Angie, even if that bed hadn't been exactly what her grandmother had had in mind.

She rested her head on the couch back, exhaled, and allowed her eyes to fill. She'd become expert at not crying while she worked at the firm, able to shut that response down. It had been the smaller part of what she'd had to make her body do, really. Now, it was more foreign for tears to come at all. Angie had, of course, noticed that, not knowing the reason. "It's okay to cry," she'd said back then with such kindness.

And Monica had, then, overwhelmed when they'd brought Celeste home, so tiny, so perfect. So unimaginable, the gift in their lives. So large, so absolute the love.

She'd not even known that she wanted a child in the way having Celeste seemed to expose a gaping emptiness that had been there all along and at once fill it. Angie had been the one to be sure. Monica and Angie had even met because of a child. Not Celeste, of course, but a child in a court case; Monica the court-appointed guardian ad litem, and Angie the social worker testifying because she worked for the agency that handled the baby's foster placement.

They hadn't had a lot of contact, both too busy, but they did meet in advance of court. Monica had gone to the agency, as an excuse to schedule herself out of the office. Angela's office was on the run-down side of town, and her office was shabby, the furniture made of pressed wood, the seat coverings showing long wear, yet Monica was struck by how free Angela had seemed, unafraid to look like herself, whatever that means, Monica mused at the time, knowing that she meant unadorned, even butch. And to show her feelings: Angie'd been unabashed about her devotion to the toddlers whose placements she oversaw.

"These kids need so much, and they deserve it. They are so beautiful, so trusting," she said. "There's so many I wish I could take home with me." She wasn't jaded, even though the cheaply-framed diplomas and state social work license hung on the tired tan wall showed she had seven—

no eight—years more experience than Monica, who was already carrying cynicism like an invisible backpack.

Two weeks later, they were upset together by the outcome of the case. Angela had been enraged.

"There is no way, just no way, that biology should trump the best interest statute. But here we go again, the judge just gives them back to the natural parent, as he calls them. He just, damn, doesn't see it. Oh god, I need a drink. Is it too early to drink? It's 3:45, that's not too early. Wanna get a drink? We can order wings and call it an early supper. Throw in a salad if we want to be healthy. I don't know, maybe they don't have salads. We can eat the fruit out of fruity drinks. Oh, I know. Olives are vegetables, but I don't like martinis. Shit, I'm babbling. I'm upset. I'm not going back to the office. Do you have to?"

"Nope. I can knock the paperwork out tomorrow. I say fruity drinks and wings sounds disgusting. But a bottle of the beer and wings, now that could work fine." It was true enough about writing it up in the morning. If she didn't get plastered, she'd go back tonight and if Darcy's car wasn't in the lot, she'd get it done. Otherwise, she'd get into the office by six tomorrow morning and fill out the damn form and write the narrative. It wasn't his thing to come in early.

"There's a place I like," Angie said. "It's just women… would you be…comfortable there?"

Monica hesitated. Would anyone from work see her? "Where is it?"

"On Third St. We'd need to drive, but you could follow me. Or you could leave your car where it is, and I could bring you back to it."

She was unlikely to be seen. "That sounds fine. Thanks, I'll ride with you, if it's halfway convenient to bring me back to my car."

Later, when Monica was on her third beer, and she had taken off her jacket, undone the top two buttons of her blouse, and let her hair loose from its bun while Angie had had her second gin and tonic, Monica leaned across the table and asked, "So how did you know? I mean, I'm sure no one at work does. I'm careful. It wouldn't exactly help me at the nice old boys firm."

"I wasn't positive. I thought you might just suggest another place, and I'd have said okay. You hide it well, but I caught you looking at me and got the vibe. You know."

"I sort of do, sort of don't. I haven't had much of a life. I mean, I've never even been to a place like this. Never had anything...real." Women were slow dancing now, locked in each other's arms in the dimly lit lounge.

"That must be so hard. The work situation, I mean," Angie said, and for just a moment, Monica thought Angie had guessed. Then she realized that Angie just meant the hiding, pretending to be straight.

"I'm just used to it, I guess," Monica said. "I was really lucky to land a position. There's a possibility of partner track down the road."

"So...it's worth it to have no life?" Angie said it with a rueful smile to convey *I'm dubious about that one.* "I couldn't do it," she said. "Couldn't do it. Well, maybe wouldn't do it. But everyone's different, I know. Oh, hey, I'm sorry. Oh, Monica. It's okay to cry. I know it's hard to even think about coming out. It's okay, you don't have to, and it's okay to cry." Her voice had been the warmest, kindest Monica had heard.

She'd gotten up and come around to Monica's side of the booth, slid in next to her and put her arm around Monica. Gentle, supporting her, slipping a napkin into Monica's hand the way a loving mother would. "It's okay to cry." Then, when Monica had stopped, and had wiped her eyes and straightened up, Angie had said, "Hey, wanna get together again? This has been fun. And you just told me you're not seeing anyone. Maybe you could have just a little bit of a life? No one will know but us unless you decide otherwise."

This time Monica didn't hesitate. "I'd like that," she'd said.

25

Deana sat, huddled over her hands, already getting upset again.

"I don't get it, Monica. What do you want to talk about now? Can't I just sign the contract? The fee is no problem. I told you that. It was so hard to tell you all this. I've never told anyone. Well, my parents knew, but not because I told them." She put her palms up in a gesture of defeat.

Monica had put herself behind her desk. A barrier to keep her from feeling too much. She didn't want to feel anymore. A hint of maybe-early spring light streaming in the window onto her desk highlighted where she'd not dusted, a ring where she'd set down a wet cup, spots where she'd missed when she watered the plant on the shelf. Too long ago, obviously. It was wilted. She could see evidence of her own carelessness, not the least of which was the client seated in front of her. She'd been stalling with this client, putting off appointments, and it wasn't right.

"Deana, I just need to disclose some things in my own background. I don't want not to have told you, in case you want someone else. I can make a referral if you feel I'm not offering objective opinions to you."

"Why? And what does objectivity matter? I want you to be on my side. Can't I have somebody on my side?"

Of course, she was right. Monica had made the very same argument to herself. But Deana's face changed suddenly as she bolted from broken to angry to terrified. Monica had no space to respond anyway. The woman who had been strong enough to work steadily, diligently, to ready herself to meet the son she'd always wanted, always loved, had come to her propelled by hope.

"Wait a minute. You're making no sense. You're putting me off again. Have you found my son and there's something you don't want to tell me?"

Oh lord, this is not going well, Monica thought. "No, no, not at all." She shook her head.

"I don't believe you. Where is he? What's happened to him? Is he dead? Sick?"

"No, no."

"Then it's Kathleen. You went to her, and she's paying you more. That's illegal. I know that's illegal. And unethical."

"Absolutely not. I would never under any circumstances do such a thing."

"Then tell me the damn truth. What is going on?" Deana was looking straight at her now, demanding. Her hand was on the top of her crutch and Monica wondered if Deana wanted to use it as a weapon. She was upset enough. And it would be fair, Monica figured, the least she deserved for fucking this up so badly.

"Deana, listen to me. It's nothing like you're thinking. I just want to keep the lines straight and make sure I only act in your best interest. I didn't tell you before because my personal life shouldn't have anything to do with what I do for you. I've just realized that it's hard for me to keep things separate, and I might tangle it up. I was sexually harassed by a boss who took advantage of me in a job. So, that's one thing."

Deana sat back in her chair, finally quiet. "Thank you for telling me. Do you think I'm doing something wrong?"

Monica sat back. So much for being honest, she thought. Fat lotta good it's done me lately.

"No, I don't think you're doing anything wrong. What happened to you was wrong."

"Then please. Please. Help me. I'm trying to stand up for myself for once. And yes, I do recognize the irony of the expression." She half-lifted her crutch. "Better late than never."

Monica closed her eyes. She knew what Deana felt, the helplessness, like being an overturned turtle needing one human hand to make things right. That Deana felt she had to plead was heartless. Worse, Monica suddenly felt like she was adding injury on top of the harm that had already been done to Deana. Another layer of rejection, another failure to support, to help.

And surely Deana had guessed that Celeste was adopted. The baby's picture was right there, and the baby was bi-racial, her enormous expresso eyes, light brown skin, and clusters of soft dark curls were dead giveaway compared with the pale tone of Monica's own skin. And Angie, holding Celeste, was clearly white. Monica wasn't about to discuss it more, and certainly would not tell Deana what she'd never told anyone and never would now.

Well, Monica figured, she'd best finish the job just in case Deana had overlooked the obvious. "I needed to make sure I was completely upfront with you, that you also know I have an adopted baby," Monica nodded at Celeste's picture with a pause and a soft smile, and then met Deana's eyes again.

"My son is an adult. He's thirty. I was coerced. I'm using an intermediary. I'm asking you again. Is there something wrong? Is that the problem?"

Monica paused, and then slowly shook her head.

"Then talk to Kathleen, explain. Return her money. Find my son. Ask if he'll meet me. Just ask. If he says a flat no, it's over. I give my word I absolutely will not pursue him or ask for information about him. If he has conditions, mediate the terms."

"All right." And Monica stood, walked around her desk, and extended her hand to Deana. The women shook.

"Thank you," Deana said. "Thank you very much."

After Deana left, Monica returned to her desk, swung her chair to look out the window and stared out for long minutes as a breeze outside set the tall maple branches in motion. How one thing leads inexorably to another, she thought, and once the path is chosen, how way leads on to way leads on to way, and then it all seems like it was preordained. Fate. But it never was. Angie was right about that. There are forks in the road all along. We confuse desire and destiny.

She could have told Angie what Spencer was doing, what she was doing. His hands all over her, his tongue pushing between her lips, the assignations after work in his office, how he liked to unbutton her blouses with his tapered fingers, the greed she glimpsed as he'd move in, pushing himself into her mouth before roughly grabbing off her underpants.

She and Angie hadn't moved in together yet. Couldn't she have told her? Angie knew she was suffering at the firm. They'd already talked about whether Monica was well-enough known by the court to set up her own office once she passed the bar. She'd said she couldn't get the references she'd need to move to another firm but didn't tell Angie how she knew that. She'd let Angie believe what was true enough, that she was miserable in the world of corporate law, that she was helping no one, including and especially herself, and she wanted to be out of it. Had to get out.

Now Monica thought, if I'd told Angie about him, and why I'd been trapped, then I could have told her I was pregnant. The whole thing was my fault. But I didn't forget to take a pill. Pill fails do happen, the nurse said when she went to the clinic in a panic. Angie might have wanted me to keep it. Hell, I know Angie would have wanted me to keep it. She so wanted a child, but thought she was already too old to carry one herself and hadn't earned enough money to do it on her own. Maybe we could have done it together.

I couldn't. I was terrified, everything to risk, everything to lose. I still think she would have turned away in disgust. And it was Spencer, who was forcing me. Raping me, but he'd insist he wasn't. And what was he going to do? Freaking nothing good, that was for sure. All I knew was a steaming pile of debt and that I was in love with a woman and pregnant by a man with power, and I had no power. Destiny isn't preordained, Angie's right about that, but nobody can control her own destiny if she has no power. It's power that gives you choices. Or choices you can endure.

Monica had gotten the first available appointment at the clinic, went alone, and missed only one day of work. She did cry then. She did bleed. It was a choice, but it did not feel much like power at the time.

Power hadn't come until she and Angela had been together longer, long enough to decide to live together. To commit. That meant that half of what Monica had been paying for housing could go to her student and law school loans. Which coincided, not exactly, but close enough, with Monica's ability to hand a resignation letter to the firm and to shrug when Spencer said, "Have you secured another position? Because you've not been here long enough that the partners will be able to recommend your work elsewhere, and I'm sorry to say we won't be able to provide—"and she'd turned away, saying, "You have my notice. I'll prepare status reports on the cases I'll be leaving."

She'd rented a small office near the courthouse and set herself up in a general practice. She got referrals from social workers, thanks to Angie's networking, so her practice was largely domestic. But those cases started to get her known by a different set of judges and attorneys and some work started coming her way. It was a struggle, but she saw that she could do it. And that was her power.

And then. And then, after more than five years, thanks to Angie's position in the foster care world, they'd had the chance to foster Celeste. A biracial baby, that made the agency consider her "more difficult to place for adoption." Angie jumped on that knowing that she herself had been considered "difficult to place for adoption," because she wasn't a baby. Who could help prepare her for whatever bigotry she might face better than Angie and Monica? Lesbians knew something about that, didn't they? Angie made a logical argument to the agency that Monica thought was as fine as any attorney could have put together.

They talked right away about applying to adopt her. Monica was at first suffused with guilt. How could she—now—let herself want a baby? But she did, the way everything asleep all winter must know it wants the growing light and warmth of early May. The news about Celeste wasn't the only reason they each took an extra day off, drove to Connecticut, got a marriage license on Friday in the shore town of Madison, but Celeste was the impetus.

A friendly judge married them on the beach, as Saturday's last sun was melting into the Long Island Sound. It was chilly and private, no parents to bless them, which overwhelmed Monica at the last minute with loneliness and doubt. "She doesn't even know," she cried in the parking lot, holding back. "We don't have any flowers, and my mother doesn't know I'm getting married."

"I know," Angie said. "We know. And we've got a license and wedding rings. Can that be enough for you? It's enough for me. And I believe we can be enough to have a daughter."

"My mother will never accept me. Or you. Us."

Angela had taken her hand then and given her a soft slow smile. "Oh honey. You may be right about your mother in most ways, and that'll have to be okay. But how many women—no matter how prejudiced—can resist their grandchild? Think about it. Will she really not want to have anything to do with loving and being loved by an adorable baby girl?"

"A biracial baby girl..." Monica muttered but smiled and shrugged.

"Yep. A gorgeous biracial baby girl who needs her mothers and grandparents to help her deal with what may come her way in a screwed-up world. We've both dealt with prejudice, right? We can help her deal with it."

"I think Dad will come around. Not right away, but down the road."

Angie squeezed her hand. The breeze whipped her hair into her face, and she used her free hand to grab and anchor it against the side of her head which knocked her glasses askew, but she didn't let go. Not until she said, "Your mom will, too. Wait and see. Can you do that? Have faith in love?"

Had it been the energy of the moving water, the changing light, Angie's persistent confidence? Or was it the ultimate redemption of the baby, the forgiveness of her own sad guilt, that brought Monica to yes at that moment, and then to I do as she and Angela stood together by the incoming tide? Or was it love? There was that. Was love an explanation? It—and destiny--had been Deana's fallback understanding of the why. Angie had invoked it as though it would be magical. Transformative.

Now as she looked out her office window, Monica remembered how that day she'd felt yes, life had brought her to that beach, that she and Angela and their baby were fated to be. But what preceded it all was the power of choice.

She picked up the phone, to call Angie. She wasn't going to like this, but for Monica it had to work both ways.

"Ang," she said, when she heard her wife's voice on the line. "I'm going to need you to wait and see. To have faith. Because I'm doing the case. For one thing, it's my practice, I have to be in charge, and I have to help her. I need to help her. And secondly, we really need the income."

She added the last to be light-hearted about it, although Angie should know it was true. But Monica wasn't pretending it was her real reason, not even to herself. Maybe it was a bit of a counter-punch, to make Angie feel some responsibility.

Angie didn't take the bait. "I guess we do what we have to do," she said. "This makes me so sad," and she hung up.

Monica sighed. Okay, she thought. Not exactly a truce but better than I thought. Not happy, but she didn't go berserk.

&

The house was dark when Monica got home, which was unusual. Even though the sky still clung to the memory of a streaky melon sunset, at least the kitchen and family room lights should have been on. Still, Monica didn't think much of it. If Celeste were fussy, Angie might even have her out in the stroller which always lulled the baby. The door from the garage to the house was locked. Monica used her key, flipped on the light and called into the silence, "Anybody home? Angie?"

She hoisted her briefcase onto the kitchen table, noting that nothing seemed to be started for dinner. With a sigh, she called out again. When there was still no sound from the house, she headed to the refrigerator to see if there was some hint of something she should get started for the family. When she didn't get any ideas, she poured herself a glass of wine and went into the family room, turning on lights as she went. It looked unusually neat.

It was only when she got to the master bedroom to change her clothes that she started to get scared. The room looked different, though she couldn't immediately identify how. When she went into the closet, though, she knew. A lot of Angie's clothes were gone. Her heart now loud in her ears, she bumped into the door jamb in her rush to get to Celeste's room, to pull open the drawers of Celeste's changing table. The contents were reduced by a lot there, too.

A wild panic initially kept her from seeing the note when she went back into her own bedroom. Or maybe it was just that the white of the paper was indistinct against the white of the linens, her two pillows propped one against the other, as if there were comfort to be had. Or hope of rest.

There was not.

Monica,

We need to be apart right now. I'm truly sorry. I love you and don't want to hurt you, but I'm hurt and scared and don't know if our marriage is what I believed. I need time to figure it out. I'm going to stay with Kathy. Celeste is fine. Don't worry, I'll take good care of her, and make sure she has her time with you.

— Angela

III

COST

26

CHARLEVOIX, 1984-1993

The pediatrician had advised them to tell their son about his adoption early, make it no big deal, explain it's just one of the ways that people became a family. That seemed right to Brian and Jennie, and so one of Daniel's bedtime stories had been All About Our Family. Jennie wrote it, fifteen pages about how excited they were when they heard he'd been born and the trip to pick him up, with glued in pictures of Daniel, three days old, swathed in a ridiculous amount of pastel blue, being put into Jennie's arms, and when they'd gone to court for temporary custody—which would last until the final decree in six months. There were pictures of the judge, the court clerk, Jennie holding Daniel, Brian holding Daniel, their car, and their front door with the WELCOME HOME DANIEL sign the neighbors had hung, blue balloons festooning their mailbox like giant out-of-season flowers. The picture Brian had taken of Jennie crying that she had captioned, "Sometimes people cry when they are SO HAPPY they can't hold it in!"

Daniel had cried a lot—sometimes incessantly—as an infant. The pediatrician said some babies were just like that although a pregnancy history would be helpful. He said, "I wish we knew had full medical information, but I guess that's not available," and they told him that all they knew was that the biological mother and father did not have any hereditary medical issues to worry about and that Daniel had been cleared for adoptive placement shortly after birth.

Later they wondered whether it was being adopted that made him so reactive as a child. But even so young? That made no sense. How could he have really understood? And he couldn't possibly have thought they didn't love or want him. The love was genuine, Brian knew that for sure. The little boy was doted on. Or was that the problem, that he was doted on? He'd been a beautiful baby to look at, even shortly after birth. Every parent says theirs is, he knew, but Daniel was classically, textbook beautiful within a couple of months. Big-eyed, dark-lashed, dimpled wrists and ankles. Downy the head that Brian and Jennie cradled into their necks when they rocked him, delicious the little feet and hands they nibbled to make him laugh when his diaper was changed.

Should they never have told him he was adopted? But the earth had tilted before then. showed itself, like a spreading crack in the earth. Unstoppable crying— was it colic?—and then tantrums had mixed in from the beginning with the shoulder rides, the laughing baths, hide and seek, the chase-me games. Brian had no idea where or how everything had gone so wrong. The wrongness had been heavy on his chest, as he'd floundered and tried to hide it as he'd seen Jennie floundering.

"I've had difficult kids in my classes, more than a couple of times," she said to Brian once, leaning against the kitchen counter when Daniel was in elementary school. Her hair had fallen into her eyes, and she hadn't even pushed it back. He'd reached over, intending to tuck it behind her ear for her, an old tender gesture. She'd pushed his hand away, irritated. Everything irritated her or made her cry.

"And you know what?" she said then. "I blamed their parents. I really thought that it was their parents' fault. So how can this not be mine? What am I doing wrong?"

"You're a good mother," he said it over and over, like a mantra. "And I'm a good father." And he meant it, even as it became a prayer, even as the crack opened in their marriage, the space where the wall had begun to arrange itself.

It would have been better, he thought, if she'd gone ahead and voiced the accusations: the first one would be *you're the one who gave up on me. We could have had a baby ourselves if we'd gone on. I told you I would. I just needed a break.* He couldn't deny that. And if she said aloud what he was sure was in her heart, next was: *and you're even the one who said we didn't need to go through an agency and know more. What if there's something terrible that's inherited? What if the mother took some drugs? Those can affect babies, right? What if, what if?*

He didn't ask her, though. Maybe he was the one who thought these things. He couldn't be sure.

That was the thing, too. There were a hundred frightened 'What ifs' that neither of them believed in asking because that's not who they were. And then the questions were pebbles raining on their heads that became stones on their separate chests and finally a rock wall between them. Sometimes he thought he even breathed separate air, stale and foul. Once the air between them had been electric—with what? Lust, he decided. He'd felt lust. He'd been young and lustful, and it had been magical. Now if he and Jennie shared air at all, it was never the fresh air of love.

"I didn't sign up for this," she said, once. He wasn't sure if she meant him or Daniel. Had he pushed her into this? Of course, he had.

They tried. They really did try, and each knew the other tried. Everything became about fixing Daniel. The best preschool, then Jennie a stay-at-home Mom after Daniel started full day school. She was the room mother who made the cupcakes and decorated the classroom with pumpkins, Santas, hearts or bunnies for school parties. She came in to help the school librarian. She worked on Daniel's reading with him, and he was a good reader.

He seemed to be musical, so they bought a piano and Jennie taught herself to play a little so she could help him. Until during one of his storms, he took a full glass of milk and poured it almost the whole length of the keyboard. Both parents were at every parent/teacher conference. There was rarely much good news about his behavior and his test scores weren't great. Still, he passed, which was encouraging, but Jennie told Brian, "Everyone passes grade to grade. They don't retain them anymore. It's not considered wise."

"Maybe he's actually pretty bright," Brian said. "I mean, Mrs. Socci says he's not paying much attention, but he's absorbing enough. Right?"

"Mrs. Socci also said she'd caught him cheating once too. Not too many second graders have figured out that they can copy someone else's work."

"Yeah," Brian said. "You do have to be smart to figure out how to cheat, right?"

They had him evaluated. The doctor said he was probably hyperactive, and 'just very immature for his age,' which was eight at the time. He didn't think medication was a good idea, though. "Let him grow out of it," was the thinking at the time. He added, "Do you know anything about the pregnancy? Was there any trauma? Drug use?"

"We really don't know anything about the pregnancy," they'd answered.

"I'm confident we'd have been informed if she'd been an alcoholdic or a drug addict," Brian added. "We would have had to consider that. We were just told that there'd been a history of good health on both sides. That he was a healthy newborn with fine Apgar scores."

"Well, keep him really busy," the doctor said."

Brian signed Daniel up for ice hockey and took him to every practice, but Daniel found it tempting to use the stick to clobber other boys. It was obvious he wasn't ready for a team sport, so Brian and Jennie invented safer activities at home to keep him busy, and it did help. It required one-to-one attention all the time, but it helped and that gave them hope. There were hours when Daniel and Jennie painted together, both of them delighted with stick people standing under a yellow-spoked sun that shone over emerald green grass. Daniel still acted out in school, though. Jennie didn't want to blame the teacher, but she did say that some were better at dealing with "super active boys" than others.

They found a private elementary school and transferred him there. Jennie drove him back and forth since it was out of their own district. By the end of one grading period, that school wanted an evaluation by their school psychologist. The psychologist said yes, Daniel was hyperactive, but then he added "It's not just that. Something's not right. Daniel worries me. I'd like you to take him to a specialist. A neurologist, or maybe a child psychiatrist." That was too much for Brian.

"He's just a little boy, damnit," he said to Jennie twenty minutes later in a nearby restaurant. He'd ordered them each a margarita and asked for the appetizer menu. It was nearly five-thirty already, and they needed to get home to the babysitter, but that would have to wait. He'd overpay her. Jennie had been crying—again—in the physician's office. The doctor had frightened her, and Brian couldn't have that, regardless of whether he was sometimes frightened himself.

Brian reached across the table and put his hand over his wife's. "Just a little boy," he said again. "We're creating a worse problem, by overreacting. He doesn't know how to manage himself."

It had been a rough month. Daniel couldn't play outside, not in the sleety-wet drear of early November, and that made him angry. Every no made him angry, though they made a practice of calmly telling him why the answer was no. Except for the times when one of them had finally had it and blew up into, Because I said no, that's why.

Then, when the house already felt like a tinderbox, winter struck in earnest. There was a blizzard, and even though in northern Michigan, they were equipped for snow, it was a doozy. School was cancelled. Jennie was home with Daniel when it wasn't a weekend; no Brian for support or backup.

Keeping Daniel busy full-time was Jennie's job and she was as wrecked as the build-a-car kit Brian and Daniel had worked on together, high-fiving their own artistry.

The two of them had been engrossed in the project, just starting to build a second one so they could race each other. Daniel had cut open the wheels of the finished one that sat, newly painted on top of his bureau. Jennie hadn't even been positive what it had been over, he had had that bad a day. She'd told him to stay in his room until he settled down. Jennie was furious about the car when she saw it. "Your father is going to be so disappointed," she told Daniel later, after she calmed down. "Why did you do that?"

"I was gonna lose," Daniel had said. "I always lose."

After Daniel was asleep that night, Jennie told Brian that had broken her heart for Daniel, but her heart had been just as broken for Brian who had so wanted that father-son good time to continue. For his sake, she pretended to believe him when Brian held her and lied, said it was no big deal, he was fine.

Now today, Brian had watched as this second doctor's advice to involve a specialist struck his wife, like a hammer blow, one from a more authoritative hand. He had to fix this. Sometimes he could bear his own anger and frustration better than he could bear hers.

He looked at his wife from across the restaurant table and conjured up a reassuring smile. "Look, he's going to be all right. Kids go through these bad stages, you know?"

He'd come up with a small earnest smile. "Drink your margarita, honey. We don't get to be by ourselves like this often." He wanted her to relax a little, to get her to mirror his smile.

There was no such reflection. "Brian, he's—for God's sake, he's been like this forever."

"It just seems that way. Some kids are harder. He's just a little boy."

"I wish I had your faith," she said.

Her voice was heavy, and her complexion looked sallow, bluish circles around her eyes. Maybe that was the dim light, though. He hoped it was the light. She'd always been such a pretty woman. It was ironic. Of the two of them, he was the sceptic by nature, the one to challenge assertions that weren't based on evidence. Now here he was, saying whatever he had to, being accused of having faith. He had to fix this. But it was true, too, he'd thought. Daniel was just a little boy. There were good times. Look at how he and Daniel had played basketball in the driveway last summer after he'd put up that hoop. Maybe he was going to be a great athlete. All kids go through rough patches. Look at how much Daniel loved Christmas. He'd remembered to say thank you on his own for almost every present when his grandparents were there, and he'd played checkers with them, on task through two games.

And hadn't Jennie just last week been lit up with delight when Daniel had brought home a picture from school that he'd drawn for her. He'd written 'I love you Mom,' on it. Jennie had put it on the refrigerator with magnets, and she and Daniel had danced together in the kitchen.

He remembered himself at the same age, playing chess with his grandfather for hours. Here he was making a big deal out of Daniel playing two games of checkers. Two whole games. But they had laughed every time Daniel got a king and Daniel had been so proud. It was a success—another good time he clung to.

27

CHARLEVOIX, 1998-2001

Sometimes she felt a hope bloom in Brian and that left her feeling more alone. A teacher would see something positive and tell them. The teacher wouldn't have known about the invisible backpacks crammed with dread that Jennie and Brian had each worn into the conference. Jennie felt Brian's eagerness to put the weight down, to believe. She was much more cautious. In ninth grade, Mr. Loomis mentioned Daniel's sense of humor and said, "He's coming along."

"Really?" Jennie said, no trace of acquired cynicism in her tone. "That's wonderful!"

"You think so?" Brian said, then quickly added, "I'm glad you see it, too. We've been thinking that maybe he missed something along the way and dropping back to pre-algebra would be a good idea."

Bullshit, Jennie thought. You've been thinking that. Tere's no "we" to it. But we'll play along until this guy calls us, too. Then she was ashamed again. What kind of mother thinks like that? She'd back up, try to climb on the positive train, and sometimes she was able ride it all the way to the next station. Still, there were days the suitcase of her disappointment in Daniel, in the whole business of motherhood was heavy, heavy. She'd heard this was the whole purpose of a woman's life. If so, it was a raw deal.

Daniel was bigger than she was now. Fourteen. He slouched, glowered, flinched away from her when she tried to do what she didn't often feel anymore: show him affection. But it was important. She knew that. She knew to look for anything to praise, and she tried. Lord, how she tried. None of this was her fault. All of it was her fault. She was a good mother. She was a terrible mother.

Only one thing didn't change: she was Daniel's mother.

"You're not my mother," Daniel said or shouted or whispered, the refrain in days that lacked melody. "You can't tell me what to do."

"I'm sorry to disappoint you," Jennie said, "but I am your mother, I can tell you what to do, and I will." It sounded much stronger than she felt. It was over stupid stuff, she knew that, but a new psychologist suggested she hold her ground after the previous doctor had said to pick her battles. It had been the doctor who'd said, "Could be just how his brain is wired. Something organic from way back, like maybe something happened in the pregnancy. You really don't know enough." He'd shaken his head, added, "He may well manage himself better when he's older. It happens," and referred them to the psychologist to help them cope.

Standing firm didn't work any better. Jennie would tell Daniel to stay in his room when he'd ignored a reasonable request, and Daniel would appear in the family room plunked in front of the television. She'd turn the television off, and he'd turn it back on. She picked up the remote and hid it in the garage, and when she came back, he'd have figured out how to turn the TV back on anyway.

She went back to what had worked with kids in her teaching days: thinking up incentives to offer. Daniel shrugged and said he didn't care. His go-to line, razor-honed, was don't worry about it, I'll be gone when I'm eighteen with beats of silence before he'd add, I'm not like you. That seemed somehow at the heart of it all sometimes. She even said it to him. "No, you're sure not," and then, even though she believed it, she was ashamed. Her apology fell on stone. "Why would anyone want to be like you?" he said.

Lonely, desperate, embarrassed, Jennie tried talking to certain of her friends. She'd say I just can't reach him, or ugh, my own son hates me or I can't get him to do one thing—and Valerie or Michelle would roll her eyes and answer, "Hang in there. Teenagers are impossible." Valerie had her own polite teenager that Jennie would never have thought gave Valerie a minute of angst, and Michelle taught high school algebra and had a son in tenth grade, so for a while Jennie would think, Oh, then this is all typical after all? Both Valerie and Michelle knew Daniel, and said he was always well-manned around them. "He'll come around, sooner or later," Valerie said. "After he drives you straight to the nuthouse. Teenagers. They're all horrible." Oh god, I hope you're right, Jennie thought to herself, then, and she'd shake her head and smile. She didn't tell them what the doctor had mentioned about brain wiring. To have them reassure her that all teenagers were the same let her feel like something was normal about her family, that Daniel wasn't a mess, and she wasn't making mistake after mistake. She repeated what her friends said over and over in her mind—that he was friendly and well-mannered toward them—and took hope.

&

He was a handsome boy, not nearly as fair haired as either of them—his was light brown, and curly, which somehow surprised them—and he had deep brown eyes under dark brows, which he used to enhance the effect when he glowered at them, in Jennie's opinion. He seemed to have friends, and Brian and Jennie stacked up reasons for and against letting him get a driver's license when the time came. They decided to wait until he turned seventeen and might be more mature.

Already, he didn't want them to know where he was and what he was doing. Wouldn't that get worse if he were driving himself rather than riding with "friends?" At least Brian could usually waylay those boys in the driveway and get a name, jot down a license number. If worst came to worst, he always said, they could call the police to track down the car. Brian said they could take comfort in the fact that most of the drivers were quite polite when he came out; didn't that mean that Daniel was choosing good friends? They did give Daniel a cell phone, for safety reasons, Brian said. Sometimes Daniel even answered it when Jennie insisted Brian call him because it was past his curfew.

It wasn't that there'd been no encouragements along the way. Like when they'd given in and let him get pick out a dog from the shelter when Daniel was twelve—or was it thirteen? "No bigger than medium," Jennie had said and, "Daniel, you promise to take care of it?" Daniel had chosen a long-legged, sweet-natured black and brown mutt and named him Bear, and mostly he did take care of him and pay attention. He never did stop taking the dog into his room with him, and there was affection Brian and Jennie hardly recognized as coming from their son when he talked to and hugged the dog.

So, the encouragements would occasionally bloom like a volunteer flower but would be poisoned by larger discouragements, and finally the memory of them would fade, too. Daniel was caught shoplifting two videos. In their small town, Brian especially was so well-known and respected that the merchant didn't press charges, wanting to do a favor for Brian, who'd straightened the merchant's children's teeth. Then two weeks later, Jennie found pornography in Daniel's room, so she told Brian to please, please talk to him. Brian did talk to Daniel, but not about the evils of pornography, which he figured was pointless with an adolescent boy. Instead, he talked to Daniel, not for the first time, about sex and safe sex.

As Brian later told Jennie, "Get this. It was just terrific. Reeking insolence and cigarette smoke, Danny-boy pointed out that there was absolutely no way that I could prove that I'd ever had sex, so as a total loser, I should shut up. A creative way of saying you're not my father. Same picture, different angle. He doesn't usually pull that one out." It was true. Jennie heard you're not my mother way more often. For a moment, Jennie thought that Brian was as worked up as she for once, that they were in the same place, but then he shrugged and gave a small rueful laugh. "If he only knew, right? How hot and hard my wife makes me."

Jennie was not mollified. She pulled away from his hand. He'd put it on her arm, to pull her to him. "I asked you to talk to him about porn—about how to treat women."

Another shrug. "Yeah, well. Teenage boys are a different species. Trust me on that." But Jennie didn't trust him. Not about that or much else. Whatever he thought he knew, she didn't believe it was any more than she did, which was nothing. She was alone. How had this happened?

"Can't you see that he treats me worse than he treats you?" she said. "He's crappy to you, but the reason you're not as upset is that he doesn't seem like he actually hates you." Brian didn't know about the time she'd let loose and yelled at Daniel, "Well, if that's how you feel, you can just get out of my house." He'd shot back, an ugly look on his face. "You'd like that wouldn't you?" and without stopping to think about it, how hurtful it might be, she'd yelled, "You're damn right I would. I'm done." Daniel had persisted, pushing her further. "You hate me as much as I hate you." She'd not had the sense to walk away. "Only sometimes," she'd said, before she got hold of herself. Later, she'd tried to apologize, but Daniel jerked away from her and said, "Forget it. I know how you feel about me."

"Oh, I don't think that's right," Brian said now. "Daniel's an equal opportunity parent-hater."

Jennie shut down then. "Okay," she said, knowing Brian wouldn't realize she didn't mean it. She turned her back, pulled the comforter close to her against another Michigan winter, and let her breathing feign sleep. One year until Daniel turned eighteen. Though he had never run away— or not yet, she reminded herself—he regularly threatened to and not come back. Would she be more alone or less if he did? Would she control her own life? Had she ever? She used to believe that she'd made choices, but now she looked back and wasn't sure if that was true. She just didn't know if she'd ever really chosen, or if she'd just always done what she thought she should.

She had that notion, and then she put it away. What difference did it make now, anyway, when there were no choices to be made? Someone should warn women, she thought, before they have a child. Or maybe before they marry. Perhaps even way before that. Sometime early she'd learned fear instead of strength; she glimpsed that much, but it was too late. It wasn't as if she didn't love her husband and her son. She did. She definitely did. Sometimes maybe not. Stop that, anyone can have a bad day, she told herself. She was sure she loved them.

They were both surprised when Daniel made it to graduation. He had the bare minimum number of credits, more than a few of them a gift from a teacher who didn't want him in his or her class again, Jennie figured. Maybe that wasn't fair, though. After Daniel had slouched across the stage, Jennie watched excited mothers wrapping their arms around the necks of tall, close-cropped sons who hugged them back. Fathers extended their hands in congratulations and once it was grasped, used the excuse to draw their boys into an embrace. Little siblings held bright helium-filled balloons. Grandparents scattered in the crowd like silver confetti. There was none of that with Daniel out on the lawn of Memorial Senior High School in the June twilight. They couldn't even find him in the jumble of seniors uniting with their families. They searched until people were leaving, congratulating the boys they recognized as friends or acquaintances of Daniel's and, finally, left.

As Brian drove them through the quieter streets of the town toward their neighborhood, they were both silent, brooding. Finally, Jennie said, "He knew we wanted to celebrate with him. We both told him we were proud. We said we wanted to take him out to dinner. He said he didn't want a party. Do you think...I mean, didn't he?" She didn't know what she was asking. "Do you think we bugged him too much about college?"

Brian shook his head. "I don't know what the deal is. Good thing our parents didn't make the trip. If I'd had no plans after high school, Dad would have had a stroke. I don't know what he thinks he's going to do. I always thought my son would..."

"I know. Be something."

"Maybe he wouldn't have pulled this if either of our parents had come? He got their cards and the money they sent. Maybe we should have waited to give him ours, and he'd have hung around. You know, figuring...."

"Shit, Jen. You just don't know. You just never know with him."

Jennie looked at him. "That's not like you."

He shrugged, and offered another head shake, lips pursed and turned down. "I'm sorry. I just thought that tonight he might… ."

"At least he walked."

"Yep. He did walk. He got a diploma. We can be grateful for that."

"It's just so—"

"Frustrating."

"Disappointing."

"Infuriating."

"Where do you think he went?"

Brian pulled into their driveway and hit the garage door opener with a forefinger jab. "Honestly, I have no idea. All his friends are with their families, aren't they?"

"The seniors, anyway," Jennie said. "Maybe some are juniors. They'd have licenses, too."

"Yeah. You want a drink?"

"No. Yes. But we don't have any. Liquor store's closed."

"I didn't actually get rid of it." Brian pointed through the windshield to the back corner of the garage, in front of Jennie's car. "I hid it in a box over there, behind the lawnmower and rakes. Not a chance in the world of Daniel messing with the stuff to do yard work."

"You've been holding out on me." She held up her hand. "High five. I'd be really mad if I weren't so happy it's there right now."

From inside, Bear barked welcome home. The garage door went down behind them.

Later, in the living room, with her legs curled under her skirt and her second rum and coke icy in her hand, Jennie said, "Do you think he's coming home?"

"Honey, I have no idea. He didn't answer his phone. Want me to try again now?"

What are your plans? How are you going to get some more education? It's not too late—we can help you apply to a college. They said it over and over. Don't you worry about it, he'd say. I'm not your problem, and one of them— usually her because she was around more—would shoot back, usually something like, "Huh. Wish that were true, but unfortunately you are." What kind of mother could possibly wish that were true, that he wasn't her problem? She didn't, of course she didn't. It wasn't like she didn't see the good in her son, how a tender heart would reveal itself in flashes. When it happened, it seemed Daniel would be all the more difficult for having dropped his guard.

"Do you think it will do any good to call again?" Jennie said. She didn't want to cry tonight. It was nice being with Brian, the way they were. Maybe they'd make love, the way they used to.

"Not really," Brian said. "But we're still his parents."

"Try again," Jennie sighed.

28

They'd only gotten him because they couldn't have a kid of their own. That was the thing. He said he hated them, and he sort of did. But Daniel figured it was mutual. His mom had even told him she wanted him out of her house, which he'd suspected was the truth all along. She reeked what a disappointment he was. And his Dad. God, his father was some kind of science genius freak. A dentist. Daniel had looked at some of his Dad's old books from when he was in dentist school and figured exactly one thing out really fast: he was nothing like Brian and never would be.

The worst people had to be his real parents who didn't want him. Unless his parents, the ones who took him, had somehow stolen him from the parents, he'd been meant to be with all along. That was the thing. How could he ever know what really happened?

Jennie (he called her Mom so she wouldn't do her stupid teary face—but to himself he called her Jennie, because that was her name, and she wasn't his mother, so what should he call her?) had told him she'd help him hunt down his real parents after he was an adult.

He'd been seventeen at the time, the beginning of his senior year. She'd said, "What do you want, Daniel? What is it you want? Do you want to find your biological parents? Once you turn eighteen, there are places you can register. Then if they—or maybe she—has registered or ever does, well, I think they help you get in touch. I'll help you find out about it anyway, if that would make you happy, I'll help you."

They'd been arguing in the kitchen while she was cooking dinner. It was a good room because Jennie baked a lot, although he didn't get the thing about having pots and pans hanging in the center over the island, and how the copper bottoms had to be specially cleaned. Leave it to her to make something unnecessarily complicated.

He tried to figure what angle she was playing. It had to was one of two things: Jennie was okay with helping him find his real parents because she'd never really wanted him in the first place, and it would be a handy way to get rid of him. Or maybe she knew stuff she wasn't telling him, and his real parents would just love another chance to throw him out. Jennie wanted to rub his face in that. What else could it be? Whatever. She wasn't saying what he wanted to hear. He didn't know what he wanted to hear.

"Why would I want to meet that bitch?" he'd said to Jennie. The way he saw it, there were plenty of single mothers, so it was mostly her fault, more than the guy's. She could've kept him.

"Daniel," Jennie said, wearing her teary smeary face and sort of moaning his name, which he hated. "Maybe she didn't have any choice."

"What do you mean by that?" Had she just admitted that they'd tricked his real parents? Or his real mother at least.

"I mean sometimes circumstances make something impossible, no matter how much you want it, you can't make it happen." Jennie had raised her hands, palms up, her whole upper body on its way into a shrug.

"Bullshit," he said. Then wondered what she was really talking about. Maybe about how she couldn't make him be worth something. Probably. It was obvious he was nothing like Brian. Who'd want to spend your life with your hands in peoples' mouths anyway? Gross.

"Wanting something doesn't make it happen. I'm just saying, maybe she couldn't raise you and she cared enough, and loved you enough before you were born, that—Dammit, the meat is getting too done. Wait a minute, I'll—"

"Never mind. It's all bullshit. I'm goin' out."

"Dinner in ten minutes."

"Don't want it."

"Daniel, you need to stay home now. I made pork, the way you like it. Just stay home."

"Going out." To underscore his point, he'd slammed the front door. He had no idea where he was going. Anywhere but here. He'd never let her see him with wet eyes. It wasn't the first time he'd taken off and it wouldn't be the last. When he turned eighteen, that would be the last.

Jennie and Brian drove him apeshit that whole year last year. Blah blah blah about making plans, his choices. Wouldn't he like to go to college? Like all they cared about was college. In the first place, they ought to have figured out that just because they wanted him to be, he wasn't smart like that. Looking at books too long made him jumpy. Did Brian seriously think he was going to be a dentist like him with his hands in people's mouths all day? Haha. What did they care anyway?

What could he do, anyway? Whatever he did was just going to be another fat letdown to them. Ryan was going to college, the pussy. Said his parents were making him, but Ryan figured he'd join a fraternity, and he could drink and party. He claimed that college girls were easy hookups, too. Daniel didn't know how Ryan got in because they had been in Civics together, and Ryan's grades in that class weren't any better than Daniel's. Ryan said, "Stupid, my parents are paying for college. As long as you graduate high school, you can—"

He'd stopped listening to Ryan. Not interested. Ryan wasn't hanging with them as much anymore anyway. Chris was going to the community college to learn heating and air conditioning. His uncle would hire him when he got his certificate. Another friend, Rob, was a damn genius at computer stuff, so he was going into some training class for internet technology.

Mike was the only other guy he hung with. Mike had been talking to a guy from the Navy. Mike's Dad had been in the Navy. In Vietnam. Mike said it like it was some big deal.

People thought Daniel should be smart because his dad was an orthodontist. He never told the truth, that he didn't have a clue what his real dad did. Probably just knocked up his mother and taken off, and he was a bum on the street now, like Brian had once said Daniel would end up being if Daniel didn't make any effort. For all Daniel knew, his read dad was around somewhere knocking up woman after woman now and Daniel had twenty-five brothers and sisters he didn't know about and who didn't know about him. Brian thought Daniel was headed nowhere. He said that a lot, and it pissed Daniel off. They'd been fighting about Daniel heading nowhere one night that spring out in the garage, and Brian had said, "No son of mine ought to act this way." He shook his head and had that mad look on his face.

Daniel had said, "Well, that works because I'm no son of yours."

He'd expected Brian to argue that point, the way Brian always had when Daniel said stuff like that, but instead Brian got all sad and said, "I guess you're not," and went into the house through the kitchen door.

The Navy was a bad idea. Daniel had been on a boat two times, and he'd felt horrible. Like barfing terrible. The Navy was all Mike could talk about, though. How his dad went to fight for the country when other people ducked the responsibility. Mike was all into watching the news, shows about the terrorists that blew up half of New York last September. Guys like us gotta stand up, go fight. That's what Mike said. Daniel had heard Brian and Jennie say they hoped Bush wouldn't do something stupid like start a war. They didn't believe in war.

That night, on his way out the door, Daniel grabbed his sweatshirt from the back of the chair in the living room where he'd tossed it when he came in. He was pissed off at Jennie for making him miss the pork. She cooked it with some kind of fried potatoes and onions mixed in, and he really liked that stuff. She had no right to talk about his real mother. He'd walked over to Mike's to shoot the shit and find out more about the military. Mike was all about the damn Navy, but Daniel finally told him about barfing on the boat. Then Mike said if Daniel couldn't do the Navy, what about the Army. Or the Marines. Mike said he could get sent maybe to California or overseas, to some action. "My Dad says Bush is gonna kick some butt big time."

If Daniel could go to California or overseas, he'd never have to come back here, which fit his plans really well. Never. That would show them that he'd meant what he said all along. They couldn't make him come back. They couldn't make him be like them. Mike got on his computer and looked up how Daniel could talk to an Army recruiter.

"Don't say anything to anybody," Daniel warned him. "Not anyone's business." He'd made sure Mike's door was shut.

"Yeah, okay." Mike was a buddy. Even though he didn't get why Daniel wouldn't tell his parents he was enlisting, he was no snitch. Daniel thought, Mike's parents are proud. Like father, like son. All that good shit.

The recruiter was pretty happy to talk to Daniel. The sergeant wanted to talk to Daniel's parents, but Daniel wouldn't give him much, just said, "It's my decision to fight for my country," and let him think his parents were against war, true enough maybe. The sergeant said, "Good man, a patriot." Daniel could sign for himself when he turned eighteen, and his plans were his to know and nobody else's. So big deal, he turned eighteen two months before he graduated from high school—which he knew his so-called parents never thought he'd do.

Daniel took their idiot test, got a 32 on it, when what you had to score was a 31, so that was cool, and when he found out he'd passed it, he went back. Then there was another test, some vocational test. Daniel didn't really understand how that one came out, but the recruiter ended up saying "Okay, looks like you could drive a truck, wanna do that? That's MOS—Military Occupation specialty... uh...Motor Transport Operator, 88 Mike. You'd get trained. That'd be at Fort Leonard Wood in Missouri, see here? First, you'll go to basic training, though. You'll find out where when you report to active duty at Military Entry Processing Station probably in Lansing. They might send you to Fort Benning or Fort Jackson. I don't know. It's up to the number crunchers. Anyway, it's nine weeks not including processing time. When you complete Basic Training, then you'll go to Fort Leonard Wood. Make sense?"

Daniel shrugged. "Cool. Anywhere but here." He signed. Right on the line, he signed for himself the day after his birthday, and it made him feel good. So what if he wasn't some geek-genius dentist? The recruiter told him to start getting in physical shape, like run and do pushups and shit and gave him stuff he was supposed to read to learn Army ranks and what would happen at boot camp.

"You know, you gotta finish and get that diploma, right?" the recruiter said, clapping him on the shoulder.

"Yeah. No problem."

"Good man. Stay in touch. I'll get your paperwork in order, and we'll get you on your way after you graduate."

It hadn't happened exactly the way the recruiter said. He'd had to wait almost a after week after graduation to go, which meant finding friends to stay with and a couple of nights he'd been on his own and had to blow some of his graduation money on fleabag motels outside of town. The bathroom in one was pretty gross.

Finally, the recruiter gave him a bus ticket to Lansing. He'd made it. If he thought about Brian or Jennie, he reminded himself that Brian had said it himself: no son of mine. And Jennie had said, out of my house. Well, now they were both right, weren't they?

He learned two things in two days. He hated buses, and paperwork sucked even worse than Charlevoix black flies in summer.

&

In Iraq, in 2003, he'd think how dumb he'd been to think Fort Leonard Wood had been hot. The summer of 2007 was the worst, though. That was his second or maybe his third tour, and in July it actually touched 124 degrees. The southern boys in his platoon handled it better, but all of Alpha Company were miserable as they rattled around in supply convoys dodging Sunnis and Shiites— it wasn't like they could tell the one from the other or that it mattered. Everyone complained continuously. The vehicles were ovens especially because it wasn't like you could roll down a window—add a helmet, armor, and

LYNNE HUGO

ammunition and it was a goddamn nightmare dripping in sweat. Not that going naked would have helped in the furnace that was Baghdad.

For the first time, though, Daniel had brothers. Their connection was visceral. They ragged on about women, about farting, about how many times a day Larsen brushed his teeth, women they've had, about fucking stupid lieutenants.

The convoys Daniel drove in were endless, moving supplies forward from a big base in the rear to smaller remote outposts and back again. They were a parade of, usually nine, maybe as many as fifteen vehicles, through neighborhoods north and west, head back south skirting the marshy places by detouring east, an alien float, a body of linked chambers with a Humvee head, three supply trucks for guts, a Humvee tail. Their nervous system was the radio, linking all of them, even though the segments of the body would be separated for safety. Did you see that? the head would say, and they'd all hear the com.

Daniel learned about what the infantry posted to those outposts did—spent their time storming doorways, flipping houses, searching out enemy. They gave kids gum, and they flex-cuffed detainees. They gave kids Lifesavers. They blindfolded detainees. Once in a while, they played ball with kids. Some of that sounded damn good. Maybe it had more of a point than driving a fuckin' truck.

There were four weeks and three days, then, when things got quiet. Nobody hit an I.E.D., and they started feeling invincible. Dominant. The power of the many was the power of the One, and the One was the alien, the USA crawling through the desert. Controlling the Sandbox. It felt safe enough that Daniel didn't mind it—not that he would have been stupid enough to argue with even the most idiot lieutenant—when he was assigned to drive the Humvee that headed a supply convoy bringing canned food plus whatever the hell was in the other trucks to an outpost. Would've been too damn much for the quiet to last.

Berger, Daniel's assistant driver, an acne-faced recruit right next to him, stuck his head out of the Humvee door. Daniel didn't have a clue why he did that and never would because a sniper got Berger just as Daniel was yelling, "Get the fuck in—"Then all hell broke loose.

&

"Hey, when your number's up, it's up. Nothin' you can do about it," Scarletti said in the barracks later.

Daniel though couldn't get the blowed up head, the crumpled body, the blood and those brain bits that had sprayed everywhere—the windshield, his face, fucking everywhere and what remained of Berger's head nearly landing in his lap. He had to lean over what was left of the kid to close the door and keep on going.

"What will be will be, y'know. Only way to look at it. If you're meant to make it, you'll make it. Ya know, it's fuckin' fate." Scarletti said later. "You were damn lucky to get close air support. They're usually off somewhere else. Or smoking crack, whatever, just not getting to us in time, all I know. Don't worry 'bout it, man. Deal me a hand and quit thinkin' on it. You 'n me, we'll be fine." Scarletti was a true buddy, like a brother.

Still, after Berger, Daniel sometimes wished he were on a patrol, when revenge might feel like hope, or cool air. Not that he wanted to kill anyone. He couldn't see that, either. It was all just so pointless.

Daniel didn't get assigned to drive the head of a convoy again, not that he done a damn thing wrong, and nobody hinted he had. Seemed like they were switching up who in the lead, but Daniel really couldn't much keep track. Things had eased up, got pretty routine. until it didn't matter what he'd thought, because he'd been tricked again.

The day the worst went down, Daniel was driving one of the long beds, but third back behind the lead Humvee. Why was he in that safer spot? Maybe it was all random, where anyone was anytime. He couldn't handle what Scarletti'd said, the crap about "meant to be."

Scarletti was assistant driver in the lead Humvee, Whitey driving that day. Daniel's truck was carrying port-a-johns. Shitters. For shit. Just like the whole, pointless war.

They were about halfway to the outpost, right on the supply route, when the radio crackled and a voice—not exactly calm—came over. "Hold up, hold up. We're hit."

"Call for close air support," Daniel barked toward the acne-faced recruit riding beside him who held the radio. That went out through the convoy, and someone else shouted. "They're not gonna show up here, dumbass. Call for evac. Fuckin' I.E.D. got 'em."

"Could be an ambush, too, asshole. Air support."

"Call for evac. They're blowed up."

"Evac on the way, hold up, hold up, all drivers halt forward progress." The radio static continued as grunts shouted to each other. Daniel heard what he needed to, "Evac on the way."

Jesus Christ, the blowed up would be Scarletti.. It was always the head that got fucked up first. Daniel did exactly what no soldier was ever supposed to do. He opened the door, jumped to the road, and ran forward. No way he wasn't going to get Scarletti, and who gave a fuck if it was an ambush. He was armed. He'd shoot. He'd kill the motherfuckers himself.

As it happened, he didn't have to. He didn't take any fire.

Daniel got to the Humvee, and one other guy risked getting out to help him when it was clear Daniel wasn't ambushed into a bloody heap. Whitey's legs were blown off, and Scarletti's guts spilled out of him. Daniel held Scarletti's head and shoulders, telling him evac was on the way, and "I will personally kill you if you don't fuckin' hang on. Stay with me, man, stay with me."

Scarletti's eyes were open, but after the first minute or so closed and opened several times. His breathing was ragged with moans. Words weren't coming. Daniel let the other guy do what he could for Whitey while they waited for the *whoop, whoop, whoop, whoop,* the deafening, blessed sound of the medevac copter blades closer and closer. Daniel didn't care if the bird landed on his own head, just get here, get here, get here. An incantation in his head, almost like a prayer.

The corpsmen's faces didn't look good getting a first look at Scarletti and Whitey when they started doing what they could with bandaging on the ground. "You're gonna be fine, bro, hear me? Gonna be fine," Daniel said into Scarletti's ear as the corpsmen lifted Scarletti into the bird for the outbound dustoff. Part of him knew he was a fucking liar. No way Scarletti was so much as making it outta that bird.

Scarletti had the rack next to Daniel's in the barracks. He'd shown Daniel pictures of his girlfriend and their little girl back in Brooklyn. Invited Daniel to come stay with them a while when they got home. Scarletti was going to have a job with Jessica's father, and he could get Daniel a job there, too. Then Daniel could get his own place. Meet Jessica's girlfriends, too. Nice girls, Scarletti knew them. Real pretty.

And that was why Daniel re-upped. It wasn't like anything was over. Nothing was meant to end like this.

It wasn't over until it was over. Not the war, of course, that was Groundhog Day. It was the boredom with its hopelessness that eroded their unity. His platoon turned on some of its own. For the most part they didn't much bother the ones who got tired of the detainees being let go in a few days for lack of evidence, when some Joes decided the Hajji could be dropped off where Shiite insurgents—or Sunnis, whichever the detainee wasn't—would take care of the matter. Nobody saw what happened to them. But some went beyond slapping the detainees around first. The anger over being endlessly shot at and ambushed and blowed up by I.E.Ds; buddies sent home missing hands, feet, arms, legs, when they were supposed to be there to bring peace to that fucking shithole desert—that anger took over and was all that mattered.

For some it was just frustration, even sadness and the failure of it all. Depression, not that any would call it that.

Some turned into oxygen thieves, retreated into the future, into thoughts of home, girlfriends, wives, packages and phone calls spent counting down the days to serve. Only the Army never retreats, just tactical retrogrades. Bunch of bullshit.

Other guys struck back. Sitreps got falsified. Insurgents who got picked up got roughed up, beat up. A few—no one knew exactly how many—got killed. Blind eyes got turned.

Some guys grew uneasy about each other, how far they'd go. Or wouldn't. Who has my back, my 6, who doesn't? A few became pariahs; either for being rogue or not rogue enough.

Daniel couldn't fit himself anywhere. Not anymore. He had plenty of anger, but not the stomach to cross some lines. But not to snitch either. He swallowed it, finished out his fourth tour and returned stateside. Tried for an early out; didn't get it. Drove a truck around Fort Bragg until he got his discharge. Honorable. Undistinguished but undisgraced and alone. Out, but no place to go.

Whiskey Tango Foxtrot. *What The Fuck.*

It wasn't like he could go back to Michigan. All the years in the Army, he'd never sent them so much as a postcard since graduation night. Out of my house... No son of mine. They probably thought good riddance. They might not even live there anymore, anyway. How would he know? It was weird. Was Bear—was he still around? Was he okay? Why now would he remember playing ball with Brian? Why not just remember how once he'd kicked a ball with ragged Iraqi kids, rubbed their dark heads, left them with Lifesavers which they might mistake for hope and made himself walk away.

Still, he found himself thinking about Brian and Jennie, in his mind calling them Mom and Dad more often than Brian and Jennie, and that weirded him out. He thought of calling them, but what would he say? "Um, hi, I don't know if you want to hear from me..." What was he to them? And that was ridiculous anyway. He didn't seriously think they'd forget him. Although he did think they might have tried.

He didn't need them, not for anything, and it all tangled like weeds that needed to be clearcut in his mind. He only thought of that because he took a temporary job working for a landscape company and ended up spending a lot of time cutting and pulling weeds.

But the way he kept checking windows of houses and businesses for a sniper made him feel a little crazy. It was always what you didn't know that had power over you, he thought, the gun pointed, bullet just waiting to explode inside your brain. Then he thought maybe it was being outside in the heat, the North Carolina summer heat, not that it was the goddamn hellhole Iraq. He wasn't in battle dress and a helmet, but he was used up on sweltering. He hated North Carolina, in the summer at least, but he hadn't anyplace else to go after Fort Bragg, and it had been easy to get a job off-base.

He heard another guy at work talking about a CDL, a Commercial Driver's License. Driving a truck. A big one. He figured if he could drive a Bradley and a Humvee, he could drive a rig. Turned out, if he started now, he could go to the school, get the license. A better job. See his own country, maybe. He'd seen enough of another one.

29

2014, PITTSBURGH

It hadn't been that hard for Monica to find where Deana's baby boy had been placed, but she had her training and research experience to call on, and Deana had had known just enough for her to use as a starting point—a dentist in the upper peninsula of Michigan. Monica had the date of birth, the name of the attorney who'd handled the private adoption because Deana had a copy of the relinquishment paper she'd signed, and the original birth certificate that would have been, of course, reissued with the names of the adoptive parents and whatever name they'd chosen for the baby.

Deana's registration with the state, making her available for her adult son to contact, had yielded nothing at all. Monica had double checked that. Monica had expected to have to hire her occasionally-used private investigator, but she hadn't. Put together, the information she'd had was just enough when she added a lot of time and persistence. And now that Angie had taken Celeste with her, Monica had nothing but time to spend on the Internet, searching through the records of dentists who were the right age in the upper peninsula, checking their biographical records, and what they'd reported to their alma maters about their families.

People are particularly proud, she knew, when they marry and when they have or adopt babies. Hadn't she announced her own little Celeste, oh the hole of her absence now don't think about it, to her undergraduate and law school magazines? It was a four-leaf clover, in a way, though: the dentist was a University of Michigan graduate. If he'd gone to some random out-of-state school, it wouldn't have worked, and private investigators are expensive. Deana had worked hard to save the money for this. Monica didn't want to spend more of it than she had to.

Was it just stubbornness? Monica asked herself. Why now? Why couldn't she let Angie's wishes—Angie's will—prevail? That's exactly it, she thought. Angie's trying to control me, to overpower me. In her way, it's not that different from Spencer Darcy. Angie would never, never see it that way, though.

They'd gotten nowhere the few times they'd spoken since Angie had left with Celeste. The shock had been visceral, a gut punch that initially flattened Monica into grief and defeat. The night she'd come home to resounding emptiness, her wife and daughter staying with one of Angie's former co-workers, when it was finally so late that Monica had known for sure that Angie really wasn't bringing Celeste home and wouldn't answer her cell phone, Monica had sobbed herself into dark hopelessness and loneliness. And anger. The voice in her head was its own argument: What have I done? Oh god, what have I done? Angie has no right to do this, no right. What have I done? She has no right. Finally, three quarters of a bottle of Chablis later, she'd settled on She has no right. She can't do this, Monica thought, and then, I won't let her do this as she looked at what she held in her hand, taken off the end table an hour earlier: a framed picture of Celeste, the baby's face an abstract painting of spaghetti sauce around her toothy delight.

At three twelve in the morning, as she sat on the couch wrapped in her wedding afghan, she'd called Angie for the last time that night, summoning enough lawyerly experience and sense to sound sober. "Angela, we can work it out. I love you. We're married. Celeste is our daughter and can't be in the middle. I'm asking you to bring her home now. You don't have the right to take her from our home." She recorded herself saying it, and date and time stamped her own message. She'd hung up then.

It wasn't like Angie had a case to justify asking for even temporary custody, Monica reasoned. Surely Angie wasn't going to do anything like that. She must just want some space to breathe and think things over. She'd know there were no grounds. What happened in Monica's office had nothing to do with how she parented Celeste. Monica was pretty sure that Angie wouldn't allege that anything adverse had ever happened to Celeste in their home. It would be a lie. I'm a good mother, Monica thought, and then she'd said it out loud. "I'm a good mother." And then, she couldn't fight it off: What if I'm not? Maybe I'm not. Wait, yes I am. Just because Angie stays home with her, that doesn't make her the only good mother. I'm a good mother.

The notion of filing for an emergency hearing made Monica sick. No, she'd wait and give Angie a chance to bring Celeste home. This was crazy. It didn't need to be happening.

Another call, another try. "Angie, I'm begging you. I know you said you were at Kathy's, and I'm sure it's a safe place, but I honestly don't know where she lives, and I have a right to know where our daughter is. I know I met Kathy, but I don't even remember her last name right now. You need to bring her home. And you. I love you. We can work anything out."

In the morning, Monica forced herself to the office, though she hadn't showered, touched her hair with a curling iron or dressed carefully. Too many tears, too much to drink, less than two hours sleep all told. As soon as she'd gotten to her desk, she'd called the two appointments she had that day and asked to reschedule, lying to both about having to be in court. Thank god I don't, she thought. She'd be embarrassed to be seen. She probably wouldn't have come in at all, but the appointment calendar was on the office computer, and she kept forgetting to sync it to her laptop, something she'd finally figured out how to do. Getting along without a secretary was still difficult, but it saved a lot of money. And she needed the money. Her family needed the money.

The calls made, Monica put her head down on her desk. Behind her, morning light revealed the dirt on the window, the scrim of dust on the bookcase, even the motes that lived in the air. How had she believed she'd escaped?

She should have known, should have known, should have known.

She woke, her neck aching, an hour later, to the vibration of her cell phone.

"It's me," Angie said. "Celeste is fine."

Monica swam to consciousness, remembering. "Angie? Angie! Oh my god. Is Celeste—"

"What? Celeste is fine."

"Where are you? Why did you leave? You can't—"

"Didn't you see my note? I've tried to explain that I've lost trust and I'm scared. I can't help how I feel."

"For god's sake, my case has nothing to do with us. With Celeste. Nothing. I'd give my life for her. You know that. I'm a lawyer. I'm sworn to do what's in my client's best interest."

"It all feels wrong to me. But I know you have the right to see Celeste, and I called to arrange that."

Monica leaned forward, shaking her head. "The right to see her? What? You don't have custody of our daughter, Angie. We're not separated. Our home is her home. You can't just take her away. Don't make me file for temporary emergency custody."

"I already filed. You know that as the full-time caretaking parent, I have—"

"You've done what? I don't believe you. On what grounds? Angie, don't do this. This is crazy. I love you. We can work this out. Don't you see, it's not right, it's not fair for you to exert this kind of control over—"

"—I love you too. But I have to do what I think is right. To protect Celeste. I went through too much, Monica. My parents went through too much. You know that."

Monica was quiet then. She swung her chair around to the window and stared out through marks from the last rain and the city dirt. She thought about giving in to Angie then. She wanted her family back.

"Who's breaking our trust now, Angie? Who left? I love you so much. And our girl. Our Celeste. And you know that." She hesitated. "I'll have to file my own motion as soon as we hang up."

But the judge ruled for Angie. It was something Monica could have predicted if she hadn't been so tired, so upset, or if she'd been thinking like an attorney rather than a parent. Other things being equal, in their county parents who have provided full-time care usually did have the upper hand. The magistrates pretty much ruled for them if there wasn't something to tip the scale the other way. And Monica couldn't come up with anything. She did, of course, get visitation and without the insult of it being supervised, every weekend Friday night to Sunday night. Two nights to Angie's five. Two days a week to rebond with Celeste, to refill the love coffer, the play-with-me coffer, the I am your mother coffer. It wasn't fair.

And, of course, she was ordered to pay temporary child and spousal support. It was going to be tight, like fitting two feet into the one shoe of her income, already stretched thin as pulled taffy. Angie knew that. Monica wondered if Angie was trying to force her into a second job, or even back to a law firm? No, Monica thought. She wouldn't do that. But then, Monica thought, I never thought she'd take Celeste and leave, not ever. I'd have bet my life on it. I'm dancing with a stranger to unfamiliar music.

The first time Angie brought Celeste for Monica to have her turn, Monica thought, I can't go on. I can't do this. Angie tearing as Celeste clung to her, as if Monica were a monster.

"It's okay, sweetheart. Mama will pick you up in two days, and we'll be together again. You get to spend time with Mommy now. You'll be fine." Angie said all the right things as the baby nestled into her neck, but she kept crying. "Take her, Monica," she said then, and dislodged Celeste partway, making Monica pull the little one away. "It's okay, she'll be okay," they'd said to each other at almost the same time.

By then Celeste was covered in snot and tears, a mass of panicked protest. It had been six days by then since Angie had taken her. Angie and the baby had been staying with Angie's friend—and, to be fair, Angie had provided the address, even with an apology that Monica had been in the dark initially, saying it wasn't her intent. The exchange was taking place in a "neutral setting," which they'd agreed could be the courthouse steps when Monica was leaving work.

It had taken just a short time for Celeste to settle down once she was in her familiar home. Monica had resisted the impulse to buy her new toys, but she gave in about cookies, and then about ice cream, even about Barney. She wanted Celeste to protest leaving this wonderful place again. Ever.

By Saturday morning, it was as if Celeste's memory fully came back—oh yes, this is my Mommy, I love her. She giggled and played. They sang their familiar songs and kissed and cuddled, and at night Monica held her daughter, whispered as she had from the first night they'd been a family, "I love you, sweetheart, I am always here, and I always love you."

But when she said it again into the baby's ear when she met Angie for the exchange back, Celeste didn't cling to Monica nor scream in protest. Monica absorbed that, confused and sad. The toddler was willing to go back. Her sturdy, heartbreaking legs and arms were wrapped around Angie's waist and neck as Angie told her, "Wave bye bye to Mommy." Angie mouthed I'm sorry, her face crumpling as she started to turn, to walk away from the courthouse steps with their daughter. Did she know it was a knife, telling Celeste to wave goodbye?

The baby waved.

&

Monday morning Monica forced herself to the office, mainly because she couldn't bear the acuity of Celeste's absence, like an unrelenting toothache she could not ignore. Maybe she could smother it with distraction, she thought. Be in a place that Celeste hadn't. And it was clear she couldn't do without the income.

It occurred to her that word of their separation would get around the court. That her referrals might dry up in the same way Monica's hope that Angie would just come home had withered. For sure, case referrals had been Angie-connected when Monica first opened the solo practice. Angie was the one who'd known the domestic and juvenile lawyers, magistrates and judges. But Monica had done excellent work—she was sure of that much—and had come to feel that she'd found a niche in the law where she could be empathic and kind. Would that be enough to put out any wildfire rumor that could burn her practice? Had she established herself separately enough yet? Angie wouldn't say anything to hurt Monica's practice, would she? One more thing to worry about.

She wouldn't, couldn't, drop Deana's case because Angie wanted her to. That's what wouldn't be ethical. Angie had it all wrong.

With something to prove about righteousness and Deana's son's adoptive parents already identified, it only took the morning for Monica to track the reissued birth certificate. Monica closed her eyes as she realized she'd found him. She hadn't been at all sure she could, and that would have changed everything. It certainly wouldn't have been the same as refusing the case. She considered right and wrong, rights given, rescinded, reclaimed. Considered power, who had it and who did not. She shook her head, opened her eyes. She went on. They'd named him Daniel.

His full name was Daniel Dirk Larsen. Son of Brian Dirk and Jennifer Dahl Larsen. Both parents were University of Michigan graduates. Brian also graduated from their dental school, Monica had already known, but now she found that Jennie (her name, spelled that way in an alumni marriage announcement) also had a Master's degree in Elementary Education with a specialty in reading. Both were retired—thank you again, alumni office—but still living where Daniel had grown up. Remarkably stable, Monica mused. What I wanted for Celeste. No, what I want for Celeste. Or maybe it's boring. Think of it that way. Daniel must have gone to school there. Let's see. Did Michigan have a high school graduation test in the eighties? Wait, check driver's license registrations in Michigan. That's easier. As she started to track Daniel, Monica made herself talk out loud to stay focused on the task at hand. Don't think about Celeste.

By Wednesday, she knew he'd enlisted, reupped once, knew he'd been in Iraq four times. And, she had a fix on the honorable discharge four years earlier, when he'd been twenty-six.

She'd lost him then. He hadn't surfaced back in Michigan, which she'd thought he would. What was he qualified to do? How would he be supporting himself? She was stymied. She started to search states for drivers' licenses and found him in North Carolina. At the time, he'd given an address near his last base, which had been Fort Bragg. And the jackpot: a commercial driver's license.

And that's where she hit the wall.

There had to be hundreds of trucking companies in North Carolina. And, she realized, he could be working for a moving company. Or a grocery chain. Or Sears home delivery. Or, or, or…. Logically, the thing to do was to ask his parents how to get in touch with him. Could she do that without revealing who she was and the nature of her mission? That didn't seem right. And yet, to go through his parents seemed somehow hurtful. Monica didn't know why. Maybe, she thought, it's the specter of Angie calling in the dark: no, no, no! You have no right. How would you feel if it were Celeste? I know about this, I've lived it. You haven't. You are doing the wrong thing.

Monica slumped over her keyboard.

She stayed that way for a half hour, straightening up when her shoulders and neck demanded it. Her mind wasn't far behind. Finally resolute, she tapped in the web address for Expedia and began searching flights to Pellston, the closest she could get to Charlevoix. She discovered it was going to be a pain to get there, involving a plane change and then a small regional airport. But she also knew it would be unkind to approach the Larsens by phone. She'd have to lie about why she wanted to see them and to get an appointment for late in the day, but that couldn't be helped. She'd tell the truth as soon as she was there.

30

CHARLEVOIX, 2014

Brian had answered the phone when the woman called and handed it off to Jennie because she'd asked for Mr. or Mrs. Larsen. He knew he was weird with the phone these days, hating to deal with it, assuming it was a telemarketer. He kept threatening to have the landline disconnected, even though they both knew they kept it because it was the number that Daniel would know, in case he ever called them. Which he hadn't. But since they'd had to put Bear down last year when he struggled to get to his feet and it wasn't fair to wait for Daniel anymore, the damn landline was like a last connector somehow.

When they'd taken Bear to the vet that last time, Brian and Jennie had both held him, sobbing. Afterward, Brian buried him in the yard, under the old treehouse. Shivering, Brian dug the grave in the thin gray of early November, and with a tender chant, goodbye, thank you, boy, good boy, good boy, he replaced the earth. When he came in from the dusk, he pretended the whiskey he drank by the fire was because he'd gotten so cold. Jennie drank to keep him company, she said, her eyes swollen.

"Jen, honey. Monica Somebody on the phone, wants Mrs. Larsen—" Brian called, walking toward her as he did, the receiver in his outstretched hand. It's time to get rid of this thing, he thought again. The junk calls are making me crazy. 'Cardholder services,' my left nut. There's no point in keeping it. Daniel's not going to call us, for godsake. Not after twelve years. He can reach us, anyway. It's not like we're not right in the same damn place as always.

All they knew for sure was that he'd joined the Army. They wouldn't have known that much except that Daniel's friend Mike was a good kid. When Daniel hadn't come home the day after graduation, Brian had gone out looking. Not to get his friends in trouble with their families, not that at all, but just what any parent would do. Even though Daniel had every right not to come home, he and Jennie knew that. Brian explained to the boys who knew him, who'd maybe believe him: we only want to know that he's all right. Most of them claimed they didn't know where he was, although Brian thought he read discomfort on a few faces and didn't believe them. Mike had been working at McDonald's part-time during their senior year, one of the few pieces of information Daniel had ever let drop and Brian thought Mike might be there as a summer job. It was worth a try.

A worker at the counter said yes, Mike worked there but had left for the day. He'd be back tomorrow. When Brian asked what time, the worker seemed to decide that maybe she shouldn't have said anything. "I don't know," was all Brian could get.

But it had been easy. Brian went back the next morning and Mike was there. He waited until there was no line and went to the counter. Brian didn't remember Mike having those shaved-up sideburns, like he might have a buzz cut under that McDonald's cap, but Brian couldn't tell for sure. The other kids didn't wear their hair that short.

"Mike, do you remember me?" he'd said. "Brian Larsen, Daniel's Dad."

Word must have gotten out that he was looking for Daniel. "Uh, yes sir." Mike said. His adams apple moved large in his throat. "I'm not allowed to visit with a customer during my shift. May I take your order?"

"A small black coffee. When would you be free?"

"One small black coffee. Would you like cream with that? I don't get off until four."

"Black. I'll come back at four."

"Oh, right. Black. Yes, sir."

Brian hadn't told Jennie what he was doing, not wanting to either give her hope or upset her more. She was trying to reconcile herself to Daniel's absence. Reconcile herself to failure, she'd said. Maybe that was best.

But Mike had come clean when Brian waylaid him as he left the fast-food joint that afternoon.

"Believe me, this is only because his mother and I are worried. We only want to know that he's okay. Do you know where he is and if he's okay? He didn't see us after graduation."

"I'm sorry, sir. I feel like it's Daniel's place to tell you."

"But you do know."

"Well...I do, sir." Mike did have a buzz cut, and his hair was so fair that Brian could see his scalp. He put that together with how straight the boy was standing, and how every sentence was punctuated with sir. This was a boy who had fallen in love with the military.

"So, Mike, what are your own plans?"

Brian later told Jennie, the kid almost lit up. "I'm following my dad, sir. U.S. Navy, sir. I go in the week after next."

"I'm sure he's very proud of you. And your mother. Did Daniel ever express any interest in the military to you?"

Eyes down, although to his credit, he still stood up straight. "Uh, not the Navy sir. Daniel gets seasick. His uncle's boat…?"

"Oh yes, yes. Jennie's brother. Well, that would let out the Coast Guard." Brian had manufactured some jocularity. "Airsickness is something like seasickness. Must be the Army then."

Mike had looked relieved. "Yes sir. He enlisted. I believe he leaves either today or tomorrow. He'll be fine."

"Thank you, Mike. I appreciate your honesty. You've relieved my worry and more importantly, you'll have relieved his mother's. You'll make a fine sailor."

"Thank you, sir."

"You be well, now. Anchors away." Brian had hidden his distress while trying to make Mike feel good, not knowing if Daniel had sworn his friend to any secrecy. There was no reason for Daniel to do this behind their backs. No reason. Like so much with Daniel, no reason, no sense to it. It was a disappointment that Daniel wouldn't at least try some more education, but Brian could have tried to get himself behind the military. He'd at least have tried. He'd gotten back into his car shaking his head. He'd had to sit there a few minutes to get his emotions in check before he drove.

Rolling her eyes at him now, and mouthing, I don't want that! Jennie took the phone from Brian in the family room. "This is Jennie Larsen," she said with some irritation in her voice. "Who's calling, please?"

Behind Jennie's back, Brian smirked in the hallway. Usually, she was able to stick him with handling junk calls. He stood and listened, wondering how long it would take her to dump this one.

"What about Daniel? Who are you?" she said, her voice sharp.

"From the VA? Is he hurt?" After a pause, pitch rising.

"Why can't you tell me on the phone?" Jennie spun around, looking for Brian. He was already behind her.

"Yes, all right, tomorrow. Any chance you could come today?"

"Yes. We'll be here." And she hung up then.

To Brian, she said, "I don't know. It's Monica Somebody—I should have made her spell her name—from the VA. It's about Daniel. She says she's not calling because he's hurt or dead but there's business concerning him that she needs to discuss in person. She'll come tomorrow. I don't know. Did you ever hear of anything like that?"

"Did you get her phone number?"

Jennie shook her head. "I should have. I panicked when she said VA. We can call the VA."

He shook his head. "Come on, Jen. And ask if Monica works there? We already know they won't give us any information about Daniel beyond what's public record. Remember?"

Jennie sat in the wingback chair and tucked her legs beneath her, huddling, though with the late fire the room was almost too warm. Brian only expressed his frustration by landing hard on the couch when he sat down. The one time he should have talked to a damn stranger on the damn phone, he thought. The one time. He'd have made that Monica person explain on the phone. He wasn't going to say that to Jennie, though.

31

CHARLEVOIX

Monica pulled the rented Ford Taurus to the curb in front of the stately colonial. It was white with green shutters and door, in a huge yard canopied by bare branches of old, thick-trunked trees. A torn basketball net hung from a backboard over the garage. She sat, her heart beating too fast in her chest, her ears. Too much coffee, she thought. And she was shivering. Why hadn't she thought to look at the weather? It was early spring in Pittsburgh, but winter in the upper peninsula of Michigan. Inches of snow on the ground. Stockings and heels with just a trench coat over her navy business suit weren't cutting it. Snow, for godssake.

She finally forced herself out of the car and walked up the driveway, grateful that it, and the walk, had been cleared. To the left of the house, she glimpsed a tree house in the back yard, which would have been hidden had the trees been leafed out. At the edge of the yard, a woodpile was stacked, precise as Lincoln Logs, beneath a three-sided shelter, completing a scene as neat as one in a magazine. This home and yard was what she wanted someday for Celeste, Monica thought, and it was what the Larsens had provided for Deana's son. No, she thought. He was the Larsen's son. Daniel. This is his home. His parents are here for him, even now. I wouldn't want someone saying Celeste was anyone's daughter but mine and Angie's. Angie's right about that, Monica thought, uncomfortable. Damn. Maybe she's right about it all.

Monica let her steps slow. Maybe she'd turn around, leave, call them with a profound apology, say there'd been an error at the VA, and they'd identified the wrong Corporal Daniel Larsen.

But he's an adult. He'll have a choice. She started to argue with herself.

She didn't have time to think it through. She'd made it only as far as the junction of the driveway and the walkway to the front door, where she'd paused when the front door opened, and a blonde woman stepped onto the porch, her face anxious. "Are you from the VA?"

"Uh, yes," Monica called back, caught. What else could she say? Later she'd wish she'd thought faster. How about "I'm lost. Can you give me directions back to Main Street?" She could have just said that.

"Please come in. We've been going crazy since you called."

Monica went up the steps and extended her hand. "I'm Monica Connell."

"Come in Ms. Connell. This is my husband, Brian, I'm Jennie. May I take your coat?"

Monica was freezing, but it seemed rude to refuse, so she took it off as she tried to gather her thoughts.

"Have a seat," Jennie said, pointing, as she handed Monica's coat to Brian. "You look cold. May I get you some tea?"

"That would be lovely. Thank you. I'm afraid I didn't prepare well for the weather."

Monica instantly realized she'd cut off her thinking time when Brian picked up the weather conversation as Jennie went into the kitchen.

"So, you must have come from a VA office where the weather is a bit warmer?" he said. For a dentist, this guy knew how to start an interrogation, Monica thought.

"I'm from Pennsylvania, and yes, spring is much more on the way there than here."

"So, is Daniel is Pennsylvania now? We're so worried. Please."

"Let's wait for Jennie and I'll explain." Monica put him off, and Brian immediately stood.

"I'll go help her," he said. "We have to know what's going on."

As he left, Monica took in the room. A fire was high and warm, so the chill was leaving her. She pulled in a long breath and exhaled. Pale teal walls, off-white woodwork, terracotta, teal and green patterned rug on hardwood floor. Peach pillows on mushroom colored sturdy sofa. A TV, bookcases, upholstered chair and recliner. Framed prints of lake scenes, or maybe they were watercolors, vaguely impressionistic. A high school graduation picture—Daniel, Monica assumed—on the mantle with pictures of a younger boy hugging a dog, family pictures with some older couples. A boy in a treehouse. An inviting, comfortable family room. They'd lived here his whole childhood.

But—Deana. Her first responsibility was to her client.

No, Monica thought then. My first responsibility is to myself. I learned that after Spencer Darcy. And I already decided to represent my client.

She breathed in and breathed out until Jennie came back, three mugs on a tray. She set it down on the coffee table and handed one to Monica, who put both hands, still chilly, around its heat.

Monica took a sip, giving herself a moment to size Jennie up. She was a pretty woman, possibly older than she looked at first glance, maybe mid-fifties or even sixty, aged by the lines around her eyes. Slender, very fair and blue-eyed, she'd taken care of herself. When she spoke, she was direct but soft-voiced. She put Monica in mind of a poised butterfly.

"We're ready, Ms. Connell. You wouldn't have come in person if it were good, but you said he's not dead or hurt, so what is it?"

Monica tried not to shift her eyes away from Jennie's. Failed. If Jennie were a poised butterfly, Monica was an insect with a stinger. She hated the feeling of shame, or was it guilt, she felt. But it had to be said. "Please call me Monica. And I'm so sorry. I couldn't explain on the phone. I'm not from the VA. I'm an attorney. I represent Daniel's biological mother."

Jennie leaned back in her seat, eyes wide. But Brian leaned forward, his eyes narrowed. As fair haired and complexioned as Jennie, now his face was reddening. It was he who spoke.

"What are you saying? You misled us? What exactly do you want?"

"Nothing disruptive or harmful, Brian, I assure you. She is only hoping to meet him. That's all." Monica hoped that was the truth.

Brian erupted in laughter. He leaned back and shook his head. "Oh, she would like to meet him, would she? That's rich. Good luck with that."

Jennie leaned forward then and reached from her chair to where Brian sat, on the near end of the couch. She put her hand on his leg. "Brian, honey. Don't."

Brian looked at his wife. "Why not?"

"She doesn't know."

"Yeah, that's obvious."

"You can be decent."

"Yeah. I can be decent. That's right." Brian shrugged, but his voice was still dark when spoke again. "Monica," he said, shifting to look at her again, "Your client—why did she send you to us? How does she know who we are?"

"I apologize for upsetting you. My client isn't responsible for sending me, and she has no idea who you are. That's confidential, and it will remain that way. I haven't been able to track Daniel, but I was able to find you. I thought that you might possibly—"

"Well, the answer is no."

"I understand how you feel. You see, I have a daughter I adopted. She's just a baby, not quite seventeen months, but I adore her, she's my life and I know how—"

"No, you don't know. You have no understanding of this." He sounded angry.

Monica stalled by drinking some tea. "Thank you very much for this, Jennie." Then she fell back on a lawyer technique. "Then I'd like to understand. Would you explain it to me?"

Brian signed and looked at Jennie. Monica saw something pass between them. Jennie nodded. Brian shrugged and gestured. "Go ahead if you want," he said.

"My husband and I go back and forth," Jennie said, speaking to Monica. "We trade positions. Only one of us can despair or be upset at a time, we've decided. It's my turn to stay calm about Daniel. Here's the thing. Daniel was…difficult. We struggled a lot trying to find our way with him." She paused, looked down, then back up at Monica, breathed in and said, "He cut us out of his life after he graduated from high school. We were able to find out he enlisted in the Army, and that he's out now. Just what's public record, but we haven't heard from him. It appears he doesn't want anything to do with us, so I'm afraid we can't help you. Although if you find him, I hope you'll tell him his parents still love him very much."

Brian sighed. "Yeah, that too." His eyes glittered, wet, as if bitterness had dissolved in the moment, and he used the back of his hand against them quickly. "I'm sure I made mistakes," he said.

Jennie picked up the hand he'd used against his face which Brian had let drop to his lap. She held it. "Doubtless," she said quietly. "Doubtless we both did." Then she looked at Monica. "We tried to be good parents. We did try hard. It just wasn't enough."

"Oh my god," was all Monica could say. "I'm so sorry." Her tears embarrassed her.

32

ON I-95, GEORGIA

It wasn't like he'd never thought about calling them. What reason would he give though? He couldn't have called at Christmas. It would seem like he wanted something. And that was after he'd already missed Jennie's birthday, that was in October, and he couldn't remember if it was the 15th or the 16^{h}, and it would be so bad to get it wrong that he couldn't chance it. He didn't want to sound like a pathetic loser. Where could he say he lived? At truck stops? In the cab of his truck? In motels? It made him sound like a drifter but it wasn't practical to pay for an apartment and furniture and utilities, all that stuff, when the cab was comfortable, and people who weren't drivers didn't know that the big truck stops had showers and all kinds of facilities for men like him. He wasn't the only one.

But maybe he was the only one with no friends, no ties, no family. Oh, he talked to guys. He'd gotten to know the ones he saw all the time on the same runs. Maybe they were friends. Sure, yeah. He could call them friends.

If he called, what could he say? I sometimes feel like shit about how I left, and I know a lot of stuff was my fault. So I thought I'd say I'm sorry and tell you I'm okay and ask how you are. I mean if you still want to talk to me at all. If you don't, it's okay, I mean, I understand. Could he say that? Would they even listen long enough for him to say it? They must hate him.

When Daniel thought about trying to get that many words out, even tried to practice it while he drove his rig down I-95 in Georgia, he got very nervous. His heart thudded and banged like something caged, something wild trying to escape. A stupid little red sportscar cut in front of him and frustrated, he pulled on the horn and flipped the bird at the driver when he saw his head tilt up to the rear-view mirror. Daniel had specifically been told not to do stuff like that. His rig had that obsequious question, "How am I driving?" in big print along with a 1-800 number on it. Daniel always wanted paste 1-800-EAT-SHIT over the number given. Truck drivers were the best on the road. Get everyone but them off and the country would be a hell of a lot safer. That was his theory. Practicing something to say in case he ever decided to call Brian and Jennie was eating the edges of his concentration. He had to stop.

And he did, for a while. But it came back. It used to happen when he was in the service, when new guys on their first tours got letters from their parents, the ones they weren't embarrassed to read aloud, the funny story-parts about a younger brother or sister. Some of the mothers were good at that and it was nice to hear. It made him remember Jennie, how she'd try to tell him stories, and he'd say they were stupid. They weren't, not really, and he didn't know why he'd said that. He'd get sad then, and when buddies asked where his folks lived, he'd shake his head and get gruff, say he didn't have any, to stop more questions. Only a couple had said, "Oh shit dude, I'm sorry. What happened, man?" Then he'd look away and say he didn't want to talk about it. If he had to, he'd get mad and walk away. They left him alone then.

He could put it all out of his mind most of the time. A piece of his life that was on a high shelf in a closet behind a closed door. Why would he take it out now? It made no sense to him, and he thought he didn't want to, but the idea came more frequently. He thought of Brian, how maybe he could call when it was Brian's birthday. That was sort of a reason, and it wouldn't seem like he wanted something from them. He didn't want to seem like he was coming around wanting something. Even if he didn't know what he wanted.

He went so far as to check the white pages. Jesus. They were still listed, same address, same phone number. He tucked the knowledge with his memories, his shame, and missing them on the shelf. The closet door wasn't closing all the way anymore.

He thought it was good they had the landline. Maybe meant they didn't have cell phones. If they did want to talk to him, would they want the kind where you could see the person? He had that on his phone and had seen people use it on the base all the time, but he'd never had anyone to use it with.

He wondered if they looked the same. He was sure he didn't. His haircut for one, though he'd let the buzz cut grow out some, it wasn't nearly as long as he'd had it in high school. Another difference was the tattoo. Jennie would hate that, but he could cover the big one up, wear long sleeves. He still brushed his teeth all the time, never did get out of that habit. His mouth felt like it was growing hair if he didn't. That, at least, would make Brian happy.

What he was sure he missed was the dog. Bear. He felt so bad when he remembered Bear. No way Bear could still be alive, could he? He hadn't even said goodbye or explained to Bear, and he hadn't always paid enough attention to him, when all Bear wanted was to play. That dog was just good, all good. And he was smart. Brian had let Daniel pick him out from a shelter, said, "It's important to adopt dogs that need a home, you know. People pay a lot of money for purebred dogs, but that makes no sense to me. It's mutts like Bear—looks like he's got some beagle in him, do you think?—that make the best pets. They're grateful."

That had wounded Daniel, made him mad and wonder if Brien was really talking about him. Not that he'd ever ask. But Bear's heart was pure gold wrapped up in forty pounds of black and tawny brown hair, with long legs and nose. He was smart, too. He loved to have the soft little valley behind his ears scratched. Or his belly rubbed. He'd roll on his back, legs up in the air for it, trusting Daniel.

Looking back, Daniel thought he'd been cold, leaving Bear that way. Brian and Jennie would have taken care of Bear and loved him, but it probably wasn't the same as him, the person who was supposed to love Bear the most forever. He wondered if Bear had forgotten him. Or ever forgave him. No way, he figured. He wasn't forgiven. Who could forgive someone for abandonment? He wouldn't, that was for sure.

Brian's birthday was in April. Too bad it wasn't on April Fool's Day, Daniel thought. That'd be the perfect day. The joke would be on him if Brian or Jennie didn't even answer after all his thinking about it. Maybe they'd be in Europe or something. They had money. Or maybe they'd hang up on him. He had a couple of weeks to mull it over. Or not. It was too hard to figure out. At night, he could go to a bar, listen to music and drink. Used to, he'd buy drinks for a flirtable woman, but not really since New Year's, when he'd met Susannah. Just as long as he was sober in eight hours. To drive. The highway could hum louder than thoughts if you gave way to its song. You just listen to that, stare at the lines ahead and keep going. Away.

33

As soon as she felt she could leave the Larson's, she'd made a show of looking at her watch and said, "Goodness, I hadn't realized it was so late. I should get going. I can't thank you enough for your time, and I apologize for bothering you. I truly hope your son calls you soon." As the Larson's front door closed behind her, Monica walked to her car feeling vaguely guilty, ashamed, and defensive, yet they'd said nothing critical. Their elegant neighborhood shuttered itself as she left. She knew she'd upset the couple, although they'd been polite, even gracious. And upset them to what end? The bullshit meter she'd developed in the domestic relations courtroom hadn't registered a word either one had said as less than authentic. These people still grieved, still wondered what they could have, should have, done differently.

They had no idea what had happened to Daniel once he'd separated from the Army. Monica knew more than they. She knew about the North Carolina driver's license, about the commercial driver's license. She hadn't told them, unsure what was right or wrong. They weren't her clients. Was it proprietary information she had no right to divulge? Would it cause them more pain? She hadn't even finished the hot tea they'd given her, though she was cold, tired and confused and longed to ask the Larsons questions about Daniel. But it would have been wrong, so wrong—unethical, really—to conflate her own agenda with her professional responsibility, because she only wanted to beat down her sudden, crazy fear for Celeste, who of late had learned to shake her head violently. Started to scream more vehement protests when she didn't want her diaper changed. That surely couldn't have anything to do with being adopted. It made no sense. Still, Monica was uneasy. Brian and Jennie had gotten Daniel when he was just days old. What she wanted was evidence that her baby was different from Daniel, very different. Unlosable

In the car, Monica shook her head. No, it can't be that, she told herself. Look at Angie. She was three, and she'd been in a slew of foster homes. Look at how she turned out. Adoption, whenever it happens, had nothing to do with what happened with Daniel. Parents lose kids all the time—to drugs, to arguments over their being gay. To divorce, she thought suddenly. To alienation. She fought that back, reasoning with herself: lots of kids have great relationships with both parents. And Angie hasn't said the word divorce. This is just a temporary separation while we sort things out. We love each other. That hasn't changed.

It hadn't even occurred to Monica that Daniel's parents wouldn't know exactly where he was, how to get in touch with him. She'd assumed. Just assumed. Once she cleared the Larsen's neighborhood and was into the upscale tourist town of Charlevoix, quiet now, before the arrival of the wealthy summer people, Monica turned into the parking lot of a local café and turned off the ignition. Her heart beat, too loud. Slow down, she said. Breathe, she said. Think, she said.

She got her cell phone out of her purse and pushed the icon with Angie's picture. She thought she should replace it with a picture of Celeste. On the third ring, Angie answered with a simple, "Hi." She didn't sound irritated as she sometimes did, and Monica sucked in hope.

"What do you need?" Not hostile, if not particularly friendly.

"I know I said I'd be gone overnight on business, but it turns out I'm going to try to change that reservation and get home tonight. I'm…I'm really missing Celeste. Would you please let me have her tomorrow night—just this once?"

"Tomorrow's not your night."

Monica couldn't quite tell if that was a refusal. Angie's voice hadn't been unkind, so she dared the appeal. "I know, I realize that. It's just that—I'd really appreciate it. I would do something back for you. Like give her back to you earlier on Sunday maybe? I think we could work it out."

"Monica, I think we should just stick to the schedule. It usually works best that way in the long run. I'm not trying to give you a hard time, but you've always told clients that." Her voice was resolute.

Two women came out of the café then. Both were laughing and the taller one put her arm around the shoulders of the other in a quick hug. The shorter one, who had brown hair and wore glasses got into the driver's seat of the car parked next to Monica, shaking her head, her grin lingering. The tall one got in the passenger seat.

In her rental car, Monica closed her eyes. "Usually both partners being flexible helps, I find that, too." She hated the pleading that crept into her own voice. Next would come the bitterness because she knew Angie would turn her down. She knew that ugly progression from experience. "But okay, if that's what you want. We'll stick to the schedule." Yes, there it was, the emphasis on the word schedule, the faint suggestion of a warning that when Angie wanted something from Monica by way of an adjustment, she'd get the same treatment back.

There was nothing to do, nothing she could think of but to work. She had clients. She had this case. She would report to Deana and let her know there was nothing to do now but hire an investigator. Deana would spend the money; she'd already made that clear. Maybe it would go cold. Monica didn't know if she hoped it would. She doubted that would make a difference to Angie. She suspected she'd burned that bridge as effectively as if she'd shot a long-distance flame-thrower ahead of herself. And for what?

She went into the café and bought a coffee to go. She was across the street from a marina; it seemed there was a lake at the end of almost every street. She could stay here tonight, take a walk on a beach. What a place for a family vacation. Boats and nature trails and curio shops to explore. Searching for Petoskey stones. Celeste and Angie would love it. Thinking of them overcame her, then. How did I end up like this? How did I make such a mess of my life? Why is it so hard to tell when a simple choice like taking a new client is going to derail the train—when I make dozens of simple choices a day and they're just that, each a single car that stays on its own track.

Angie was right, she thought then. Destiny has nothing to do with anything. It's all our choices. We think that the choices are right when we make them, and maybe they are. Except our own history shapes what we believe we must do, and so our lived moments, days, years become our destiny? Is there any such thing as pure choice?

No, she wouldn't stay here asking herself questions that had no answers. It wasn't a bad drive to the Pellston airport. If there was still a flight out tonight to Detroit, she'd see if she could still get on it. Otherwise, first thing tomorrow. Tomorrow. At least she'd be at the hotel in Detroit tonight. There'd be room service. A hot shower. She'd order a bottle of Chablis and drink to how beautiful, how fragile a built life is, and broken easily as crystal by a choice. A choice that wasn't necessarily a bad one. Except for the cost.

34

The hang ups to their landline started sometime—neither Brian nor Jennie were sure—after April first. The first one had been that day, which had made Brian think it was some kid's idea of an April Fool's Day prank. It wasn't as if they hadn't had them before, though. Everyone gets hang up calls. Usually, their caller ID would show it had been a telemarketer, or occasionally someone local who hadn't the manners to apologize for dialing incorrectly. But the caller ID was blocked. Or it was a private caller, whatever that meant.

After the fourth time, it was Jennie who said it, although Brian later admitted he'd had the same thought. They were in the glassed-in sunroom that converted to a screened porch in warm weather, which this wasn't, not yet, but the first signs of spring had started in the woods behind the house, and they were having wine. "Nice that it's staying light later every day, isn't it? I love daylight saving," Jennie said, elaborately casual. "You know, the phone thing? You don't imagine that that attorney maybe found him and told him what I said…or something?"

"Oh God, honey. Let's not go there, okay? She's a decent person, you could tell. She'd have let us know. But we answered the phone. If he was calling and we answered the phone, for God's sake, why wouldn't he say something? That doesn't exactly make sense."

"Oh. Right. Well, I was just thinking."

"Jen…seriously." It was still his turn to be negative. He'd switch off when she got melancholy or upset. He read her like a book. By now it was like being in college and picking up a beginning reader. It kept them sane. An hour ago, Jennie brought up getting another dog, and he'd pretended to have to think about it before agreeing. She wanted to go to the shelter tomorrow to look for one. Maybe that golden retriever/Lab mix she'd seen in a picture the shelter put in the local paper. If Brian would hurry up and go with her while the dog was still there. He'd go. He'd tell her after dinner and let her talk him into going first thing in the morning. A dog to train—and love—would be good for both of them.

&

There were two more phone calls the next week. Then another the next week. Hangups registered on their Caller ID. "The do not call list is for shit." Brian said. "I think these are those damn computer calls."

"Can we report it somewhere? Like the phone company? Or just get the damn thing disconnected? We don't need it. It's a waste of money, you're right."

"…robocalls that hang up when the machine answers," he said, still musing. "Some company's glommed on to our number. Supposed to be illegal—but nothing stops them."

Over the past several weeks, they'd each answered the phone, and no one was on the other end. That, too. But he wasn't going to push about disconnecting the landline, something he'd already argued for. Let her get annoyed enough to come to it herself now. "You got anything on for today? Who's on dog walking duty when? I thought I'd run in to the office at lunch and see how Tom's doing."

"I'll do the puppy," she said. "I still think you should do that volunteer stuff at the clinic. They need a dentist. It's not that far to drive."

"Helluva long time since I did any general dentistry, y'know, before ortho, honey."

"Don't you think anything would help the clinic patients? I mean even what if all you did was identify mouth and throat cancers early. But they told you they have donated equipment just for filling cavities. You can do that. Like riding a bike. Say no root canals or extractions."

"I suppose," Brian said, draining his coffee mug. "I'll see if Tom wants to donate any supplies. Tax write-off anyway." He unfolded the paper. "When you gonna teach her to go get the paper?" he said, pointing to the retriever with his chin. The dog's head popped up from where she'd been curled nose to tail on the rug in front of the sink. "I don't see actually the golden in her. Tail's not bushy. Looks more yellow Lab to me. What else did Dr. Raghu guess might be mixed in? Please, not beagle. They're nuts."

"Let sleeping dogs lie," Jennie said, and she laughed. It was good. Brian didn't like it when the burden of finding hope or meaning or any cheer was on him. He liked it when it was Jennie's turn. Neither one of them had brought up Daniel when they talked about the phone this time. That ship had sailed.

35

I-40, NORTH CAROLINA, 2014

It was like being back in the desert, only alone, waiting for an IED to go off, no buddy there to have his back. He used the recall on his phone to call his parents' (now trying the term cautiously) number again. The number that used to be his, too. He imagined it ringing in the kitchen, and, at the same time, on the extensions on the sunporch and upstairs, in their bedroom. A couple of times the machine had answered, and he'd hung up quickly, before it could get through the outgoing message. But once Brian had answered. "Hello? Hello?" then a long pause, waiting. Then a final "Hello?" and then he'd hung up while Daniel was still holding his breath, trying to work up to saying something, he couldn't think of what right then, everything he'd practiced had suddenly been wrong, and he didn't know if Brian? Or Dad? sounded stupid. Both did. Obviously some other guy wouldn't be answering the phone.

It didn't matter. Brian or Dad, it didn't matter. He'd hung up.

Daniel shelved it for almost a week while he drove a Route 1 trip that was annoying. He could think much better on the freeway. He tried again. It had weirded him out to hear Brian's voice, he decided. He'd just say, "It's me, Daniel." That wouldn't be stupid.

That time Jennie answered the phone. Shit. Why hadn't he prepared for that? Brian had sounded pretty much the same, but Jennie's voice (it must be her, he told himself) wasn't familiar, like the smell of roast chicken or chocolate chip cookies he'd know anywhere from when he lived there. She used to do the voices of the characters, even animals, in stories when he was little and she read to him. He'd made her cry when he was a teenager, and she used to get really mad. She'd always had a teacher voice. He used to mock it. He remembered those voices of hers, but when she answered the phone, she just sounded like a nice lady he might have met before, but might not have. Daniel was the one who hung up.

Why was this so hard? It's not like they can do anything to you, he told himself. They don't know where you are. What's the big deal? If you don't want to call them, don't. If you do want to, then freaking do it. Stop being a moron.

He decided he'd call on Brian's birthday. Again tried to remember the right date, if it was the twenty-first or the twenty-third. Decided it was better to be early than late, and he could say, "I thought I'd call to wish you a happy birthday," and it would be best if he did it on the twenty-first. If one of them said, "It's not for two more days," then he'd say, "I remember that, but I wouldn't be able to call then, so I'm calling now," and they'd probably let it go.

He hoped it would be Brian who answered.

He prepared by calling himself insulting names about being a coward while he drove all day, practicing what he'd say. He called up every gross insult the guys in his unit had flipped at each other when they were on tour and used them on himself. Except the ones about their mothers, which made him uncomfortable right then.

Still running the east coast between Jersey and Georgia, he stopped for the night outside of Wilmington, North Carolina. It was late April warm, stuff blooming everywhere, making him sneeze. Not like the upper peninsula of Michigan, where the arms of trees might have a faint green aura or might not yet. It's a late spring there, but when it comes, there's nothing like it. Nothing so pretty in the world. Cherry blossoms came to his mind. The lace of them used to be everywhere, hadn't it been in early May? He'd like to see that again sometime. That, and how they smelled, like God had spilled pale pink lemonade at a wedding in heaven, or he'd think that if he believed in God, which he only sometimes did. He'd been to a wedding by a cherry orchard once with his parents, and there was lemonade for the kids. He hadn't wanted to go, and then he'd had fun playing with other kids and didn't get into trouble that day. Maybe his parents remembered, but if they didn't it would be stupid to bring it up. He really wanted to know how Bear was. Please let Bear be okay. Let something be okay.

There was a good stop he'd found before, off of I-40. He took a shower, ordered roast chicken and mashed potatoes to keep the right mood going even though it was hot outside. Then hit the bar to calm his nerves. No more than two shots. Jack Daniels. He had to have a clear mind. Just two.

He'd call from his cab. No background noise there to distract him. He'd go through with it. One way or another, he'd get it off his mind. If they hated him for good now, at least he'd know. He could figure things out from there. He touched redial on his phone.

"The number you have reached has been disconnected. Please be sure you have the right number in mind and have called or dialed it correctly."

Daniel pulled the phone from his ear and stared at it in his hand. This was a mistake. He'd called that number and gotten an answer six times in the past several weeks. He'd heard their voices. He tried again, not using redial but touching the numbers separately. When he got the same recording, he listened all the way through, shaking his head before he hung up and checked the white pages online. The listing was still there. He wrote the number down on his scratch pad and checked it against what he'd called. Tried it again.

He gave up when the recording got to "disconnected."

He laid his head back. He was small, stupid, ambushed. They'd figured out it was him probably. Wanted nothing to do with him. He couldn't blame them, he guessed. His stomach hurt, and he felt wet in his eyes. He hadn't cried when Scarletti died, never made it home at all, and that was the worst time. So this made no sense. What was the big deal? You don't have to act like you were blown up. It's not a goddamn IED, he told himself. It just felt like it. He closed his eyes against the tears to shut them down. Took a deep breath. Another and another. Blew out. Got himself back. He made himself get out of the cab and walk toward the bar where there'd be people. He'd have to control himself in front of people.

It was staying light later as the year began to reach for the solstice. Through the entry door to the bar, a lit beer sign glowed and the sound of rock music thumped, though Daniel already knew it wasn't live. Maybe there's be a woman to sit by and he could buy her a drink. That's how he'd met Susannah. Not that he'd seen her a lot, only when he was at the terminal, and it had only been since New Year's. And he couldn't even see her too much because she had a kid, and she made it clear that the kid always came first. He hadn't met the kid, hadn't been invited to and hadn't asked if he could. Kids scared the crap out of him. But he liked Susannah. She didn't push, push, push like other women. Just easy. She only went out when her parents could stay with the kid, who was five. Wouldn't leave him with anyone else. She was crazy about that kid. Good crazy, not psycho crazy.

He went into the bar and took a stool. A long-haired blonde with enormous boobs looked up at him from farther down the bar, her eyebrows possibly suggesting a question. He wasn't sure. He kept his face blank and when the bartender approached ordered only his own beer, not adding …and another round for the lady over there. He could have, but he was enjoying thinking about Susannah.

He usually only called her when he was in town or at least the times he'd been there since New Year's. It wasn't like it was a rule for godsake. No real reason he couldn't just call her tonight was there? He probably wouldn't, though. What if she didn't answer either?

The bartender slid a Bud Light in front of him. He had a handlebar mustache. Daniel remembered Brian used to hate those. Said they were why he decided to work on kids—so he'd never have to work around mustaches. "Not even a woman's mustache like Grandma's," he'd joked, and Jennie had slugged his arm.

"Run a tab?" the bartender said. The mustache bobbed. Brian was right. Those big mustaches were stupid.

"Yeah. Thanks." Daniel didn't look toward the blonde at all. The music was loud for so early in the evening. It was giving him a headache, or maybe it was from being tired and thinking too much.

When he first saw Susannah, he hadn't looked away. She had copper-colored hair that was long and wavy, and blue eyes, not that he could see her eye color right away. She was with two other women, but she was the one who attracted him, like something shiny and rare, a piece of mica surrounded by dull stone, he just wanted to look at. When the two other women got up to dance and she sat alone at their table, he did something he'd never done before. He went over to talk to her. He started by complimenting her hair, and she said that red hair and blue eyes is the most rare combination and probably why he found her utterly irresistible. She was just joking—he could see that in the way her eyes danced—but he thought it was possibly true and nodded seriously, like a dork. Later he thought approaching her might have been the single bravest thing he'd ever done. When he told her that a month later, she didn't believe it.

"What are you talking about? You've been to war!" They were spending the night together. Her son was with her parents overnight, and she'd let him come to her apartment. Daniel had three condoms with him. He didn't know if she was on the pill. Everything was new, awkward. He'd tried to get a look at the bed, but the door was closed. The apartment was small, unremarkable. But it was a home, and he'd been sad for not having one himself.

"It's true, though." Then, he sang, "Oh Susannah, don't you cry for me, though I've been to a giant sandbox with a banjo on my knee," meaning to be funny.

"Old tired joke," she'd said. "Did kids call you Daniel Boone when you were in school?"

"Nope."

"Really? I thought all kids had their names made fun of somehow. What did you get made fun of about?"

"Being adopted," he said, shocking himself. He'd never done that before, told anyone. And it was a lie. He'd never been teased about being adopted, not once. No one that he knew of thought it was any big deal. He did, though.

"What?"

"Yeah."

"Daniel, that's terrible. That's not funny."

"What's terrible?"

"Why would someone tease you about being adopted?"

"Oh, I thought you meant it's terrible to be—"

"No. I mean, was it?" She'd taken his hand then and held it in her lap. They were on her couch. A little boy's truck was over in the corner and there were crayons on another table, the one with the lamp. He'd seen a child's picture, complete with a yellow circle sun with spokes protruding all around and emerald lollipop trees, taped to the refrigerator. Jennie used to tape up everything he'd done.

"Yes. No. I dunno. I don't want to talk about it."

"Okay. I hope no one was bad to you."

"I'm fine."

And then he was furious with himself because he'd completely killed the atmosphere. He could write a book on how not to have sex with a hot red-headed chick who has blue eyes and curly eyelashes that he really just noticed. A handful of freckles. And a good body. He was seeing new things by the minute. Her fingernails were short because she was a medical assistant, she said, and the doctor she worked for wanted her hair out of the way and short clean nails. Her ears were pierced, but at work she wasn't supposed to wear earrings unless they were little studs. So her parents had given her real diamond ones when she graduated and got the job, and she didn't bother to change them. And he'd seen the bed when he went to the bathroom, and he'd mapped out the route and had a plan in his head. And then temporary insanity had overtaken him and he'd blurted out that crap about being adopted. And lied about being teased. Kill me now, he'd thought. You flaming idiot asshole.

He shook his head remembering it now, pissed at himself all over. Why had he told her that? Still, even that night, after he'd been so stupid, she'd kissed him goodnight and it hadn't been a peck on the cheek either, but a real kiss, long, with tongue and heart in it. Later he wondered if it was because Susannah felt sorry for him, but then he thought, no, that wouldn't account for the tongue.

He'd reminded himself of the tongue, that she'd given tongue, the next time he was back at the terminal. And that she'd said, "Call me when you're back," so he'd dared to call her. But no more mistakes. He wasn't making more mistakes.

Which was why he stayed at the bar for two more beers and didn't call Susannah. Because it could be a mistake. And after the mistake-night of no sex, the next time he'd been in town, when he'd called, she'd been able to get her parents to babysit. He'd had her pick the place and had taken her out to dinner. It wasn't fancy because he didn't own the clothes for it, but that was all right by her, she said. It was nice, not too loud, and afterward, they'd gone back to her place, and she'd given him one more beer, and she'd had another glass of wine. And he could tell that it was okay that he knew where the bed was. Before he touched her, she said, "I'm on the pill. But it's best if you use a rubber, too. Better safe than…" She had them in the drawer next to her bed, which made him wonder if there were other guys, and even knowing he had no right to it, he didn't like the idea. He'd taken her breast in his mouth and, though it had been long since his last time and his body was eager, he told himself to slow down, slow down. Slow down.

He hadn't let himself go until he felt her core shuddering over him, and then, still inside her, he pulled her close as she lay the length of herself against his length. He'd held back so long he almost couldn't, but she moved to help him and finally, Daniel gasped.

And this had happened, too, which he was still pondering. As they got up, standing there naked, Daniel had picked up the framed picture on her dresser to study it. A little boy with an older couple. The little boy had red hair, like Susannah. "This your son," he'd said.

"Yes," she'd said, simply.

"He's really cute. Looks like a great kid." Daniel had instinctively known he should compliment her child, though who knows what a kid looks like until you see them in person.

"Now you're just sucking up." She was naked, too, and had come over and fondled him.

"Am not." Of course he was. Best to shut up.

"You telling me he's not cute or he's not a great kid?" His voice teasing.

"Oh shut up." She'd laughed, teased him back, picked up his boxers and threw them at his head. He picked up her bra and hung it from one of his ears.

No gears had been changed until he looked back at the picture, still in his right hand, and said, "These are your parents?" and when she said yes, he'd said, "So what are you, an alien? Where'd the red hair come from?"

And Susannah, calm and clear as a good summer sky, what had she said? "Oh, that's from my biological father. But blue eyes come from both sides. Blue eyes are a recessive gene, gotta get those from both sides."

"So..." Daniel had been flummoxed.

Susannah had waited for him, and finally said, "My stepfather adopted me."

All Daniel had been able to summon had been an "Oh." He'd put the picture down then, as if it were suddenly radioactive.

"Daniel," she said. "It's no big deal."

He hadn't answered. One of the things he really liked about her was she wasn't push, push, push like other women.

IV

MOTHERS

36

It had been a difficult month, Monica's own fault. Finding Daniel's parents was merely challenging for a good researcher, which she was, a greased slide into the idea that she could complete an intermediary role between Deana and Daniel the same way and get the hell out of this case. Maybe repair her life. But locating his parents had turned out to have nothing to do with finding Daniel. Even the private investigator she'd hired nearly a month ago, with Deana's approval, hadn't turned him up yet.

At least Deana wasn't blaming her. Not yet, anyway. Even though Monica told her they were billable hours, Deana came in person once a week to grill her: what had the investigator done? How many hours had he spent? Where was he? What had he tried? Had he considered X or Y?

Deana was a contradiction; her voice stronger, more resolute even as Monica thought she had seen her age in the last—lord, what was it? Almost six months since Monica had first met with her? The woman who sat in front of her now looked more gray. Maybe Deana's hair was just dirty, though. That made gray show more. It certainly did in Monica's own hair, which needed both washing and a trip to the salon again. Not that she was anywhere near Deana's age, but there were shots of gray here and there, and she needed highlights to hide them. A cut would help. Her brows could use work, too. The arch on the right looked like it had been drinking. When had she started letting herself go? As soon as Deana left, she'd make an appointment. She wished she could afford a facial, not that she thought it would help the webs around her eyes she'd noticed recently.

Seeing the changes in Deana now distracted her. Monica leaned away a bit instead of forward as Deana leaned forward in her chair, undaunted by what Monica told her. "As soon as Daniel's located, I mean, I'm sure he will be, I'd like you to go ahead and pay Kathleen back all the money," Deana said. "Maybe you should get that done now? So there's no hold up with your contacting Daniel?" She wore a sleeveless dress, and flaccid skin beneath her arms showed her age. Today, for the first time, she was using two crutches, the kind with a brace around the lower arm. They rested against the front of the desk now. Monica wondered, but didn't ask Deana: was her bad leg worse? Did that happen with age or stress? Or had something happened?

"Please trust me, that's not a good idea."

"Why? I think that—"

"Because there's the possibility that Birmin won't be able to find him, and then we'll have stirred the pot for nothing. There will have been no point—"

"I told you, I don't care about that. He has to keep looking until he finds my son." Deana's eyes were red-shot, and getting watery, dark-smudged beneath. Struggling for composure.

"Pfffff." Monica blew out sadness on a long sigh and looked down at her desk.

"How can you not understand? You're a mother. What would you do if you lost your baby?" Deana's voice was rising.

"It's not that I don't under—"

"You'd do everything you could, wouldn't you? I know Daniel's not a baby now. But if you made a mistake, if you got lost and didn't know what else to do and didn't have anyone. You have no idea what that's like. I feel like you're not..." She shook her head and stopped.

Monica was silent a minute, weighing what she could bear. She spoke softly. "I understand. You think I'm saying that you might want to think about giving up. Maybe I was saying that. But remember it's my job to remind you of your options. And the costs and benefits of each. The decisions are yours. I'll help you with whatever you decide. I'm on your side. I'll advocate for you." Monica had never been this tired before. She needed Deana to leave.

Deana fumbled in her large navy purse. Monica stood, reached for the box of tissue that was on the far side of her desk, slid it to within Deana's reach. She would have liked to give way to tears herself; there was pressure behind her eyes and her nose prickled. Her throat was tight. If she could just lie down, she'd be all right.

But Deana pulled two tissues from the box and let go. Not about to leave, that much was clear. Monica took a breath. And another. She reached forward, through the shaft of afternoon sun that split the air between them. Put her hand lightly on the other woman's upper arm, careful that there was nothing in the least suggestive of anything but kindness in the touch, which there wasn't. "We'll do it in order," she said. "As soon as we get a fix on where Daniel is, I'll go straight to Kathleen. I promise, nothing will be held up. It's just the best way to do it, that's all." She should have said that in the first place.

As soon as Deana cleared the office door, Monica sank into the chair she'd just vacated, the comfortable one reserved for clients. It still held the warmth of Deana's body. Cold, she burrowed back into it, laid her head against the back. Breath became sigh, and another and another sigh that became, finally, silent sobs.

&

"You look tired," Angie said. It was Wednesday night, and they were meeting on the courthouse steps for Angie to turn Celeste over to Monica when she finished work. Their neutral meeting place. This had been going on since the judge had agreed to Monica's request for another night each week. The toddler patted Angie's hair. Although she'd been happy enough to let Monica kiss her, she'd not leaned out of Angie's arms for Monica to take her. "Would you like me to keep her tonight? Skip the visit?" Angie added.

"You'd like that," Monica muttered under her breath. Then to Angie, brightly and overly polite. "Oh, no thank you. I'm fine." Then, cleaning it up. "Maybe the three of us could catch something to eat as a family? I think that would be good for Celeste." She had to keep trying. "It's nice enough to go to Vinny's."

It was a café with an outdoor patio, and live music. They'd eaten there before in springs past, the two of them, laughing, finding each other brilliant and funny, and now it had come to this, another soft early-May dusk. The last red and yellow tulips were still joyful, even as merchants were starting to put out planters with the first summer flowers. At first, warmth and blooms had comforted her briefly with a familiar inevitable sense of life coming back. Like the way Angie's face had softened when heard heard 'Vinny's' as if she, too, were remembering and longing for that easy delight. But now, quickly again, it all seemed like an illusion.

"No thanks. I don't think that's a good idea. Don't want to confuse her," Angie said, unnecessarily pointing with her chin toward Celeste.

"I don't see how…"

"I think it's best."

Angie looked put together. Not ragged. How was she managing to clean up? She looked—well, she looked good. She was wearing tight jeans that made her legs look sexy. Did she have eye makeup under her glasses? Angie had never been one for makeup. "Are you seeing someone?"

People and relationships die. Not everything gets worked out. Some things get fixed and some can't be, Monica warned herself. Do not cry now. Do not.

"Monica, look at me. No, I'm not. There is nobody else. This isn't about that. It's about what we each believe about this baby. Nothing's changed about that, but we're still married." She took a step toward Monica, starting to dislodge Celeste from her hip. "Time to go to Mommy, honey."

Celeste buried her head in Angie's neck, her arms tightening their grip. She shrieked. It sounded like nooooo. Was she saying "No!" now? That clearly? Was refusing Monica going to be her first clear word, before she said Mommy?

"Yes, come on, honey. I'll see you later. This is your time with Mommy." Angie was clear and firm, and Monica was grateful, ashamed of herself.

"Thanks for that," she said, coming and taking the toddler, who shrieked again. "Hey, Miss Minx. You want a bubble bath tonight? What story shall we read? Ohhh! I know. *Goodnight Moon!* First let's have some yummy spaghetti."

"She had spaghetti for lunch," Angie said evenly. "And she's already had her bath. I thought it might help out. You might have time to just play…"

Monica could smell the baby powder, the lingering scent of the baby shampoo on the squirming little body. Celeste was dressed in a new pink dress that was beautiful with the olive and brown and near-black tones of her skin, hair and eyes. Her hair was a mass of loose curls and Monica caressed the baby's head, careful not to disrupt the bow on one side.

"Oh, no spaghetti for dinner! Let's have some…I know. Let's have chicken and peas and…" She was too tired to think.

"Mashed sweet potato would be good." Angie smiled when she said it.

"See what great ideas your Mama has, Celeste? Mashed sweet potato it is." Monica was confused by the help. What did it mean? She had no idea. It was like a small window in Angie's wall. Or was Angie just showing her that she was the one who knew what to do with Celeste, she the better mother, the one who could cope? No, Angie wasn't like that. It was an offering.

37

William Birmin, the investigator, had come well-recommended for being ethical and persistent. So far, Monica was trusting that his ethics were up to snuff, but she didn't have to rely on trust about his persistence. She could already endorse that he was persistent. Maybe more than Monica wanted. She no longer knew.

She was required to act in her client's best interest. There was nothing illegal or immoral about what Deana sought, but Monica felt her own commitment faltering as her life faltered. She'd been sure she was doing the right thing. Was it supposed to cost her everything? She found her thoughts slipping toward a welcome defeat.

Maybe Birmin won't find Daniel.

I could tell Angie I'd dropped the case. Not exactly lie, just tell her I'd withdrawn. Would she accept that or do her push, push, push thing? She doesn't know anything I don't tell her. I'll burn that bridge when I come to it.

She thought about the person she used to be. Before

Angie. Afraid. Not who she was, not real. Also, absolutely alone.

How do you cross a burning bridge?

And, then it became easier, because the possibility of a lie was removed, which also made it more difficult and more explosive.

William Birmin called on a Friday afternoon. Monica saw his name on caller ID and considered not answering, not picking up the message he'd leave. Maybe she'd listen on Monday. She shook her head, sighed, and answered, swinging her desk chair around to look into the four o'clock light, dappled as it filtered through the leaves of the tall maple in front of the building.

"Mr. Birmin," she said.

The investigator had a bass voice. He wasn't a social talker, for which she was grateful. All business.

"I've located Daniel Larsen. Or, more accurately, located his employer. Works for Middlesex Trucking. They're an over-the-road outfit, distance runs, mainly east of the Mississippi, headquartered in Philly. I apologize it took so long. The problem was he doesn't have an address. It seems he lives out of his truck and just uses motels, truck stops, and terminals between runs. Rather strange. However, I do have a cell phone number for you, and I know where he'll be next, the terminal, I mean. No telling where he'll stop."

"Anything I need to know? Arrests?"

"He's clean. Not picking up traffic tickets, and nothing else showing. Didn't check all fifty states, just the east coast, but that's where he mostly runs. Do you want me to make contact for you?"

"No, thanks. Can you email me everything you've got? I'll figure it out from here. I'll need a final bill from you, too. You did great work. I appreciate it a lot."

"Pleasure's mine."

Monica broke the connection. She really wanted the weekend with Celeste. Deana would want her to follow up now. Yesterday, if not sooner. But she'd have to see Kathleen first, get that taken care of. She should have asked Birmin to postdate the bill. And now she had to think through how to contact Daniel. She sighed and stared into space, then studied her hands. Her cuticles were dry and ragged, and idly, she tore one off with her teeth. It stung, and blood appeared. She licked it off.

Tired, tired, she opened her laptop. Damn. Already, her inbox showed the email from Birmin. Along with his invoice, a separate attachment showed Daniel's cell phone number, the history Birmin had gathered, and Daniel's run schedule end points for the month. The next one was Saturday. He was due at his company main terminal in Philly, where his rig would have its regular safety check and service. Monica went to MapQuest. It was on the edge of the city, still over a four-hour drive. Damn again.

Not allowing herself time to back out, she picked up her cell.

"Angie? I'm so, so sorry to bother you. Something pressing has come up with a client and I'm wondering if you're available to keep Celeste if I need you to."

The desk was cool under her arm and free hand as Monica laid them on the exposed wood. She moved her laptop aside and put her head down. Celeste. Angie. I miss you, she whispered. Sleep my child and peace attend thee, all through the night... she sang it softly, the lullaby by which she'd rocked Celeste since they'd had her. "You're the one with the pretty voice," Angie used to say. ...I my loving vigil keeping, all through the night. She finished the lyric, eyes closed.

38

PITTSBURGH, 2014

Kathleen opened the front door of the big house in the upscale neighborhood. Monica had gotten the address from Deana and hadn't asked how she'd obtained it. Paying Kathleen back had been Deana's plan for years, she'd said, though the idea of Deana having tracked Kathleen's whereabouts probably wouldn't please the other woman. Monica didn't plan to divulge it and hoped Kathleen wouldn't think to ask about that.

It wouldn't have required a hurricane to knock Kathleen down; it looked like a brisk breeze would suffice, she was that slight a figure now, with something of a hump in her spine. Heavily highlighted hair, with drawn-on eyebrows, her pink lipstick was just slightly crooked, but her smile was warm. Monica assumed she received a smile because it was a woman at the door, no threat, although there was a question on Kathleen's face too. Seeing how frail the older woman looked, Monica felt guilty. It would have been much easier to deal with someone robust.

"Mrs. Hamilton?"

"It's Mrs. Pierce. Mr. Hamilton is deceased. Actually, so is Mr. Pierce. But it's Mrs. Pierce."

Oh my god, Monica thought. Did Deana not bother to mention that? "I apologize, ma'am. My name is Monica Connell. I'm an attorney, and I'm here about a legal matter that I didn't think was appropriate to discuss on the phone. May I speak with you?"

Alarm spread on Kathleen's face. "Oh my. A legal matter. Well, it would be best if you come back when one of my sons could be here. My oldest son handles my affairs. Perhaps you could give me your phone number and I'll have—"

"Mrs. Pierce, I don't mean to alarm you. There's not a problem. There's nothing you need to do."

Kathleen's face did not smooth out. "Then what?" She cocked her head when she asked a question.

"Really, why don't you let me just quickly tell you, and then you can decide about calling your son. I'll be happy to explain to your son with you right there. If you want him."

Uncertainty hovered over Kathleen's fear. "Well, I don't know."

"It's up to you. It won't take long. It's actually about Mr. Hamilton's…death." Monica tried to infuse her voice with reassurance. She arranged a kind smile on her face and kept her hands relaxed, where Kathleen could see them, one of them holding her briefcase, the other easy and visible at her side. She stayed back, giving Kathleen plenty of space.

"Tony?" Kathleen's eyebrows tented. And that head cock again.

"Yes, ma'am."

"That was, goodness, that was over thirty years ago. What on earth…?"

"Ma'am, it's a delicate matter, which is why I'm not positive you want your son in on it, although that's entirely up to you. It's actually about the child he had with Ms. Wilkes."

Kathleen took a step back into the house and for a moment, Monica thought she was going to shut the door on her. But now she was registering fear—or was it disgust?

"No!" she said. "My sons don't—you can't." Her voice was two levels higher. It was alarm, Monica realized.

"Please, Mrs. Pierce. It's nothing like that. No one is going to bother you or your children. That's why I'm the one who came. Would you please let me explain?"

Kathleen stuck her head outside the door and glanced in the direction of the houses on either side, which were heavily landscaped and at a good distance. The house was on a wooded cul de sac, across from a park-like center island. The notion that anyone was watching was ludicrous to Monica.

"Come in," Kathleen said.

The house was elegant. Either Kathleen had impeccable taste, or a professional had done it. Monica snuck furtive glances at the room, guessing at which of the pieces were antiques. Oil paintings: were those originals? Hardwood floors, oriental rugs, upholstered furniture, a grand piano, French doors out to an umbrellaed patio surrounded by roses. Did anyone live here? Monica couldn't imagine Celeste's sticky hands in this room. "What a lovely home, Mrs. Pierce. The décor is gorgeous."

"Thank you. I'm afraid I didn't quite catch your name."

"It's Monica Connell. Here."

Kathleen studied the business card Monica handed her. She breathed in, exhaled, raised her head and looked directly at Monica. "What are you here for?" she said steadily, a challenge. And then just waited. This woman could stare me into the ground, Monica realized, thrown by Kathleen's ability to summon an old strength.

&

"No. I do not want her money. I do not want her to do this. She made an agreement."

"Mrs. Pierce, you do know that the child isn't a child. He's a thirty-year-old man. Deana only wants to return your money out of a sense of moral obligation, not because she's breaking an agreement. She doesn't want to disrupt your life or your children's lives. Not at all. She is deeply remorseful for the pain she caused you and wishes you well. All she wants is to connect with the son she gave up."

"Has she thought about his parents? This is one more family she's messing with."

Oh god. She sounded exactly like Angie. "Yes, ma'am. She cares about and appreciates their rights and all they've given. She doesn't want to disrupt them in any way." Was that true?

"How can this not disrupt them?"

"I'm so sorry you feel this way. She just wants to return—"

Kathleen made a stop sign—the same kind Angie hated when Monica did it--with her hand too close to

Monica's face. No wonder Angie hated it. Monica had to pull back a little. She scooched a little farther away on the couch. She could have used a glass of water, but Kathleen hadn't offered anything. She would have also appreciated a bathroom but didn't want to ask. She wanted to be done with this now. Kathleen looked stronger and stronger there in her pressed gabardine slacks and—probably—cashmere blue sweater.

"I told you, I don't want it. I'm not letting her off the hook. We made an agreement. I kept my part. You tell her I expect her to keep her part."

Now, Monica tucked her hair behind her ear and smoothed her skirt. Was her suit dowdy? Sometimes she hated her job. What was she doing, arguing with an old lady, twice a widow, in her own home? She straightened her back.

"Ma'am. She has every right to contact an adult. I'm to be an intermediary, and he can say no, also, which she'll respect if he does. That has nothing to do with—There's always a bridge between them and that extends to you. That's not something you have a choice about."

"I'm telling you, I burned it. It's long gone."

"Ma'am." Monica felt herself backing down. "I apologize if it seemed—but the thing is, my client has every right to contact an adult—"

"I think I've made myself clear. I refuse her money, and I expect her to leave the boy alone. It's time for you to leave now."

Monica bit her lip. She tried again from another angle, not seeking agreement. "I have a cashier's check for you, Mrs. Pierce. It's for the full amount you paid, I mean donated to my client, plus interest. Perhaps you could pass it along to your favorite charity if you don't wish to have it yourself." Monica opened her briefcase and withdrew the check. When Kathleen wouldn't glance at it or take it from her extended hand, she laid it on the coffee table in front of the couch where they sat, several feet from each other.

"If you leave it here, I will destroy it. I will accept no responsibility for that money, do you understand me?" Kathleen's mouth was hard, set now. The crooked pink lipstick slanted down.

"That would be an enormous waste," Monica said softly, pleading.

"Then I suggest you don't leave it."

Monica hesitated. Deana had spent years saving this money. She'd done it to buy her freedom, a squirrel sacrificing acorns to save them, during every long winter since she'd signed those papers. To get her son back thirty years later. Monica couldn't let it be thrown away, no matter what. She sighed and picked up the check, put it back in her briefcase, and rose to go.

"Thank you for hearing me out. If you change your mind, the offer will stand. And I'd be glad to speak with your son anytime." She set her business card in place of the check on the low polished table.

"That will not happen," Kathleen said. "Absolutely not. You stay away from me and my family." She picked up the card and tore it in half, then tore those pieces, then tore the pieces again, keeping her eyes on Monica's face as she did.

"Thank you again for your time," Monica said, and before she could be more thoroughly defeated, she walked to the front door. Kathleen followed her. Neither said goodbye, although Monica turned when she'd stepped onto the cement porch. Kathleen shut the door loudly before she got the word out.

There was nothing to do but tell Deana the truth. Monica had gone back to the office and called her, not wanting to, but equally not wanting to tell her in person. Maybe she could edge Deana toward dropping the whole thing, a moral obligation to continue to honor Kathleen's wishes that she not contact Daniel. Did Kathleen have that right? Monica wasn't positive, but Deana had made an agreement with her, that was true.

She could have figured she wouldn't get that lucky with Deana anyway. Another bad card drawn, another chip not falling.

"Well, I'll not keep the money," Deana said. "That wouldn't be right. I like that you mentioned giving it to a charity she supports. She could have done that. I could do it in her name, couldn't I? Of course, I could give it to Daniel if he needs anything. Or I wonder if his…the Larsens need anything."

"Whoa," Monica jumped in. "They are his parents, remember? That would be so wrong." Angie would have a heart attack if she knew Deana was thinking that way, as if the Larsen's had been boarding Daniel for Deana and needed to be paid. She was getting very uneasy. Had Angie been right all along?

But then Deana said, "Oh, I understand. I just want to do the right thing. More than that, I want to do something good. You told her I am sorry for the pain I caused her, right? Did she…?"

'I'm afraid not."

"Oh. Okay."

"Maybe you want to drop the matter at this point?" Monica said hesitantly. If she'd offered a recommendation, could she have swayed Deana? Later the notion that she should have pushed bothered her.

"I want the chance. Just a chance, that's all. She's wealthy, I knew she didn't need the money. I'll think about how to do what's right with that. But I still want a chance with my son. You're not quitting? You said you'd help me." The words in themselves were a question, but Deana's tone was an expectation, even a demand. Not that Monica had never refused an expectation or a demand. She had, and more difficult ones than this.

But Monica was a mother involuntarily separated from her child; because she understood loneliness, understood sadness, and understood loss, now she heard herself say, "I'll help you."

39

PHILADELPHIA 2014

Daniel was tired. He'd driven an hour longer than he was supposed to, Frankenstein, the terminal manager was pissed, and Daniel still had to complete his paperwork. Driving the big rig in city traffic was never a favorite of his, and though it was Saturday, there was some fuckin' festival downtown that had half the streets closed. Just his luck. At least he didn't have to look for a motel. There was a 66 he could catch a ride to easy, and a bunch of decent places to feed his face right near it.

Oh Jesus. Frankenstein was heading right for him, his acne-pitted face all weird, staring at Daniel like a giant question mark. Then he stopped not in Daniel's personal space but still too close, and a square stance, like he wanted to fight. "Hey, Larsen. There a broad here t'see ya."

"What?"

"A broad. Askin' for ya. Don't much look like the type for pleasure, ya know what I mean. But do your business elsewhere."

"I got no business, Frank." None that Frankenstein would ever know about, that was for sure.

"Yeah. Whatever. I told her to wait. She's got a briefcase, looks official. You in trouble?"

There was no way it was Susannah. He'd told her the name of the company he worked for, but it was hardly something she'd even remember. And she wasn't the type to own a briefcase anyway, at least far as he knew, but how many medical assistants carried briefcases?

"No."

Frankenstein peered at his face. "They'll yank your CDL, y'know. Better not be a cop. The boss won't keep ya."

"I didn't do anything. There's no trouble, I'm telling you," Daniel said, shrugging. He was getting mad now. He was hot, tired, and didn't like being questioned. He swiped the sweat off his forehead with the back of his hand. He wanted a shower and something to eat. He wiped his hand on the T shirt that said Middlesex Trucking—he wore it because they'd given him two of them for free. He needed to get out of here, clean up, and later on, to wash his clothes. He made a show of swinging up to get his duffel bag from the sleeping area, which was almost a sweet little studio, of his cab. "And my paperwork is done." It wasn't, but he wanted to get Frankenstein away from him. "I'll have it to you in a couple. Gotta take a leak and wash my face. I'm roasted," he said and gestured with his chin toward the bathroom. "Change my shirt."

"Long as there's no trouble. She's gonna wait on you, ya know. Y'oughta get out there."

"Yeah, got it."

Daniel watched Frankenstein turn and walk down the cement of the cavernous terminal floor. He put his duffel down, took his paperwork off the driver's seat where he'd left it, hurriedly finished and signed it. It wasn't really like him to have lied about that. That guy just grated on him. He'd always hated being told what to do.

After Daniel turned his paperwork in to Frankenstein, the nosey terminal manager pointed with his chin toward the office, which was nothing to speak of. There wasn't an actual receptionist, but then, why would there be? Just a desk, a bunch of filing cabinets, and Patti, who answered the phone.

"Better not be..." Frankenstein muttered as Daniel turned away.

"Stuff it, Frank," Daniel said, irritated. Then, thinking better of it, not wanting his next run delayed in retaliation because Frankenstein was like that, added, "There's no trouble. Have a good day off."

Frankenstein shook his head like a warning and hitched his pants up. Daniel walked toward the office without saying more.

Though the glass in the office door, he spotted the woman who was waiting for him. She was wearing a suit. There was no place for her to sit, and Daniel wondered how long she'd been there. She was leaning against the wall, her head tilted back and resting against it. As he opened the door, Daniel spotted the briefcase, upright on the floor at her feet. Frankenstein was right about something for once. She was a pretty lady, not pretty like Susannah, but nice-looking. Her brown hair was in a bun like the kind Susannah wore to work, and she had gold hoop earrings, a white shirt. He cleared his throat to get her attention.

"Are you looking for me?"

"Are you Daniel Larson?"

"That's right."

"My name is Monica Connell." She looked at the secretary, Patticakes, the drivers called her behind her back because her cheeks were so big. "It's a private matter, Mr. Larson."

"Uh, what's this about?"

The lady looked over at Patticakes, who was completely interested in this conversation now, having heard that it was private. "I think it would be—"

"Yeah, okay," and Daniel nodded at Patticakes. He opened the door, gesturing to the woman to follow him.

When they'd reached the sidewalk, the woman said, "Mr. Larson, this is a personal and sensitive matter. I'm very sorry to have come to your place of employment. It was the only way I could find you. The phone wasn't appropriate. Could we possibly go somewhere to talk?"

The sun was sharp on her face even though it had started its afternoon slide down the sky. The lawyer squinted, facing it, facing him, and Daniel guessed at her age. Maybe forty, with those lines around her eyes. She'd looked younger in the office where the light wasn't so good.

"Not unless you tell me what this is about," he said. "Is there some problem? Who are you exactly?"

"I'm an attorney. Please call me Monica. Here's my card. Is it okay if I call you Daniel?"

"Goddamn. You're a lawyer? Am I being sued for something?" He knew his voice was rude, and that it mixed harshly with the traffic noise. That was all right with him.

"Absolutely not. There is no problem concerning you whatsoever. This concerns your mother."

"What?" He took a step backward at the same time he side-eyed her.

"Please. Please just hear me out." She reached out a hand and he jerked away.

"My mother! Did she send you? How did you find me? Did something happen to her? Did my father die or something?"

The woman—Monica—her face changed. "Oh, Daniel. I'm so sorry. I've confused you. Please, this is so personal. We're standing on a public sidewalk, and I just think it would be good if we could sit down and I could explain. No one is dead or sick, though. It's nothing terrible, I promise you."

He'd been hunted down, like some kind of criminal, or maybe an animal. He took another step back, so he wasn't within arm's reach of her and narrowed his eyes. "What do you want?"

He saw her take a breath and wait. "Nothing, really. Nothing. To give you information about your mother. Your choice what you do with it."

That raised his hackles. "There's nothing bad to say about her." Daniel felt like punching someone, his insides too wild for his body to contain.

The Monica-lady sighed, put her head down a moment and then looked back up. "I don't want to be doing this here, but it seems you won't give me a choice." She glanced around her and waited until no passersby were near on the sidewalk. Still, horns honked and busses exhaled loudly, forcing her to raise her voice. "It's information regarding your biological mother. She'd like to meet you."

40

PHILADELPHIA

Disaster. Monica had done the best she could, and it had still been a disaster. Daniel had said words to the effect of fuck you, fuck her, fuck whoever he was, fuck it all. Tell her no, not now, not ever, no how, no way. Not interested in her now any more than she was interested in me when it counted. Not those exact words, but his message had been clear: he was angry, so angry. Monica had handed him the carefully prepared printed information she had with her: her own office address and phone, Deana's address and phone number, anticipating exactly what happened: that he'd crumple it in his fist to throw out. Daniel had made something of a show of it, too, but—and she'd respected him for this—instinctively looked around himself for a trash can, and seeing none, stuffed it in his pocket.

"Please, if you change your mind, I'm in the yellow pages under attorneys. Pittsburgh. Monica Connell." She wondered if he'd remember that he'd put her business card in his shirt pocket before she told him why she was there.

His back was already turned, though. He was walking away.

"Daniel," Monica called after him. "I know you served in Iraq. I just want to say thank you. My grandfather and Dad were military. They were in—" She was interrupted by a cacophony of sirens.

He probably hadn't heard her. The street noise was fierce. She took a few steps to rush after him, calling "Daniel" when she'd realized he wasn't going to stop, but then realized she was gathering curious glances from people. She wanted to say *Oh, you're got it all wrong, it's nothing like you're thinking.* She'd straightened her face then, wiping it of disappointment, smiled at the woman who'd just slowed down to stare at her, and headed directly to the lot where she'd parked her car.

She'd have to tell Deana that she'd done all she could, that she'd be sending a final bill. She'd given Daniel his mother's contact information; it wasn't up to Monica to tell Deana that he'd only put it in his pocket for lack of an available trash can. She would tell Deana only that it was unlikely that Daniel was going to call her. Surely Deana understood that Daniel could have found her on his own if he'd wanted to, since Deana had registered with the state. Angie had been right. And the worst of it was that Monica hadn't thought to tell Daniel that Brian and Jennie loved him. How much they missed him. She could have at least done that. Maybe one good thing could come have come of this. Maybe he'd have called them. She could have at least done that, not that they were her clients. On the other hand, he was so angry, nothing she said would have made any difference to him. And it was Daniel's choice. Everybody had made their choices, hadn't they?

41

PITTSBURGH

A ngie pushed End on her phone and sighed. So, Monica would be back late tonight, huh. And wanted to know if she could possibly have Celeste tomorrow. And maybe get together to talk. She sighed again, this time to angle a breath toward her forehead as if to blow hair from her eyes, although none was falling forward at the moment.

She looked around Kathy's apartment. "Baby girl, do we need to get our own place?" she said to the toddler who was playing, surrounded by wooden blocks on the carpet. Kathy, as dear a friend as she was, didn't really get it either, why Angie had left Monica. "That's a little irrational, isn't it? I mean, you're welcome here, it's not that. But she's just doing her job, isn't she? We know Monica's a good mediator, for God's sake, she's even certified. Judge Price loves her."

"What does she have to mediate?"

"I can see this could be delicate. I mean, maybe the mo—I mean the biological mother is trying to work something out. The kid is like thirty, right? So not a kid."

"I don't care, Kath. Celeste and I should come first. She knows what happened to me and my parents when I was a kid."

"Of course. I didn't mean to offend you. I just meant that I think you can trust her to separate her personal life from her professional one." Kathy—Angie's friend first and a social worker second—had backed down then. She'd given Angie a hug and run a hand through her own short brown hair ruffling it back and forth. Angie knew Kathy didn't agree, but would let her stay, although Kathy wasn't used to an extra person and a toddler. She was, after all, single, and liked her orderly space. She'd smiled at Angie and straightened the stuff on the coffee table that Celeste had scattered.

It wasn't that she and Celeste couldn't stay longer but Angie wished Kathy really understood. But Kathy didn't know how Angie had put her full trust in Monica and why it was shaken now, and Angie wasn't about to compound the wrongs by telling her about Monica's past. Would it matter anyway? And Angie couldn't have Celeste go on sleeping in a pak n'play. So why was she hesitating? Why not just go out and get an apartment?

Maybe because everything Kathy said was true. Monica was a good mother—and a good wife. Just as it was also true that when Angie let herself feel the implications of splitting up their family, having Celeste not raised by her own two parents, solidly together, it was unfathomable. She'd had Rose and Bill, an intact set of parents who loved each other and opened the largesse of that love like a tent over and around the three of them keeping them safe.

But then the specter of the woman outside the fence of her elementary school would come into her mind and the old panic would set in, nearly visible, a darkness around the edges of her vision, and the sound in her head would be no, no, I can't, no. Now, as she remembered the woman approaching Rose in the grocery store, the police coming, she had to shut it all down again and she said it out loud. "I'm sorry, I'm sorry. I can't."

And what else didn't she know about Monica, the wife she'd been sure she knew inside and out? Angie shook her head again. She whispered, "I just can't."

The little girl ignored her, absorbed. Angie shook her head as if to shake out old pictures. She leaned over to focus on Celeste's face and lightly scratched the baby's scalp with the five nails of one hand, then smoothed her curls back in place. "We'll be okay. Right, cutie?"

&

It was Angie's first memory of Rose, how she'd comforted her by putting her hand on Angie's head and lightly scratching her scalp in a way that made Angie close her eyes and breathe, unmoving, not wanting Rose to stop. She'd done it the first time Angie had been brought to the house, yanked from another foster home that hadn't worked out. She remembered she'd been crying in the car because the social worker hadn't brought the teddy bear that she'd had from two foster homes before. There had been shouting all the time there, but Angie had a bear. Rose had been quiet, just said, "Hello, sweetie," all easy, and had put her hand on Angie's head for a few seconds and then scratched Angie's head with her nails. The social worker said, "Rose and Bill, this is Angela. I'm sorry. She's upset because we didn't bring her teddy bear, but honestly, it's best if I don't go back. There was some turmoil. If you'd like, I can—"

And Rose had interrupted the social worker. She knelt and looked at Angie. "I'm so sorry, honey. It feels bad not to have your friend with you. I understand. We got you a teddy, but if the one on your bed doesn't look like a good new friend, we can go to the store and maybe you can find one that looks like your old one. I know it's not the same, but I'd like to help."

Bill stood back a little bit from Rose. He smiled and said, "We're happy you're here. Would you like to wait or go check the teddy bear situation now? We could all go together if you want." Nothing to scare her. When he moved toward her, she didn't even duck because when he smiled his eyes got squinty like grownups did when they were mad, but his mouth turned up and his voice was nice. Angie remembered how she'd thought these things, and how he was bigger than Rose and walked like a bear, but he never once scared her.

It hadn't been long before Angie would come around to slide under Rose's arm and pick up her opposite hand to put it on her head, silently asking her to do it. It felt so good. There were lots of little things Rose did that were like that, Mom things Angie called them to herself. Rose sang the same song—Sleep my child and peace attend thee, all through the night—every night, and after she listened to Angie read, Rose always stayed to listen to whatever Angie wanted to talk about. She made cookies.

She was nice and funny to Angie's friends after Angie started making some, and her friends could always play in Angie's yard.

When Angie thought about Rose, she tried to list all the Mom things that had made Rose her first and only real mother. Rose was always there. Rose kept her word. Angie asked herself over and over: Am I like her? She wanted to be like Rose, who'd told Angie that she wouldn't let anything hurt her again. Rose was the first person who hadn't let Angie down. That was it, Angie thought now, that was the real Mom thing: Rose was fierce about putting Angie first. Bill had been, too. Angie remembered what it was like to not come first. Her own kids would always know they came first. It was the only way she could make sense of what she'd lived and then the gift she'd been given: she was meant to be make sure foster kids got good homes, and to watch over them. She was meant to be a parent herself.

Angie'd believed she was meant to do that with Monica. No, that part had been a choice, she corrected herself. It had been a choice to teach Monica the lullaby, the comfort song. Oh, she knew Rose would advise her to forgive Monica. Rose had even told her it would be good if she could forgive her biological mother, just in her heart. She hoped she hadn't let Rose down by not doing that. Maybe she could forgive Monica, from a distance. But trust her again? She didn't see how she could do that. Trust was the rare bloom of their marriage, and Monica hadn't just cut it back. She'd uprooted it. Kathy would say that most plants will survive being uprooted if they're put back in the ground carefully, surrounded with good soil, fertilized and watered. Didn't that depend on how broken the plant was? She and Celeste wouldn't always come first. Was she wrong to need that? Kathy would say she was thinking in the past, not the present. That talking and listening and putting yourself in the other person's shoes for a few minutes aren't ever a mistake. Was that true, though?

42

PHILADELPHIA

Daniel didn't call Susannah when he got to his cheap motel room. He couldn't possibly have made his voice sound normal. First Frankenstein had pissed him off, and he'd forgotten to take his stuff with him after he threw his duffel back in the cab while he finished his paperwork. Then instead of going back for it, that woman got him more mad, and he'd just left. Maybe mad wasn't the right word for it. Worked up. He didn't know. Now he was as aware of the crumpled paper in his pants pocket as if it had been smoldering. He wouldn't touch it, but rather took his pants off and sat in his boxers on the one chair on the other side of the room, and flipped on the television, to watch what his mom—she came to mind—used to call mindless crap, while he drank four of the beers from the twelve pack he'd picked up. He ate a bag of pretzels and some stale chips that came with a chemical-tasting dip that he got from a vending machine in the cement outdoor corridor of the motel. He wished he'd thought to buy a sandwich at the convenience store when he'd stopped for the beer.

Daniel considered calling Susannah as he'd wanted to, and told her he would, but what could he say tonight? And now, headed to six beers in, he was getting shit-faced, and that alone would make it a bad idea. She'd said she couldn't stand shit-faced men, that her biological father had been a drunk.

He tried to think about what the lawyer-woman had told him. He didn't get far. He just knew he didn't want anything to do with some chick who couldn't be bothered with him when he was born. What the hell did she want now, when he was thirty damn years old? She had a nerve. He drank two more beers while he watched women's bowling and then a cartoon, which was pretty funny. He needed something to eat, but he'd have to put on the pants. They lay on the bed, radioactivity emanating from the pocket. He felt the toxicity coming at him. Only one thing to do: burn that paper once and for all. He didn't want to know who that lawyer was or the name of the person who said she was his mother, but obviously she wasn't because Jennie was, and he'd tried to call her, but she hadn't answered the phone. No, that wasn't right. It was disconnected. But maybe he should take some time off and go up there. He felt bad, just bad. His head hurt.

He got up to search around the room. Shouldn't motels have matches in them? They gave him soap and shampoo. There should be matches, shouldn't there? And he couldn't go out to get matches without putting on the pants, and then he might put his hand in the pocket. He might take that paper out and look at it, which he knew he did not want to do.

&

Daniel had a week coming to him before his next run, the first time in a year he'd had any time off, but what was he supposed to do with a week of down time, for godsake? It wasn't like Susannah would spend every night with him. She had her kid to think about and she'd never ask her parents that often, no matter how close she was to them. Calling them her parents got him thinking about the picture of them she kept on her dresser—there was another one, he'd noticed, on her refrigerator, stuck there with magnets along with ones of Kyle and a lot of his drawings (which all looked pretty much alike—the kid was no artistic genius, that was for sure). It seemed like she never even thought about being adopted by her father, more like she just was fine with it all. It stuck in his mind like a song that repeats, one to which he couldn't make out the lyrics except for a word here or there.

He called her the next morning, when he was sober although his mouth felt like something had died in it and his head was cotton, but he was sober enough to sound like it and to hope it wasn't too late for her to ask her parents to babysit that night. She liked to give them plenty of notice. She was thoughtful like that. Sunday night she usually had to get herself ready for the work week, she'd told him once, but maybe she'd make an exception.

When she picked up right away, he realized he should have thought through what to say first. All he came up with was, "Hi, it's me."

"Hi, you. I thought you'd be back last night?"

"I, uh, well, I was held up."

"What happened? You okay?"

Daniel looked around the room, which was decorated in shades of dirty green and baby shit tan, casting for what to tell her. "Yeah, I'm fine. Y'know. Logjam on 95. I thought it was too late to call when I got in." He sure wasn't going to tell her he was waylaid by a lawyer who told him to meet up with a stranger who claimed to be his real mother so he'd gone to a motel and gotten drunk.

"Daniel. Here's a clue. Your cell phone works from the freeway. You can use it to call me." Her voice wasn't really annoyed, though. More like, next time, here's what I want you to do.

"I'm really sorry. I should have. Next time I will." There, that was better.

"That'd be nice. You know, I wondered if you were…"

"Just not going to call? Shit, Susannah. I wouldn't do that to you." He closed his eyes and jumped off the cliff. "I care about you. And besides, I'm not the type."

"I didn't think you were…"

"Any chance your parents might babysit tonight? I mean, I know it's Sunday and that's not a good night for you, but if you could—"

"I'll call them right now and call you back."

Maybe he hadn't blown it, even with the lie. If he told the truth now, though, she'd wonder what else he'd lied about, wouldn't she? Daniel laid his cell phone next to the television, and switched the TV on, flipping through several channels before turning it back off. What if he missed her call because he didn't hear the phone go off? His pants lay on the one chair, still emanating radioactivity. He was going to have to put them on if he wanted to see Susannah. He picked up the shirt he'd worn driving yesterday and sniffed it. Not entirely disgusting, but not exactly daisy-fresh. He couldn't get into the terminal today, either. He'd have to buy a new shirt if Susannah said yes.

He probably would have broken a window in order to have some glass to chew if she hadn't called back in under five minutes.

"They'll do it," she said, skipping a greeting. "But here's the thing. They're busy this afternoon, but willing to come over after their thing—it's a neighborhood association meeting—and stay with him."

"Uh...so, um," Daniel stammered. "You can?"

"Yeah, sure, tonight. But they're busy this afternoon."

Daniel kept his mouth shut. He hadn't even asked about the afternoon, knowing she spent the weekend days with her son.

"I was thinking maybe you'd like to do something with Kyle and me this afternoon. Mom and Dad said they'll come over here to watch him. They can get here by 5:00, she said, so we could still get out for supper by ourselves. They'll feed him and put him to bed."

"With Kyle?" Incredulous. "I thought—" She hadn't let them do activities as a threesome, worried that Kyle would get the wrong idea, get overly attached. She said it scared her.

LYNNE HUGO

"Things change. But would you like to?"

"Sure. I mean, yes, I'd really like to."

"Great. Why don't you come over at one? Maybe we'll go to the zoo and let him get ice cream. You can suggest it, I'll hesitate, and you can say, oh, come on Mom, I think ice cream would be great, I'll relent, and he'll be your best friend for life. The only thing he loves as much as ice cream is my dad. Maybe me, but dad for sure…"

Daniel laughed. "Deal." He hung up and was immediately terrified. What did he know about little kids? He'd done fine during little interludes before their dates and then they'd take Kyle over to Susannah's parents' and Daniel would wait outside in the taxi. It had been unspoken that she'd not wanted to introduce Daniel to her parents, but he knew. Now he was going to spend the afternoon with Susannah and Kyle and meet her parents? In one day? And oh crap, he still had to shower and find a nearby place to buy a shirt, then take the bus to Susannah's.

&

"You're great with him," Susannah whispered. They were leaving the zoo, where Kyle accepted Daniel's outstretched hands and let himself be lifted forward and up toward the monkey when Daniel was the one to first spot one asleep in a tree.

"He's really neat," Daniel said and meant it. Then, on the way to Susannah's car, they'd come to a grate in the sidewalk. Kyle was afraid to walk on it, and Daniel said, "Hey, buddy, we can swing you over like a monkey." He'd held his hand out for the second time and the sticky-handed little boy—chocolate ice cream on his chin and Superman T-shirt—had slipped his hand into Daniel's. With Susannah holding the other hand, they'd swung him over, with Daniel making publicly inappropriate monkey sounds that Kyle found hysterical. Of course, from then until they reached the car, Kyle found multiple nonexistent impediments on the sidewalk for which the monkey swing was a must.

Daniel never even thought about what was in his pants pocket through the afternoon. It didn't occur to him until Susannah's parents arrived and before Daniel could get a real look at them, Susannah was in the way, hugging her dad. She kept her arm around his back when she said, "Daniel, these are my parents, Ben and Barbara Morrisson. Mom and Dad, this is Daniel Larsen." Susannah stroked her mom's shoulder as she said her name.

An overweight, short man with gray hair that started about a yard back from his forehead stuck his hand out. Daniel reached to take it, but the shake was interrupted by Kyle launching himself at Ben's waist. "Grandpa," he shrieked. Then, "Grandma, can we watch Lion King?"

Barbara, who was taller than Ben by an inch, looked nothing like Susannah except for expressive blue eyes and the same arched brows. She wasn't as fair skinned, and her hair—salt and pepper now—had never been red. "Oh no, not again!" she said, slapping her forehead in mock horror before she put her arms around him and Susannah at the same time. Susannah sure had her laugh. And her straight nose.

"It's Grandpa's favorite. And we went to the zoo today." Wheedling, but not whining.

"Grandpa, what do you say?" Susannah said, clowning in an exaggerated hands-on-hips way.

"Well, it is a mighty fine movie," Ben said, winking at Daniel and again, sticking his hand out after the aborted first attempt. "Nice to meet you, Daniel."

"Yea, yea, Grandpa says yes!" Kyle said, jumping around. "Yea, Lion King. And popcorn," he tacked on.

"We should get going, Danny," Susannah said. No one had called him Danny except Brian and Jenny sometimes, when he was little. He'd always gone by Daniel. "Mom, I'm sorry the place is a mess. I didn't get to—"

"It looks like a five-year-old has been living here...." That laugh again. Their laugh.

"A five-year-old wrecking crew," Susannah said. "Yep."

Daniel called up manners Jenny had taught him, so rarely needed now. When he thought of her, the paper in his pocket felt like something alive and dangerous. "It's a pleasure to meet you, sir," he said to Ben, and then, to Barbara, "Really nice to meet you, Mrs. Morrisson. So nice of you to let us go out."

Susannah went out of her apartment, Daniel behind her. On the way out, Ben followed as if he were needed to close the door. He shook Daniel's hand again, looking at him straight on. "You be good to my girl," he said. "Because she's solid gold."

"I know that sir, and I promise you."

&

When Daniel and Jenny came home after dinner, he chatted with her parents, finding it easier, even though

Susannah sat on the couch between them, and he was the outlier, across the room. But they were warm, and drew him in. Barbara had established order in the apartment, and it felt nice, homey, he decided, the four of them there and Kyle asleep in his room. He really did like that little boy and what it felt like to pick him up. What would it be like to have a son? Susannah had said, "I can't pick him up anymore. He's too heavy." When Barbara asked about Daniel's folks, he didn't tell them he'd been out of touch for twelve years. He said his dad was an orthodontist and his mom had left teaching to stay at home with him. That they were still in the upper peninsula of Michigan. He hoped that part was true.

"Isn't that fantastic that she could do that? They adopted him when he was a newborn, too," Susannah threw in. Daniel was silent, the paper in his pocket smoldering, but he hadn't needed to say anything because Ben patted Susannah's leg.

"I only wish I'd had you from the first day," he said. "Couldn't love you more, though. Always hated that I missed any part of being there."

"He always makes it sound like I was twenty-five. Dad, I was three."

"You were three years, four months and two days." Ben laughed. "That's what I got cheated out of! It's all your mother's fault."

"I love you too, Dad," Susannah said, then, looked over at Daniel. "What'd I tell you? Best dad in the world."

"Pfft. Made my mistakes," Ben demurred.

"Sounds like you hand-picked her," Daniel said. "Makes sense to me."

"Oh my, that I did. As you say, who wouldn't? Well, I did get Barbara, too."

"Oh, nice of you to remember that," Susannah's mother chimed in.

After Ben and Barbara left, Daniel said, "I bet you need me to go, too. I know tomorrow's a workday." He wasn't going to push for more.

"For you, too, Danny," she grinned. "But I really don't want you to leave right now," and her hand was on his belt, unbuckling.

The first time they'd been together, which didn't happen all that fast, he realized later she hadn't meant to make him feel weird when she whispered, "Danny, are you real?" She'd meant it in a good way, that she was glad about what they were doing. But his mind had gone right where it always did, that he somehow wasn't real, maybe a kind of imposter. The wrong parts of him had stiffened when she said it, and, of course, the wrong part had gone soft.

"What's wrong?" she'd said, going up on an elbow, whispering, even her hand whispering across his naked chest, not embarrassing him by moving back down. "Did I do something? I'm so sorry, Danny, I—"

"No!" he'd said, too loud, and then, finally, looked her in the eyes, though there was scarcely any light in her bedroom. "No, I mean, it's not you. Just give me a minute. You're—you're perfect." That was true for him.

"Tell me, what's the matter, please."

"I don't...I don't feel...like I belong anywhere sometimes, and when you said that—" So he told her, but didn't really tell her, so was that a lie? Was everything about him a lie?

276

"Is it from being on the road all the time? Not going back home for so long?"

'Maybe." Well, for sure that was a lie. Or not entirely. He'd jostled his body then, as if resettling himself to be more comfortable in the bed. Really, he'd wanted to be either closer or farther away from her and it made him crazy that he didn't know which. For once, he tried closer. He liked her more than he'd ever liked anybody.

"Maybe you need to make a home of your own? Have you thought about that?" She'd kissed him then and nestled in his arms on her old sheets that were worn as water, asking nothing more. He'd just breathed her in, one hand on her breast, asking nothing more of the night. They slept, and the next time they'd been together, more than a week later, the accumulated disappointments in both their lives had turned into raw hunger for each other. Outside her apartment the night sky cracked and spilled summer stars through the window where she'd left the drape open to moonlight and air. Her bed was a boat, and their glistening bodies rocked a violent tender rhythm until they each dissolved, liquid together. Susannah's eyes were also wet but Daniel did not disappear.

&

"Where you headed out to? How about calling me while you're gone," she said afterward.

Her bed was a mess, he noted, resolving to straighten the sheets out and get her spread off the floor for her before he left. She wouldn't want him there in the morning, not with Kyle home. There was that picture on the dresser. A close family. She was an only child.

The notion had come to him when they were at the zoo with Kyle. He'd dismissed it at first, then when Susannah said what she did about how he'd been a newborn, and praised Jennie for staying home with him, anger had joined hands with need and fear and their dance was frenetic, circular, too close around him. Maybe he'd go to Michigan. Could he do it?

"I've got a long run coming up next. Not sure of the schedule. I'll get it in the morning."

"Oh, okay." She sounded disappointed. "You didn't mention that before. Where to?"

"Not positive. Mighta been Texas. They switch us up all the time, though. Didn't pay a lot of attention. Y'know. It's a guy thing. We're idiots. I'm sorry." He remembered how the kids in either third or fourth grade had learned it, and ground it to bits from overuse: liar, liar, pants on fire. He wanted it to stop. He wanted to stop it. He wanted her. There was hope in his raw, urgent hunger for her, for this quiet, open place. But was it meant to be? Who had he been meant to be? Who and where?

In the morning, they woke to the six o'clock alarm Susannah had set, and Daniel put on his clothes, kissed Susannah, and whispered, "I'll call. It might not take the whole week, I dunno. But I'll call. And I'll be back."

"You better," she said, climbing out of bed, her hair loose, fiery against her pale skin and wild from sleep, one strap of her nightgown falling off a shoulder. Daniel put it back in place, and then pulled her to him, held her against his body for a long moment, closing his eyes and resting his chin on her head. "Can I send Kyle a postcard?" he asked.

"He'd love that," she said. What he wanted to hear was "He could love you." But then she added, "Come home soon," and he tucked the words into a pocket of his mind for safekeeping.

Within the next hour, Daniel had gone to the terminal and retrieved his bag, then headed to the motel to check out, pay the bill, and catch a bus to the airport, the simplest place to rent a car. He had no idea if he could do this, or what he was going to say if he did.

V
HOME

43

PITTSBURGH

Daniel had parked at an angle across the street from Deana's house. A Pittsburgh street address, not in a fancy part of the city was all he could tell. He checked the house number again. That was it: a small, yellow one-story with a detached single car garage just to the left, a handkerchief yard that a teenage boy was mowing now. There were no flowers or anything around to fancy it up, though many of the jammed-in neighbor houses had bright plantings around their tiny porches.

Daniel stared at the kid behind the mower; could that be that his brother with the backwards cap for godsake? His pants were about to fall off his ass. He remembered how Brian used to get after him for that. A bike was on its side in the driveway. The white paper the lawyer had given him, its wrinkle marks deep and permanent, uncrumpled from his pocket now, was spread on the passenger seat of the rental car. The GPS had brought him straight here, in just over four hours with one stop to pee and get a gas station Coke, to what he either didn't or did want to do, and now he felt less real than Captain Kirk.

The name on the paper was Deana Wilkes. He hadn't even thought—when he'd stood there on the sidewalk like a statue in the sun outside the terminal—to ask the lawyer: what about the guy, the father? Does he want to meet me too? Does he know? Do I have brothers or sisters or both? Do they know about me? They didn't dump me.

Daniel thought every one of those questions now, though. He sat there and watched and wondered about the kid who was mowing Deana's lawn.

Fifteen minutes later, the kid went to the door and knocked. A kid who lived there wouldn't knock, would he? Daniel peered through his car window. Someone—it looked like a woman—came to the door, then left the kid on the porch and came back maybe ninety seconds later. The door opened again, and a woman came outside on the porch. She was hunched over two crutches. Daniel stared. No way. She looked old. Was that her? She handed something to the kid. It looked like they talked, and the kid pointed to something on the patchy grass, but Daniel couldn't tell what that was about. The woman nodded, shrugged, and went back inside. Then the door closed again, and the kid put the lawnmower in the little garage, to the right of a dark sedan parked in it, got on his bike and rode off.

Daniel's could hear his own heart, too loud. Too much. He started the car and put it in gear.

&

He really didn't have a clue what he was doing except making everything worse. Behind the wheel still, now parked outside Monica's office under a large shade tree twenty minutes later, Daniel put his face in his hands, then looked up and shook his head. He sat and stared at the entrance for a few more minutes.

He got out of the car, locked it, and entered the building. Monica's office was on the second floor. He wondered if he could get by the receptionist.

The outer door said, simply, Monica Connell, Attorney At Law. There wasn't a receptionist, not even a receptionist desk in the small waiting room. A window in one wall overlooked the street where his car was parked. Another door, partly open, lead to an interior office. Someone was there; he heard voices.

Daniel shut the outer door loudly enough to make his presence known and stood, awkward, knowing he shouldn't be there unexpected, defiant and ashamed at the same time. It would be too hard to come back another time.

She came to the inner door. A baby was in her arms.

"Daniel?" The lawyer was startled. No, frightened. She turned slightly as if shielding the baby from him. "What do you want?" She wasn't pleased to see him, he sure got that.

Daniel put up one hand and didn't move. "I'm sorry. I don't mean to be…uh, rude. I, uh, I should have asked a couple…I mean, I didn't mean to startle you." He was aware then that he was larger than she, taller, broader. He'd picked up some weight since leaving the military.

"I'm not working right now. I just came by to pick up some paperwork," she said. The baby waved chubby arms.

"Whose baby is that?" Daniel asked.

"She's mine," Monica said. Wary. "As I said, I'm not working right now, so I need you to leave. I'll be happy to talk to you another time when I'm not busy."

The baby was black. Or biracial. Daniel tried to put it together in his head. "Oh. She's very cute."

"Thank you."

"I can see that I startled you. I apologize. I just wanted to ask a couple of questions."

"I already told Deana your position, if that's what you want to know about," Monica said. Daniel watched her work to keep her body in front of the baby's. Now the little one played with Monica's hair and then made squirmy motions like she might want to be put down. Monica patted the baby's leg, shifted her weight on her own hip, but wouldn't put her down.

"Uh, is your baby yours? I mean—"

"Daniel, yes, she's mine. She's adopted. Same thing. That's not why you came here."

"Who's the person on the crutches?"

"Oh my god, Daniel. Are you spying on that poor woman?"

"Is that Deana?"

"Yes. Either contact her directly or leave her alone. I will be honest with her. She's my client, not you."

"What happened to her?"

"You'd have to ask her. It was before you were born, though."

"Is my father looking for me too?"

"No."

She'd hesitated, so he persisted. "How do you know?"

"Because he's dead."

"Holy shit. For real?"

"Yes."

"Did he dump me too?" Bitter. But still, a question.

She shook her head. "He never knew about you." Her voice was even, but she still looked wary. She wanted him gone. "He died first. This story is not mine to tell. If you want to know, you should be talking to Deana."

"What happened?" He took a step forward, now wanting to know, yes, he did want to know, and he saw that like a mirror of his movement, she took a step backward, protecting that baby. Her baby. That baby was first to her.

"I think I will," he said.

"Daniel, there's something I didn't tell you when I saw you and I should have. When I was looking for you, I met your parents, and they asked me to please—"

"You met my parents? Brian and—you went to Michigan? Or did they come—" The afternoon light coming through the waiting room window was filled with dizzy motes, and the motes were his whole history coming for him.

"Listen to me. They said if I found you to tell you that they love you. You really should call them. That's all. I'm sorry I didn't tell you before. Now I need to get my daughter home."

He ignored the last. "Where are they? Phone's disconnected."

Her shoulders went up slightly and she cocked her head. A little defensive. "Well, they were there two months ago. No, closer to three now, but they were in the house I think you grew up in. It was in March."

"You were there?" He was eager now, his brows tilting in surprise.

She nodded. "I visited them."

"In Charlevoix? On Wikeman Road?"

She nodded again. "That's it."

"They're there?"

She nodded again, adjusting the baby who was getting fussier. "I really need to go," she said. "If you'll excuse me, please."

"Was there a dog?"

"I saw a dog bed," she said. "And a couple dog toys."

"Bear," he whispered. "Bear," he smiled.

44

When Deana went to the door it was already twilight, too late for the mailman. When she opened it, she left the chain in place. It wasn't as if she were expecting anyone. A vaguely familiar man stood on her porch. He had short brown hair combed to the side, and clean black brows that arched distinctively. A straight nose between high cheekbones. The man's full mouth was unsmiling, and she wondered if he brought bad news, but Buster the cat was inside, and her car was in the garage. She thought she must recognize him from her street, that maybe he was a neighbor whose name she should know, but she kept to herself so much that she never really did know any of them. She leaned her face through the opening.

"May I help—?" And then it came to her in a wave, even though this man was taller than she remembered. "Tony? Tony! No, I mean…Are you…are you? Daniel?"

He nodded. "My name is Daniel Larsen, ma'am. May I speak to you for a moment?" So formal it was excruciating.

Deana fumbled with the chain, setting one crutch against the wall to free her right hand. "I've hoped for this for so—come in, come in! Please come in!"

"Thank you."

She tried to put her arms around him, tottering a bit as the crutch she was using left the floor. A mistake. She felt it immediately as he stood, stiff and unresponsive, hands at his sides.

She let go and backed off. Embarrassed, she retrieved the second crutch, slid her arm into it and said, "Please, I'm sorry. Sit down, won't you? Would you like something to drink?" So strange, so bizarre. As if she hadn't waited for thirty years for this moment, she was offering him something to drink, as if he were a stranger, not her beloved son.

"No thank you, ma'am." He sounded as if he were in the military, addressing an officer he didn't like. He reminded her of her father that way.

"Sit down, won't you, though?" She switched on a light so she could see him more clearly, gestured him to the couch, and made her way to her own chair, which was the right height for her to get up and down more easily using the arms. She rested her crutches each against a side of it. Deana saw her son take in the small room, still dim though the table lamp nearest the couch was on. Shabby, he'd doubtless think. Someone raised by a dentist would have been grown up in a house with money. She'd put hers into savings but also, furniture wasn't important to her. Hers was dated, blue slip-covered now, and Buster the cat had sharpened his claws on one end of the couch, disdaining his scratching post. How had she lived here so long and done so little with it? She'd been much more interested in helping her clients, in tutoring and mentoring kids, but of course, she could have redecorated, too. The pictures on the wall were, well, boring generic flower prints from Target. The gray carpet should be replaced, though she'd had it cleaned.

"You don't need to call me ma'am. Please. I am your mother after all." Deana said, and saw his face harden. "I just mean, I was your mother, your biological mother. I know you have another mother, and I'm sure—"

"You don't know anything about me. I just came to ask a few questions."

She saw she could lose any chance, so she said, "I understand. What would you like to know?"

"What happened to my father? I mean my biological father. The lawyer said he died and he didn't know about... me. Or, I guess I should say, you."

"He was killed in an accident. He was hit by a car." That was true enough.

"What was his name?"

"Tony. Anthony, really."

"Anthony what?"

Deana was quiet and closed her eyes for a moment. Then she shook her head. "I can't tell you that."

He registered shock. "You don't know?"

Deana put her face down on one hand. She sighed, then looked back up. "It's not that. I'm sorry, the thing is, he was married, and his wife was very, very hurt and angry, and I need to make sure that...nothing...I just need to make sure."

"Sure of what? You said he's dead."

"I made a promise."

"What difference can it make now for me to know about him? I don't get it." Daniel's voice was rising, agitated, demanding, his full lips working. He looked so much like Tony that Deana could barely endure it, those dark eyes under the black arches that weren't bushy at all, almost feminine they were so clean. Deana couldn't take her own eyes off him, though he didn't seem to be studying her at all to look for resemblance. Maybe just as well. She didn't see much of herself in his face.

Deana kept her voice as even as she could. "Daniel, we worked in the same place. It was an insurance company. He was a good man. He was married. He was killed in an auto accident before he or I knew I was pregnant. We loved each other, but he was married. I don't know what would have happened. I don't know his medical history or details about his family. He died before we could...uh... work anything out," She hoped it would be enough.

Daniel sat for a minute, taking in what she'd said, and Deana thought maybe she'd satisfied him. She wondered if he'd ask what had happened to her, had she been born handicapped, or had something happened to her.

"Who'd you make this promise to? What's that about?" Another challenge.

She hadn't thought this through. Deana shook her head. "Daniel, I can't. I just can't. The rest just doesn't involve you. He had children, and—"

Daniel stood and loomed over her. Upset. "Are you telling me I'm not an only child? I have brothers and sisters?" Maybe that was anger in his voice, she couldn't tell.

"Well, his, not mine, I never had any others, so technically, there's some—"

"All this time I was alone, I didn't know, and you never tried." His eyes widened, but more. He was shaking his head, too, his neck reddening the way Tony's had the few times Deana had seen Tony infuriated at the office. It hadn't been at her, though this rage was.

"You don't understand. There's no connection there, it's not—"

"Don't. Don't even." He put up a hand as if to put a barrier between them.

She tried another approach. Speaking very quietly, Deana said, "You said you've been alone all this time. Weren't your parents good to you?"

"Yes, they were good to me. Very good. That's really not the point here." His eyes were wet. "I can't do this," he said. Daniel stood a moment looking at her as if he were memorizing her face before he turned and left, pulling the door shut behind him.

And Deana thought then how she'd tried to take charge of her life after so long and it had briefly felt so good, so right to make a choice and to live it.

45

Daniel sat behind the wheel of his rental car in the parking lot of a crappy strip mall maybe ten minutes from Deana's house. He'd left abruptly, angry, or maybe it was too sad, not leaving his phone number, too upset to ask Deana stuff he'd meant to ask. Had she even considered keeping him? Had she cared what happened to him? Was she born crippled like that? Did she have a job? Did he have aunts and uncles? She didn't look like she was married. He'd only found out she didn't have any other kids. Really, though, what difference did any of it make now, anyway.

He really hadn't considered the possibility of siblings before, which he now thought had been stupid. And Deana flat refused to give him any information, any details. Said she didn't have the right. He was so mad, as mad as he'd used to get when he was a kid. Everything was worse. He wished he'd never gone to see what's her name, the lawyer, or Deana. He wanted to call Susannah but didn't know what to say about what he'd been doing because he wasn't exactly where he'd said he was going. Or even headed there.

Liar, liar, pants on fire. Like mother, like son. Was that the deal? The thought made him sick.

He slapped his hand on the steering wheel and swore. How he hadn't called Susannah, ought to do that and to send Kyle a postcard, but not from here. His mind was circling, like Bear, the way he used to chase his tail, which had been funny then.

There was a bar tucked in toward the far end of the string of storefronts. Darkness came late these days, though the solstice had passed, but there was some action going on there. He got out, locked the car, reminded himself which pocket he was putting the keys in, patted his back pocket to check for his wallet and walked toward the lit sign.

It was almost three in the morning when he found the car again. He'd turned left instead of right after last call at the bar and had no idea where he was. Alone, he unlocked it on the third try after opening the trunk twice with the electronic key fob and jostled himself onto the back seat, willing himself to pass out, no music here to hold back how he'd argued with Deana and gotten nowhere. Nowhere, like it was his permanent address.

Susannah and Kyle came to him again, how he hadn't sent a postcard. Why? He needed to be someplace else to do that, someplace he was supposed to be instead. He swam through the boggy water in his head. Find the boat, find the oar, row. Row. Row. You can get there. He remembered Jennie singing to him, Row, row, row your boat. Jennie. Mom. Yes, they were good to me. They were good to me. He'd rather be like them if it wasn't too late. He was alone in the car, hungry and his head all sloshy with swamp water, and he cried. Taking on water, drowning, he cried. I can't do it. Row, row, row your boat, Jennie sang, gently down the dream. You can.

Then he did pass out and slept there until the sun, his need to pee, and his headache woke him.

Coffee, he thought, then, immediately, his stomach said no. Water then. Yes, water. He was parched. Water, aspirin. A bathroom. You're okay, you can do it. He heard Jennie in his head. It was bizarre to him, after so long, but he heard her, the way she used to say it, her voice kind and encouraging. He was ashamed. He was going to call, absolutely he would. Susannah or Jennie. One of them for sure.

Or neither. She was wrong about him. He couldn't.

What he could do was drive. One thing he was good at. After a while, after he'd found a fast food place, drank water, peed, washed his face, drank coffee, peed again, he could drive more. Not that he knew where. It didn't matter. He didn't care. Anywhere but where he'd already been. He told himself he wasn't running away because he had nothing to run from any more than he had anything to run to. He slept in his car. Once, in the parking lot of a mall, a cop rapped on his window and startled him awake by barking, "Show me your license and registration." When Daniel was able to produce those, and the rental car papers, he was told, more politely, "It's not allowed to spend the night in the parking lot, sir. I have to ask you to move on."

So, Daniel moved on, to the parking lot of a twenty-four-hour grocery store. That was after he'd been to the second bar. Or maybe it was the third. It was hard to tell them apart. He didn't ask himself what he was doing, what about his job, when he'd run out of money if he wasn't employed. He remembered to call the car rental company during the day, after he'd gone into a deli and gotten a sandwich and caffeinated soda. A couple aspirin with that made him feel better an hour later and he'd thought clearly, but only about what was right in front of him and only enough to remember to look at the rental paper, when he was supposed to return the car, and ask a passerby if he knew the date, which the guy did. He called about the car, made that right, and that was okay. He saw the missed calls from Susannah, and the texts, but he didn't read them before he turned the phone off again, because what would he say?

He wanted to get somewhere he'd never been, or didn't remember being, and crossing the open palm of Indiana, how alien windfarms seemed to have landed on its treeless surface, he achieved what he thought he wanted: the disorientation he felt made sense. He got off I-70 at the next exit. Any bar would do, which was a good thing because there wasn't a big choice.

"Sorry, buddy, cash only. Unless you got another card. This one's declined."

"It's fine. Been using it right along," Daniel said to the bartender. "Run it again, will you?" Behind the bartender the beer sign winked at him. One letter had gone dark. It was a garish touch in a dingy place; outside the mid-afternoon was brilliant, the green hands of field corn reaching out of dark earth beside the highway into town.

"Dunno, man," the ruddy-faced bartender came back a couple minutes later, looking irritated. "This one's no good here. Gotta have cash upfront now unless you got a card that works." He was square shouldered, with big hands and Daniel wondered if the two big rings he wore on his right hand had anything to do with punching deadbeats. He'd avoided the irritable assholes in the Army, the ones who'd whip out their fists, mainly because they were usually the batshit crazy ones. He didn't have cash; he'd used the last of it in vending machines over the last couple of days. But the credit card should have been fine. The bill wasn't overdue, he was sure of that.

"Give me a minute," he said. "I'll step over there and call the company. The card's good. Let me see what the problem is." He took the card out of the bartender's hand, and drew his cell phone from his pocket, turning it on. Another text from Susannah. Couple other messages he didn't listen to from a number he didn't recognize. He switched over to the phone function and turned the card to the customer service number, stepping away from the bar but nodding to the bartender who hadn't agreed. He stood, eyeing Daniel from behind the bar, and finally shrugged and pointed at the phone.

Daniel pushed the numbers, listened to the menu, trying to keep his voice low, which was pointless because no one was near, he repeated his credit card numbers into the phone, pushed two more numbers, and waited for an actual person. Then, again, he had to give his credit card number and then the last four digits of his social security number.

"Let me check on that for you. Please hold a moment," the woman's voice said pleasantly, after he demanded an explanation.

"I'll need to verify your identity, Sir. Can you give me your security answers?"

"What are the questions?" Daniel found this infuriating. How was he supposed to know their damn security answers? The bartender glanced over again, like he had nothing to do but be suspicious of Daniel, which Daniel was also starting to find infuriating.

"I can give you hints about what you set up as replies, Sir," the credit card lady said. "The street or road you lived on as a child?"

"Wikeman."

"Thank you. Your mother's maiden name?"

"Dahl." He spelled it, enunciating the letters into the phone.

"Thank you. I have verified your identity. A fraud alert was put on your card because our system recognized spending well out of your geographical area and you didn't respond to phone calls questioning if the charges were legitimate, Sir. If you approve these charges, I can cancel the alert now."

So the fraud alert was cancelled because he knew the street he'd lived on growing up and his mother's maiden name. He went over to the bartender, gave him the card, had a beer with no chaser and nursed it while he thought about how funny it was. That credit card lady had asked him about his mother and right away he gave them information about Jennie, without even thinking about it. Jennie. His mother. And then he was sitting at that damn bar crying. Not even drunk. Too overcome to have the wits to get up and leave right away, too embarrassed to ask for a napkin.

He got hold of himself enough to get out and make it to his car. He sat there and let the evening fall on him, his phone on the seat next to him, blank-faced and speechless.

He had to backtrack east and head north. Another night on the road, and he'd thought he could make it to the upper peninsula by nightfall of the second day, but his eyes were too heavy, and he was too experienced a driver not to recognize when he had to stop. Daniel didn't think about either what was behind or what was ahead, or why, only driving. He reclined the seat and slept a few hours at a time in highway rest stops, used those rest rooms toilets and sinks, got cash from an ATM and ate from vending machines.

Driving into Charlevoix the next morning was like opening a present. How could it be so familiar, so unchanged? It was his in a way it never had been when he'd lived there. He shook his head once: how had he not known that he'd missed home?

And then his street, all the same. The old colonial houses with their shutters and tire swings, the neighbors, the cars in the driveway, the big old trees! His address, his house! His old treehouse behind the garage, still there. All of it home. Home.

He pulled into the driveway and turned off the car, deciding what to say. He smelled himself then, sour, rank. He looked in the rear-view mirror. His reflection was scraggly, unkempt. Scary wasn't an overstatement. He needed to go clean up first. What had he been thinking?

He turned the car back on; he'd go find a cheap motel, clean up and come back.

The front door opened, and a blonde woman took one step onto the porch. Stared at the car, a question on her face. Daniel thought he should put the car in reverse and leave quickly. He looked terrible, terrible. This was all wrong. She couldn't see him a mess like this, he'd have to come back later. But he hesitated, and it was too late. She started down the three stairs, using the handrail. She'd never used a handrail before. He turned the engine off and got out, to go to his mother.

46

PITTSBURGH

"He showed up. You said he refused to meet me, but he just showed up. Daniel. My son showed up and he was so angry." Deana was sitting in Monica's office. She'd left a message on the machine twice the night before and again before Monica had gotten to the office the next day. She needed to talk, she'd said, her voice ragged. But Monica had known without talking to her what had happened, and, when she called back, she'd suggested Deana come to the office. There would be no charge.

Monica faced her, their knees nearly touching. She'd pulled her chair from behind the desk. It wouldn't be fair to hide behind it. "I'm so sorry. I should have called you," she said. She was alarmed by Deana's appearance, gray-faced, eyes veined with pink and hooded. "He showed up here, too. I didn't know he was going back to your house, or I would have."

"Back? He only came once, but Monica, I think he hates me," Deana said spilling the words that came like blood from a deep cut. "I never thought—oh, it was such a mistake. I never should have. It was terrible. Terrible. He wouldn't let me say anything to him, nothing. I'm sorry, I shouldn't be bothering you, and now I don't even know why I am." She paused for breath and seemed to remember what she'd heard and try to put a sequence together. "Did he come here after he was at my house?"

Monica wondered how to put any balm on this fresh wound Deana brought her. She kept her tone soothing though she, too, was upset. And about to make things worse, but Deana had to know. "He hadn't spoken to you, apparently. He'd seen you from a distance. I assume at your house, but maybe not. He wanted to know what had happened to you. I told him to either see you and ask you himself or to leave you alone. He also wanted to know about his father." As Deana visibly reacted, shaking her head, leaning in, starting to interrupt, Monica continued, "No, I didn't give him any information about his father or your history. The only thing I've provided him is your identity and contact information and that you'd like a chance to meet him. Nothing else. That would have to come from you."

Deana slumped back.

"Oh, wait. I'm sorry. I did tell him that his father is deceased now. He was pushing me hard and my baby was here with me. I was uncomfortable and wanted him to leave." Monica was exhausted, sick of everything about this case that she should never have taken. Deana looked like a wrecked ship. How would she go on? Could Monica even say now, after all, that Angie hadn't been right?

"I guess it doesn't matter that he knows that," Deana said, her eyes glittery-wet now. She lifted her large purse from the floor to her lap and rooted inside. Monica guessed what she wanted, stood to reach tissues from where they were out of Deana's reach and passed the box to Deana, who took it and whispered thanks. "I know I can't betray Kathleen. That would be wrong of me, and I don't know what he'd do. He didn't seem altogether…"

"Rational? I know. Right now, he's not going about things in a calm way. I respect your approach to Kathleen's wishes, Deana—and you've got to know that everything you've told me is confidential."

"Do you think he'll be back? I mean, is he sort of spying on me?"

Monica sighed. She'd taken this on, and now she was responsible and didn't want to be. Outside the office a horn blared, brakes hard-hit, tires on pavement. The horn again like a punishment. That damn intersection needed a light. "He was angry," she told Deana. "I thought it was more at me for not giving him information. I truly don't know. He seemed very focused on wanting to know about his father, what had happened. I'm sure when he slows down some, he'll have questions about you, too. That just makes sense."

"Sometimes I feel he has a right to know that he does. Have the half-siblings, I mean. Maybe he's meant to have siblings. You know."

"For what it's worth, I think you're right to keep Kathleen's information private."

"I take it you don't agree about the siblings, his having a right."

"I used to. For sure, I used to." Monica shrugged and shook her head. She felt an unliftable weight of sadness.

Deana swiped at her eyes with the tissue and balled it in her fist. Monica looked away from Deana to the picture that had replaced the one in the frame on her desk. A professional had taken it on picture day at Celeste's new daycare. Angie had taken a job. "Not now," she said when Monica asked if they could talk about working things out between them. "I'm not ready for that. I'm too confused about what I feel."

When Monica said, "Let's deal a new hand," since that seemed to be Angie's favorite metaphor of the moment, Angie had replied, "I'm not sure."

What was that supposed to mean? "It's up to us, isn't it? We can shuffle the deck any time."

47

CHARLEVOIX

Daniel had thought Jennie was going to faint on the driveway. She'd approached the dusty rental car, keeping a bit of distance but coming close enough that she didn't have to shout, "May I help you?" She probably thought—as would be like her—that a visiting friend or relative was looking for one of the neighbors. That used to happen now and then, and Jennie would be quick to help. Daniel thought then of how she'd always been quick to help. A breeze ruffled her hair. She searched his face as he stood, cautious, by the car, maybe seeing a resemblance, but not reacting to it.

"Mom. It's me." He realized again what a mess he was. How could she recognize him?

"Daniel? Daniel? Oh God, my Daniel come home?" She'd closed her eyes and swayed, off balance.

She hadn't believed he'd come back when he said, "I'm just going to go clean up, and I'll be back in a couple of hours. I should have done that first."

"You'll do no such thing! You're home. Did you forget that we have bathrooms here? Did you think we rented out your room or something?" She laughed but kept holding the sleeve of his shirt. She'd aged, he saw, and suddenly felt terrible that he'd done this, made the years pass hard. Losing Kyle would kill Susannah, but he couldn't think about them now, nor the unanswered texts on his phone. How many lives would he mess up in the end?

"How's Bear?" He'd asked it on the way up the porch stairs, eager. He'd later think of this initial half hour home as his headfirst dive into the cold bay of regret.

"Oh Daniel, honey. We kept him going as long as we could, but then he couldn't get to his feet one day. I know how you loved him. We all did. He felt like my living connection to you, and—" Her eyes had filled as she spoke.

"No," he said, remembering that the lawyer had said there was a dog bed. "No, that's not right. When?"

Jennie's arm went around his back, but he didn't yield. "It's been close to a year, Daniel, he would have turned sixteen in April." Then a slight trace of something else, "What did you expect?"

Against his will, tears. He stood at the front door then, waiting for her to open it.

"Go ahead in, honey," Jennie said, pointing. "It's still your home." She gave a half-shrug and smiled with a small head shake. "Always."

Inside, there was the shock of another dog, a not-Bear dog, that looked like mainly yellow Lab, one that hadn't barked a warning, but bounded up to Daniel and jumped, paws to his belt, a big lolling tongue ineffectually swiping in the direction of Daniel's face. Bear didn't do that.

"This is Taffy," Jennie said. "She's a very sweet girl. We're working on her manners. "Off, Taffy. Off!"

"Off, Taffy." Daniel repeated, using a knee to block the persistent greeting then relenting and ruffling her ears. "When will Dad be home from work?"

"Honey, Dad is retired," Jennie said. "It was early but, oh well, he had a number of reasons. But right now, see—"

"Retired? He's way too young, I mean, you both are young."

"We were actually older when we became parents, remember? How old do you think we are?" She laughed. "Anyway, he's at the doctor right now. He had a blood clot in his leg, it was scary, and now he has to give himself shots of blood thinner in the stomach. This is a follow up, he can drive himself now. He's going to be so happy you're home. I want to hear all about—" She stopped then. "I don't mean to pry. "No conditions on anything. We just want to be in your life."

"A blood clot? Dad? Is that serious?"

"Well, it can be very serious if it breaks off and goes to the lungs. Or the brain or something like that. It can be fatal. But his was really painful, and we got him to the hospital in time. Now it's all the follow up to make sure it's dissolved. The neighbors—you remember the Olsens?— have been a huge help."

He hadn't known there was an emergency. They'd been relying on the neighbors. Hadn't known his dog was dying. What had he expected?

The new dog followed them everywhere, tail sweeping the air behind them. It was a miracle that so much of the house looked the same, he supposed, though he'd never imagined it as possibly changed. The kitchen had new paint, she said, and yes, then he remembered it had had some weird wallpaper. Some of the living room furniture was new, but he recognized the old tables, stuck here and there. The family room was also repainted, and with new track lighting and new insulated drapes on the sliding doors, which he wouldn't have noticed if Jennie hadn't shown him. New porch furniture out back, rattan, Jennie said, not that Daniel would know the difference, as he pointed out. They had the screens in already. It had been his job to wash and put them in. He'd hated doing it.

"Oh, those are new windows," Jennie said. "Look. You just slide the window up, and there's the screen. No changing them! Your dad thinks they're the best thing since sliced bread. Which he claims is an expression he made up himself." Daniel looked at her face. Did she mean, See, we didn't need you after all? Well, if she did, he deserved it.

He snuck a look at her face, but there was nothing to read there. Maybe she was just showing him the windows. Maybe she'd forgotten the arguments.

His room might have been a time capsule. "I only come in here to dust and vacuum every now and then," she said by way of explanation. "You know, I didn't want to… change anything. I thought you might want…." There was no finish to the sentence.

Well, what would he do with high school junk? Lord, his clothes were still in the closet? He wondered, idly, if the porn was still stuffed deep between the mattress and the box springs. That would be a trip.

"Would it be okay with you if I shower and shave?" He heard his voice, polite, and formal now. He didn't mean it to be, but better to make a mistake that way than to assume anything. Brian wasn't back yet. Dad.

It seemed none of them wanted to touch the subject. Where had he been? Why hadn't he called? It was a nuclear wasteland in the spaces between them, a place no one would chance going for fear of contamination. It was enough that he was there. Daniel was careful, behaved as a guest. When he didn't know what to do, he hugged the dog. He could see that Jennie, in particular wanted more from him, but she didn't press. Didn't ask. She, too, was careful not to overstep.

Brian had come home while Daniel was in the shower. At dinner, he'd said he'd come into the house wondering who the hell was blocking the garage, and Jennie had met him at the door with a smile like the sun. "He's in the shower! He's home and in the shower," she'd said and then she'd cried all over his shirt. "And it was clean just two days ago," Brian joked. But it was he who raised his wine then and said, "Welcome home, son. We've missed you." And then he said it again. "We've…missed you," like he couldn't find the words he wanted. Daniel, horrified by Brian's hairline, that he wore glasses, had hair in his ears, less chest and more stomach, raised his beer and clinked Brian's glass, then Jennie's wine.

"I'm sorry," Daniel said. It wasn't a proper toast, he knew, so he shook his head to try again. "I mean, thank you. I'm glad to be here. I…missed you, too." There, he'd said it.

48

That night Brian and Jennie whispered as they got ready for bed in their room. They knew exactly how long it had been since they'd had to think about being overheard. Brian knew that Jennie had no wariness about Daniel's return, but he did. Not that he wasn't happy about it; he was. Taffy lay curled into her tail on their bed, eyes open and tracking their movements to make sure that at least one of them remembered to give her a treat before making her get down for the night.

"I wish he'd stop asking me things like he's a stranger," Jennie said. "Did you hear him offer to stay in a motel?"

"I did."

"That's ridiculous. Why would he even think of that?"

"Maybe he's feeling his way? Not sure if he belongs or something?"

"Well of course he belongs. We're his parents."

"Jen, honey. He hasn't exactly behaved like a—"

"Shhh! Keep your voice down. And he's here now."

Only one light was on, plus the one in the master bath, which Jennie had already used, and now as she put on her nightgown in the soft circle of light next to her side of the bed, she looked delicate and breakable to him, and he thought how over and over they'd switched positions on everything about Daniel.

"We've got to know what he's got in mind, hon. Of course, he can stay here as long as he wants. No problem. He can move in, I suppose…." He was reassuring her now but wanted to establish some parameters.

"I don't think we should ask him questions. I don't want to scare him off."

"Jen."

"Don't Jen me. We need to give him time." She was going to hang tough here. That meant he'd go it alone. Wouldn't be the first time.

"I hear you. Keep your own voice down, babe. Can you give Taffy her treat and get her down?" His tone was agreeable, but he hadn't agreed.

Brian's opportunity came late the next afternoon. Jennie, reluctant to leave, said she had to make a trip to the grocery store and Brian didn't offer to do it, which he normally would. Instead he said, if you don't mind, hon, I might lie down for a bit, which was total bullshit. Daniel volunteered to walk the dog. Earlier, he'd been going through the old stuff in his room. Astonished, sad, recognizing and not recognizing the angry boy who'd been and failed to be.

"I'll go with you. I'd as soon stretch my legs as lie down, actually," Brian said, and patted his gut. "I could do with burning a couple calories, I guess."

"You look okay, Dad."

"I'm not blind, buddy, but thanks." He wanted to tell Daniel that he'd pay for him to get a haircut, but he resisted. There were more important things. "Leash is in the—"

"Pantry," Daniel completed the directive. "Where Bear's was. All the dog stuff. I know. Not that much is changed in the house." He got the leash out of the kitchen pantry where it hung above the bin of dog food and snapped it on Taffy's collar.

"You need a jacket?"

"It's pretty warm out, but thanks. I like this dog."

"How much stuff do you have with you?" Brian asked as he followed Daniel out the front door, thinking it was a cagey way of asking how long Daniel planned to stay.

"You want to know how long I plan to stay, right?"

"Jesus, Daniel. I didn't mean it that way, not like we want you to leave."

"What then?" Daniel said as the dog pulled on the leash, and he moved ahead of Brian on the road as they walked the neighborhood. Brian couldn't see his face. He lengthened his steps trying to catch up, to read if he was right about that first edge of the old Daniel in the tone, exactly what Brian feared. Jennie would say he wasn't being fair. This version of Jennie, anyway, the Jennie who'd been destroyed by Daniel's desertion. The Army used to shoot soldiers for what Daniel had done to her. To them.

"The opposite. She needs to know you're going to stay."

"She?"

"We. We need to know you're not going to just disappear again. I guess I'm saying your mother needs to be in your life or out of it. She can't go through it again. I mean I sure as hell don't want to, but she can't. I want you to stay. I don't know where you've been, except about the Army. I'd like to know. Your mother says not to ask you any questions. She's afraid of driving you away. You've got her that scared. It's not normal."

"Yeah. Not normal."

"What's that supposed to mean?" Brian was irritated now. He'd laid his cards on the table and Daniel still held his close, secret. Same old same old. All the effort was coming from him.

"Nothing. Sorry. I'm sorta freaked out I guess. A lawyer came to see me. I guess she'd been here. She said—"

"Yes. She was looking for you. We didn't tell her anything. Couldn't." Brian didn't much like cutting remarks, and now he'd just made one, and when Daniel had finally said something honest. Stop it, he told himself. The sky was so clear, too, as if everything in the universe were transparent and lovely, coming to life again. Let it be so, Brian wished silently. A squirrel scurried across the road and up a sycamore in the Burrough's front yard. Taffy tried to dislodge Daniel's arm from his shoulder and then Brian felt almost proud of Daniel's easy strength, holding Taffy back without having to brace himself.

"Yeah, I know."

"She said...someone else...hired her to find you." Brian wasn't sure what to tell or ask. Jennie was better talking about sensitive issues, when to plow ahead and when to shut up.

"Yeah." Pissed off.

For sure, Daniel's tone was bitter. No maybe about it. So, he'd better leave it there, Brian decided "Is it okay if I ask what you do for a living," he said.

"Oh Jesus, of course. I'm a truck driver. Since I got out of the army. Not much to brag about, I know. Over-the-road stuff."

"Where do you live?" Brian asked it as lightly as he could, not risking a look but checking out the mailbox that Taffy was sniffing with such interest. The breeze was lifting the new leaves overhead as the afternoon lengthened their shadows out ahead of them now, two tall figures stretching under the aging sky. How much longer could this go on?

"I'm embarrassed to say. Nowhere, really. Sort of, well, I'm based in Philly. Philadelphia. I have a big sleeper cab, see."

"Oh. Okay." Brian didn't know what to say. It sounded horrible to him. "You can pretty it up some when you tell your mom. You know she'll want all the details."

"I've made a mess of things."

"I take it the lawyer found you and that's why you came here."

"No. Well, yes. I'd actually called before that. The phone was disconnected."

God. They'd waited for years. Years. He'd finally prevailed because of all the junk calls. "I'm sorry about that," he said. "We only just did it a couple months ago because it was all those damn robocalls. We both have cell phones and, we didn't think you were—"

"My fault," Daniel said. "Like everything always was."

LYNNE HUGO

Was he bitter? At them? This was like separating grains of sand. Was Daniel blaming him or himself?

"Didn't mean it that way, son. Look, I'm sorry. We were getting all these junk calls. Constantly. We'd kept the line hoping, and then it seemed…pointless. Didn't mean it was your fault. Sorry I—"

"Neighborhood looks pretty much the same," Daniel said, as if to change the subject. "Except the cars in the driveways are different." He gave a small laugh.

"You always did know cars. Better than people."

Daniel looked at him and Brian kept his face neutral. Taffy zagged onto a manicured lawn to pee and Daniel stood, waiting. "Who lives here now?" he asked.

"You wouldn't know them." He didn't mean anything crappy by that, but somehow it sounded like a swipe. Well, maybe he had swiped, a little.

"Okay, okay. I get it. I know. Come on, Taffy, good girl. You're not Bear but you're a good girl," Daniel said, and leaned to caress the dog's head. He wore a T shirt and jeans that both fit him closely, nothing that Brian could get away with anymore, and Brian saw the difference in their bodies now, remembered how he'd used to look like that, and wished he did again. Jennie was always bugging him to join a gym again. Maybe he would.

"You're right. I probably wouldn't know them." A clean up attempt from Daniel.

"Well, really, a lot is the same, though," Brian said. "The Rotherby couple moved, thank God. Nice new family in there now. Got young kids. We even have a black family. Feature that. A little diversity at long last."

"You oughta see Philly."

316

They were both making repair attempts, Brian sensed. Maybe it would be okay. And he knew a little bit, but nothing about Daniel's intentions. They'd covered the entire neighborhood now; he could see their garage door was closed as they approached the house, completing the large loop, so he couldn't tell if Jennie was home yet. He hoped not. He didn't want her spotting them from a window and coming out to join the walk. "Let's keep going if Taffy isn't bothering you. You said you'd tried to call. Did you need help? Or do you? Is that why you came? Are you in some kind of trouble? We'd want to help..."

Daniel shrugged. "Not legal trouble if that's what you mean."

"Is there a baby involved? Like...on the way?"

"It's not like that. No."

Brian tried to hold Daniel's arm to stop him from moving ahead so he could look at him, right there on the road, but Daniel walked on, the dog pulling him. Brian knew Daniel could have stopped. "Money?" Brian said, stopping himself, then having to catch up. "Jesus, Daniel. Don't make me play twenty questions. You can tell me."

"I don't want something. I dunno what I want. I should probably go."

Brian thought Jennie would kill him dead so dead if she knew about any of this, so he hoped she never would. "How's that going to help? Why not stay and sort things out?"

"Gotta...job n'all. People." Daniel said.

"But you must have taken vacation time or something. How much longer do you have off?" They were rounding the top of the loop, passing what used to be the Rotherby's again, he couldn't remember the new people's name, with that damn dead cherry tree that Ed had been too cheap to take down for the past three years right there in the front. Jennie would likely be back. Brian had to move things along.

A long hesitation. Brian made himself wait it out.

"I gotta call. And there's a woman."

"Oh," Brian said. "I see." Now he was getting somewhere. "And you're in love?"

"Maybe. I've messed up, though." He shook his head. "Wasn't meant to be."

"Meant to be? Gimme a break, son. That stuff is crap. People use it as an excuse is what I'm saying."

"Timing then. That lawyer came, and it messed with my head..."

"Upset you?"

"Sort of."

"So you came here. I'm glad you did, son." He hoped Daniel could tell he meant that. Risked saying it again. "Really glad you're back."

"Not right away. Not here right away, I mean. I went there first. To the other...person."

"Your biological mother?"

"Yeah."

"Oh. How did that go?" Brian asked. He'd been furtively scanning down the road for Jennie's car on it or turning into their driveway. He hoped she was taking longer, especially that she wouldn't be unloading and derail him, just as the train was heading for the What The Hell Is Going On station. When silence followed his question, he turned his head so he could see Daniel's face. His son might have been six again for the tears running down his face, that same naked need for help and fear of getting it.

49

The worried messages from Susannah had stopped appearing on Daniel's phone the previous morning. No more voice mail, no more texts. The last one had added if this is your way of breaking up, I'd have preferred you just tell me. You've confused me and Kyle both, but I hope you have a good life. At first it had been a relief, but now he just felt hopeless about it. Over and over he kept leaving, traveling into a desert of freedom.

Out walking the dog together, he'd told his dad—it felt strange to tell him, but it was okay, it felt more right than not—more than he'd planned. Not that anything about being here was planned, but he'd kept asking and Daniel felt himself releasing, as if strings trussing him were loosened. But then he'd started to fall apart just mentioning Susannah. Then they'd been back home, right then, Taffy all excited to see Jennie in the driveway where she was unloading groceries, like it had been a month instead of an hour, worthy of wild jumping and delighted face licks. He remembered how Bear had loved him like that. And, come to think of it, how Kyle ran to him for hugs when he went over to Susannah's. Used to go over to Susannah's.

The only thing his dad had said was, "Some things can't be fixed, that's true. But more things can than can't. If you broke something, tell the truth, tell what happened. Step up. Say you're sorry. You'll make other mistakes, but don't make that one again. It'll get you through life, son. I've had to do it more times than I care to remember, and I know there are more coming. Don't mind telling you I'm sorry..." And out there in the driveway, he'd put his arms around Daniel. And then they were in the house, and he let his mother put her arms around him. He put his around her and laid his cheek on top of her head, the way she used to put hers on his, before he was always too angry.

&

The rental car wasn't a problem. That company was happy to take more money. Frankenstein, however, was apoplectic. "How the fuck am I supposed to find a driver for the South Carolina run tomorrow if you're just now telling me you're too high and mighty to bother to show up. How much time do you think you got, Mister?" It was a rhetorical question, Daniel assumed, since it was a shouted statement, and he knew perfectly well that Daniel had no way to provide an answer. But Daniel had occasionally done an extra run when he was supposed to be off, picking up work from different companies who were shorthanded, and he assumed that there were drivers on the roster who'd pick his up. Or maybe a retired guy who'd kept his CDL and just occasionally took a run for some extra income.

He realized now that he'd come to take refuge when he couldn't think of any place else to go. Or, to learn whether there was still a final refuge left him in the world. Perhaps that was more like it.

"Don't do this to your mother again," his dad had said, a postscript to what he'd said about how some things can't be fixed, but many can. "Or to me." Daniel took it as a warning. Maybe it was forgiveness, too.

Later, after the groceries were unloaded, while Jennie was cooking and Brian was making salad, Daniel came into the kitchen and handed them each a small piece of paper. On each he'd written his cell phone number and Daniel. Underneath that was Middlesex Interstate Trucking, Philadelphia and another phone number with (dispatch) next to it. "I don't really have an address," he said. "My cell phone is the reliable way to get me, but this is the company I work for, well, if I don't get fired for not being there now, and in an emergency, dispatch will know where I am. You know, if there were an emergency or something. I mean, if you needed me." He looked at them then, standing together, each holding what he'd given, standing together still after so much, so long. He was embarrassed to have said it.

But his dad understood. He just said, "Thank you, Daniel. This means a lot." His mother looked at the paper, looked at Daniel and back down again. She closed her eyes and just said, "Thank you." Then she went over and stood on her toes to kiss his cheek. "Thank you," she said again, her voice soft. "Do you think you might call us, I mean sort of talk now and then?"

"How about most Sundays," Daniel said. "If something comes up and I can't do it, I'll shoot you a text. You seem like you're pretty good with technology, you two."

"Not dead yet," Jennie said. "That would be so good. So good."

He still hadn't brought up leaving, and he had to. The rental was eating money now. If he got back by the end of the week, he could maybe salvage his job. Not right now, though. Not yet. He'd do it after dinner, he decided. And then he didn't, seeing the pride on his parents' faces when his mother, who'd not questioned him about anything, hesitantly asked about his military service and he gave them a few details. "You really grew up," she said. "Good for you."

It was the first time he remembered—though it probably wasn't really the first, was it?—that he'd made them proud. He didn't want to spoil that.

After breakfast the next morning, Brian went to the garden shop to pick up some flagstone. He wanted Daniel to help him replace a couple of pieces out back that were cracked, "while you're here."

Daniel berated himself: I could stay for six months and help him every day and never make up for all the father-son things I never did. While Brian was gone, Jennie asked him if he'd carry the goose down comforter to the attic for her since they wouldn't need it again until late fall. "I worry about your Dad on those ridiculous pull-down steps," she said. "You know how steep they are. He's got a bad knee. I can do them fine, but the comforter's so bulky." Then in Daniel's head: I bet she's hoping I'll be back to get it down for her in the fall. She didn't say that though, and he didn't mention it. She followed him to the attic to pull the chain on the naked lightbulb in the ceiling.

The light was yellowish, the walls unfinished, and boxed and unboxed stuff in stacks up to where the roof started its slant toward the peak above them. Hooks were rigged from some of the cross ties and heavy plastic zip bags held treasures like Jennie's wedding gown and veil. They stood on sheets of plywood, in the center, where there was enough overhead space to be upright and move around. Under the naked attic lightbulb, her hair was as much silver as blonde. It startled him.

While Jennie worked the puffy comforter into a huge plastic zip bag, Daniel poked around. "Lotta stuff up here," he said. "Wow."

"I know, honey."

Daniel spotted something familiar, took a few steps and squatted to reach, pulling a puzzle off the top of a stack. "You saved my toys? Seriously?"

"Well, not all of them. But some favorites. You know…I thought you might have kids someday, and…" she laughed and shrugged. "Like they might want something here, or be here to visit, or you might want, I don't know. I just saved some."

"I can't believe you've got this. I actually remember this puzzle, the one with the trucks." Daniel thought of Kyle with his trucks, how he loved them. Of all Kyle's puzzles, too, Daniel didn't remember one with trucks. He moved some plastic. "Oh my god, you've got my books, too."

"Well, Daniel. I was a teacher, you know," she teased.

"Oh, no, really? I had no idea! Eyes wide in mock surprise, teasing back as if being together wasn't fragile as melting ice. A person could fall in and be trapped, drown, because it wasn't warm enough yet to swim through. But then she laughed again, easy as the stream water bubbling over rocks, like where he'd played as a kid, so he dared more. "Do you think, I mean, would you mind if I take the truck puzzle with me?"

"Daniel, it's yours. It was always yours."

"It's to give to a little boy."

"Dad mentioned—you have someone." She wasn't questioning him, though, and she half-turned, busying herself with something that probably didn't need to be done.

"Not now. I messed up. But I want to send something to her son."

"Is he special to you?"

"Yeah. He is." Then he just said it, wanting her to know, though he couldn't think why. "Kyle. Such a neat kid."

She'd turned around and was looking at him, he felt it, though he was still squatted down in front of the books and puzzles. "Daniel, if she's as special to you as he is, try again," she said. "Keep trying. That's how you make a family. You make it. You love them, and you make it. There's your unsolicited advice from your mother. Your mother who made her mistakes and wants you to know she's really sorry for things she said."

He sensed she was going to say more, but it was too much to feel right then, those words from her. Daniel plunged on, surrounded by his own dusty history, poorly lit, but there, all there.

"I went to see...Deana,' he said. "You know. The person the lawyer said wanted to meet me. I didn't want to. You're my mother." His forgiveness, only way to say it.

Her hand went to his shoulder and stayed. "I figured you had, and you'd tell us if you wanted to. Was it okay?"

"No. She just made me mad. She wouldn't tell me anything. She's crippled, did you know?"

"Honestly, we don't know anything. Things are often done a lot differently now. We just knew we wanted you. Always have, still do, always will."

"So you didn't have a choice? You just got stuck with me," he said, thinking how Ben had known exactly what he was getting into with Susannah.

"Of course, we had a choice, honey. We chose to have a baby. Isn't that what people do? Well, I mean, we hope that's what people do. It's sure what we did." Jennie laughed a bit, almost off-hand about it. Like it was obvious. Then she said, "What did you want to know that she wouldn't tell you?"

Daniel had to backtrack mentally to figure out that she had gone back to talking about Deana. "Oh...about who the guy was. What happened. I just left. I don't want to talk about it"

She ignored that, he noticed, but somehow it was okay that she did. "Did she say why she wouldn't tell you?" Jennie spoke softly.

"Not really. I sort of blew up." He mimed an explosion with his hand and a Kyle-worthy sound effect.

Had she just rolled her eyes a little? She used to do that sometimes when he said something that she knew wasn't right.

"Nothing? And no reason. Huh," she said.

"Well, something about his being married with kids and she didn't have the right." He was getting mad again, but not at Jennie. At the whole idea of it. "But that lawyer told me he was dead now, so what difference could it make." He was afraid to say the rest.

But she guessed. "Were you thinking you want to know about those kids of his? I take it she doesn't have other kids?" She got down beside him and put her arm around his back, firm and brace-like there.

She didn't act like it hurt to talk about. "Don't I have the right?" he said.

"I don't know about rights, honey. I don't know what that means when it comes to crossing boundaries that might or might not be there for a reason. But maybe you could think about making peace with her? Would that be easier for you in the end?"

He shrugged. "I don't know." But he didn't think so. "Mom, I've got to take off. Not because we…talked about anything. I'll help Dad with the stones and then I've got to head back. I don't want to go but the rental car is costing a lot, and I'll lose my job, maybe I already have." There, he'd managed to say all the worst things and he was still alive.

Disappointment flashed on Jennie's face before she smiled and said, "Of course I understand, and Dad will, too. We know you have a life and work. But now we know where you are, and everything is a thousand times better and we're so glad. So grateful." Now both her arms went around him as she said, "I love you. We love you." She was good like that. Didn't she used to be good about a lot of things? She'd said that thing about out of my house, sure, and the other stuff about what a problem he was. That was true, too, and he could tell her he'd left because he couldn't stand to keep disappointing them and being disappointed by them. He could tell her he left because he couldn't be like them, couldn't be what they wanted. He could remind her of it if he wanted to hear her say it right out. I'm sorry, Daniel, I'm so sorry. Hear her blame herself. What was the point of that now after what he'd already heard? Hadn't something like forgive me been asked and answered between them? Maybe he could be enough for them now, and they could be enough for him.

Beneath them the garage door rumbled open. Brian was back. Daniel could stand up and get started on the rest of the work.

50

PITTSBURGH

Deana didn't like it when the doorbell rang. It always startled her. Oh, for sure, it was usually innocuous, like Diana from next door, kind to bring her a piece of peach pie she'd baked, or the lawn boy, either collecting money or asking something silly like was it okay if he put gas in the mower. (As opposed to what? She wanted to ask. Vodka? But she always just said certainly, knowing that as always, there was a gas can in the garage, it was full, and he knew it. But whatever, as the kids next door said to each other. She'd heard them while she sat on the porch last summer. They were getting toward teenagers, now.) The thing was, though, she was never really expecting anyone, never prepared.

But dammit, she wasn't even dressed when it rang at ten fifteen in the morning, so it not only startled her, it irritated and embarrassed her. It was probably Nan from across the street and two doors down, recently retired, lonely, looking for something to do with herself, a talker.

She'd showed up twice before in the morning inviting herself in for coffee, bringing two pieces of home-baked cinnamon coffee cake, which Deana found on the dry side, and the conversation full of side stories and way too many details. Usually Deana was dressed by now, but she just wasn't today, and was in no mood for Nan anyway. She ignored the bell.

It rang again, insisting. Then, a knock.

Okay, she'd say she was ill. Deana made her heavy three-beat way to the front door.

"Daniel! I'm sorry! I was just…getting in the shower and heard the door. I didn't expect… Please—come in."

"I'm not staying," her son said, but not unkindly this time. He looked better than the first time she'd seen him, less ragged. He'd gotten a haircut and wore an open-neck plaid shirt that looked crisp, maybe new, and dark jeans. Deana took this in.

"That's okay, I'm glad to see you. You look good," she said, not sure what was okay to say that wouldn't stir a toxin into this better air between them. She was embarrassed that the blinds were closed, keeping the room unnaturally dark for mid-morning. He wouldn't know she had work to do this afternoon, quarterly taxes for several small companies due soon. She must look like a batty recluse. Then, she thought, well, if the shoe fits…. "Really, I'm so sorry I'm not dressed. If it's okay with you, I'll duck in and just put on some clothes. Maybe you'd like some coffee?"

Daniel hesitated. "That's okay, ma'am." She noticed how he held his body as he stood just inside her front door, his hands behind his back, feet slightly separated.

"You don't need to call me ma'am. Deana is fine if you like, and you can be at ease, soldier. I recognize parade rest. My dad was a marine. Maybe you'd like to know something about him and my mom?" She avoided calling them his grandparents, wouldn't be foolish enough to go there.

Again, the hesitation. "All right. Thank you."

Deana counted that a win. "Follow me into the kitchen, then. Maybe you would pour your own coffee after I get you a mug? There's a pot made. Milk's in the fridge, sugar on the table. Meanwhile, I'll be quick about some clothes."

The bedroom mirror confirmed that she looked scary: wild gray hair messy as used steel wool, a ratty faded robe. Her decent slacks were dirty, of course. She'd have to wear the old gray ones. The damn brace took too long to get on. How long would he wait if she went in the bathroom after changing to fix herself up a little? Her one tube of lipstick and her eyebrow pencil were in the bathroom cabinet. No, she couldn't lose this chance. It could be her last. Deana finger combed her hair, licked her fingers and smoothed down her eyebrows, cleaned sleep sand from the corners of her eyes, spread some of the petroleum jelly she kept next to her bed on her lips, and re-emerged from her bedroom, not sure if Daniel would still be in the kitchen.

"Coffee okay?"

"Yes, thank you."

"Would you like to be here or in the living room?" Deana asked. Nervous, she pushed on to get it said. "I'll answer anything I can." She'd worded that carefully. "I'm guessing that's why you came."

"Here's fine," Daniel said, from his seat at the table. "My mother didn't think I'd been fair," he said. "I do want to know about…the guy. And his kids. I mean, I'd like to meet them, since he's dead. I don't get why I can't do that. Makes no sense."

"I'm sorry," she said, resolute. "It's what I've said. He was married, I got pregnant, he was killed in an accident before either of us knew I was pregnant, before… anything." She gave a slight shrug as her eyes shut and she shook her head. Then she inhaled, and opened her eyes to meet her son's, earth-brown and searching. "I'm sorry, that's all I'm willing to say. I gave my word."

He looked deflated, even defeated, and it was unbearable that she would keep to herself what he needed. Daniel leaned forward with a last attempt, his eyes, as intent with hunger and want as Tony's, the dear earth-brown that had been her best home, their sparks of light her hope. They would be lost to her again.

"What does that have to do with his kids if he's dead? I don't get it."

That gesture, the forward thrust of his head when he wanted something, that, too, was her Tony again and Deana wavered. Was he back, coming through his son, demanding Tell him! He's mine, too. She tried to breathe through confusion. Everything was in her hands, nothing was in her hands. The stars she'd believed in were falling around her head. But who was she to decide her son's future, Kathleen's sons' futures.

After a long silence during which neither of them gave in, Daniel sighed and said, "Your dad was a Marine?"

"Yes. The Second World War and Korea. He was still

in during Vietnam, but I guess he was too old for combat. He was never deployed there anyway. Would you like to see pictures?"

"Sure."

Deana brought her mother's album into the kitchen and showed Daniel her parents and grandparents. He asked questions about where her father had served. "Daniel," she said. "I have his Marine ring. I'd—I'd like to give it to you. There's no one else."

But Daniel shook his head. "That doesn't feel right. I have things from my grandparents that my mother is giving me, see, and I have, had, grandparents on both sides. You should give that to someone in your family."

Deana was silent. This was how she was to be punished. All right.

"All right," she said. "I understand."

They talked little more after that. Buster prowled the kitchen as Daniel guarded information about himself, telling her minimal information about his time in the army, that he was a truck driver, didn't really have a girlfriend, not right now, although he'd hesitated before answering that which made Deana suspect there was maybe someone. She told him she was a CPA and he shrugged, said math had always been his worst subject. He said he'd think about staying in touch, but he wasn't sure about that, and didn't offer his address or phone number. He said, "I have yours. Are you planning to move in the future?" Deana acknowledged that she wasn't.

"If you do, you can let that lawyer know, okay? I'm sorry, I need to be going," he said, pushing his chair away from the kitchen table. He took his mug over to the sink.

"Thank you for your time. I truly apologize for how I acted when we met." His tone was still formal. Although now he stood at ease, nothing he said sounded easy.

Out on her porch as he was leaving, Deana called after him, "Daniel? Please. When you talk to them, will you thank your mother and father? You don't need to say it's from me. That's all, just thank you. I can see they have a fine son."

He'd turned to see what she wanted when she called his name. When he heard, he smiled and she realized it was the first time she'd seen his smile. "Yes, ma'am. I can do that." And then he was gone.

&

Kathleen had moved the year after Tony died, but Deana had always known the new address, just as she'd known where Tony had lived—not that she'd have ever thought of intruding there. But, before he'd died she'd driven by his address, easy to find in the phone book, when Tony had told her on Friday that he and Kathleen were taking the boys to a baseball game the next afternoon and he hoped they weren't too young to appreciate it. What harm was there in that, she'd rationalized. She'd wanted to know everything about the man she loved. She didn't tell him she'd done it.

When Kathleen moved, the new address was on the check she sent for Deana's living expenses the second year, along with her tuition money. Deana had kept her word. Kathleen kept hers. It was a wonderful arrangement. It was a terrible arrangement.

Deana knew Kathleen was still in the big house she'd bought after Tony died. She'd driven by that one, too, though for a different reason than she'd driven by the first. It was, by then, dawning on her what had happened; the enormity of the settlement Kathleen had received, what she, herself, might have had to raise her child.

Still, Deana had kept her word.

Now, she'd considered calling, but it wouldn't be right; she would look Kathleen in the face, beg if she had to. She had to do it while her son's need was clear in her mind, while she held his image so clearly in her mind, her Tony almost alive again, returned to her from long ago, from when she was happy.

She made her ponderous way up the Kathleen's walk, having parked on the road, thinking the driveway presumptuous. Deana sighed. Three steep steps up. At least there was a handrail, though it was on the wrong side to be useful. That meant Kathleen must not be particularly arthritic—or she had a more accessible entrance elsewhere. Deana went up the steps on her rear, undignified at best, awkward at worst, but she was used to that, and then used the rail as an overhead hoist from her left, grabbing her crutch with her right hand.

She stood and breathed in, breathed out. Inhaled, exhaled. Rang the bell. Hoped this was not for nothing, hoped Kathleen was at least home.

She'd have known Kathleen anywhere. As soon as she opened the door, an aggrieved expression on her face, Deana saw the difference between the two of them. Kathleen had aged, too, but the way years were kinder to rich people whose hair color is mixed and adjusted just so by a stylist—rich people who would know what and how much to eat and what classes to take at what private gym, who have had the money to buy the clothes—even the dark slacks and fern green sweater to wear around the house—that would cling easy over her breasts, skim her waist, and drape over her hips. Kathleen's nails were manicured, a pale pearl, and she was tastefully made up, even now. Deana's gaze flickered to Kathleen's eyebrows, beautifully smooth, no wandering strays.

"Yes?" Kathleen said, her tone chilly.

The recognition was not mutual. Maybe that was best.

"Mrs. Hamilton? I apologize for bothering you. I'm—"

"Mr. Hamilton is deceased. Unless you're looking for my daughter-in-law. But what do you want?"

"I'm looking for Kathleen. Kathleen Hamilton."

"It's Kathleen Pierce now. Again, what do you want? I'm not buying anything." Impatient. Irritated.

"May I speak with you privately a moment? I apologize for intruding on you. I just want to speak to you about Tony's son." Deana saw confusion cross Kathleen's face as she tilted it slightly, a question, even as she shook her head. Deana realized what wasn't registering and added, "I mean...his other son."

There was that squint-eyed confusion for a few more seconds, and then Kathleen knew. And then Deana saw something that frightened her as Kathleen stepped out of the house onto the front porch, forcing Deana to step backward. Kathleen grabbed the handrail close to where Deana had been hanging on to it. Deana had slid her own hand back to make way. The heavy door clicked definitively behind Kathleen, as if demonstrating denial.

"You're..?! You're her?! How dare you come to my home? Our agreement was complete years ago. There is nothing more you can extract from me." Kathleen stage-whispered. There was no one anywhere near who could have heard. The neighbor's homes were at a distance, blanketed in shrubbery.

Not to upset Kathleen further, Deana dropped her own voice to a whisper, though it felt stupid and unnecessary. "I know our agreement is complete, and I thank you for that. I have kept my word to you, I assure you. I'm not here to break it now."

"I know who you are. What do you want? That lawyer you sent was already here, and I told her the same thing I'm telling you. No, no, no. Get out and leave me alone."

"Would you hear me out, Kathleen? I am not here to upset you."

Kathleen looked over Deana's shoulder. A car drove by on the road and she immediately put up a hand in a cheery wave, flashed a smile. "Step inside," she said, when the car had given a light honk in greeting and passed, and her smile had vanished.

Kathleen let Deana manage the door by herself. She led her into a formal living room adorned with framed oil paintings. French doors opened to a furnished patio. Kathleen pointed Deana to a wingback chair while she seated herself on a loveseat, a coffee table between them.

"All right. What is it you want," she said, her voice more impatient than questioning.

"Tony's son is named Daniel. I'd wanted to meet him, and that's how the lawyer got involved. I thought there'd be a connection, but...I don't know. Anyway, I told him about my own family. Nothing about Tony, not who he was, nothing about the accident. I did tell him that Tony was married and had children, and I had no right to divulge anything about them and wouldn't. I also told him that Tony had died. That's all."

"What does this have to do with me?"

"He keeps asking who his biological father was. I don't think that's really what he cares about though. It's his half-siblings he wants to meet. I think he sees me as guilty, and probably Tony as guilty. But those half-brothers, not that he knows they're brothers, I never told him that, I promise you, I think maybe to him, they are as innocent and uninvolved in our tangled choices as he is."

Deana couldn't tell if it was horror and repulsion that kept Kathleen silent now, or maybe that she was listening, but she took a breath and went on. "Kathleen, since he can't ask you himself, the one thing I can do for him is come to you and ask. Now that your boys are grown, would you consider telling them that they have a half-brother? They never need to know my name. I will never interfere or insert myself, and I will never bother you again. All I'll do is let Monica Connell—that's the lawyer—know and then I'll stay out of it. She knows how to get in touch with Daniel. I don't even know."

"Huh." Kathleen muttered. "You don't know?"

"He said he wasn't sure he wanted to stay in touch, and I respect that. He has parents."

"No other kids, though." Kathleen seemed interested despite herself, her curiosity getting to her.

There were framed pictures on the side table next to Deana: Kathleen and a man who wasn't Tony, next to a wedding picture of a grinning young man and a bride in a strapless gown with a train, yards of white netting edged with lace around her head. On the table next to Kathleen's chair, another frame held a closeup of a young man with Tony's eyebrows, maybe his eyes, and something of his nose, too. He looked like Daniel, or maybe she meant like Tony. Not that Deana had any pictures other than the ones in her mind. Here, though, a son of Tony's was propping up a poodle puppy, a laughing girl with picket-fence teeth beside him, the puppy's tongue extended, straining to lick the girl's face. Deana wished she could hold the pictures and ask, "Are these the boys," though she knew they were. But Kathleen wouldn't like her touching anything. It wasn't as if she were a welcome guest. She didn't have a picture of Daniel. It was all more sad than she could stand, seeing Tony's boys, missing her own, and now, maybe forever.

"None that he mentioned. I think not."

"You don't know much, do you?" Kathleen sounded faintly critical.

"I didn't want to intrude. As I said, he has parents." The truth was, Deana had wanted to know everything about Daniel's life but there was information that wasn't hers to have, a bridge he wasn't going to cross. She'd never created a family with him.

Kathleen was softening in some barely perceptible way. Maybe she could give Tony's other son one gift.

"I want to look you in the face and apologize for the pain I caused you. I am truly sorry. Your sons were hurt—in his way, mine was too. He's Tony's son as much as the other two. Would you consider letting them meet if yours want to?"

Kathleen closed her eyes. When she opened them, they went to the framed pictures in turn. "I've been widowed twice now, you know," she said.

"No, I didn't know. I'm so sorry."

"The boys are all I have."

"I understand that. I'm glad you have them." That was sincere. Deana was embarrassed that her eyes were tearing now. For whom was she crying? Her own son, lost to her? Tony? Kathleen's grief, or her own lost life? Deana had no tissue with her and was reduced to sniffling and trying to clear her eyes by blinking. "Kathleen," she whispered, hating that she was pleading, but pleading anyway. "He looks just like Tony. Daniel does." She said nothing more for a long moment and neither did Kathleen. Deana thought maybe she'd found the key. She tried it. "Your boys would recognize him. It would be like they had..."

Kathleen looked at her then, and the look stopped Deana cold. She'd said exactly the wrong thing.

"I won't do it," Kathleen said, resolute. "One of them is engaged, they're planning their wedding. The other one's married and they're expecting a baby. I will not let you—or this Daniel person—destroy their image of their father. They almost worship his memory. He was a great husband and father, and I'm not letting you take that away from any of us."

Deana wasn't pleading now. "That image of Tony? You all weren't the perfect family. Not that any family is, but Tony was flawed. He was a flesh and blood man, and maybe your sons ought to know that, too. Mine already does."

"You know nothing about who my husband was." Kathleen was righteous, sitting straight, suddenly furious.

Deana shot back. "I know everything about who he was. I knew he was married, I knew about the boys. You didn't know about me. I loved him, and I knew he loved me." Immediately she thought: oh god, I've blown any chance of bringing her around. "Look," she said, forcing false calm into her voice. "Back then you said you were trying to have another baby when he was killed. I didn't know I was pregnant. We could have both ended up pregnant at the same time, and I'll be honest. I have no idea what he'd have done. What choice he'd have made. I know what he promised me. You know what he promised you. He was just a man, Kathleen. He wasn't what either of us thought, but we both loved him."

Kathleen hunched over her lap now. The indignation drained. Deana didn't look at her when Kathleen spoke next.

"I tried so hard." Then Kathleen was spilling tears. "Neither of my boys got close to their stepfather. I mean, they were in their teens, and that wasn't good timing on my part. You can have the lawyer tell Daniel none of this is his fault. Tell him Tony would want him to have a good life." Now Deana wiped her own eyes, knowing where Kathleen would end this. "Please, please. Leave them alone. I know you found me, and you could find them. Don't do that. You have the power to do the right thing this time."

"I don't know what the right thing is. I...I want to make something good come of all this. I was thinking, that might be the something good, you know? Or maybe it's something else that I can't see."

"Or maybe it's not there," Kathleen said. "I don't know. Don't overestimate your own power."

"I'll honor your wishes." Deana swiped at her nose with her hand. She needed a bathroom but didn't want to ask. There was no more to be said, only dignity to be lost by begging or more arguing. Grateful that the hostility was gone, she began the struggle to her feet.

"I know you've suffered, too," Kathleen said. "You've suffered, too." She'd sat while Deana arranged her crutch on the rug, used the arm of the chair and the crutch to work herself to a stand.

When Kathleen stood to follow Deana to the door, Deana stopped, looked her in the eye again. She'd risk it. "Would it be all right with you if I contact you in five years to ask again? Maybe there'd be a reason to have changed your mind. Maybe you'd have given it more thought."

"Five years?" She hesitated, then nodded slowly. "All right. That would be all right."

Deana said, "I don't want to give up hoping that there's something…bigger that makes sense. Thank you, Kathleen. It was kind of you to hear me out." As Deana made her way onto the porch, she heard the heavy door close behind her.

51

Monica sighed. How had this case opened such a fissure in her marriage? Had it been there all along? Angie was back to work now, Celeste in daycare, something they'd said they didn't want for her, and yet she seemed to be thriving, picking up vocabulary. Angie loved her job—she'd always loved her kids—and seemed to be doing all right. Monica was miserable, missing the comfort of coming home to her wife, and Celeste's absence was a gut punch every morning, every night. She hurt when she saw the toddler look to Angie for help with anything she needed during their tradeoffs.

But Angie had said she was confused, and it seemed she'd backed off any legal move. Monica clung to that. She didn't bring it up when they met. It wasn't like Angie couldn't think of it on her own, but Monica wasn't going to put it in Angie's mind if it wasn't there.

And now, Deana wanted to talk again. She'd gone to see Kathleen on her own and was bringing in some written instructions "for the future," she said, "in case something happens to me before five years." Bizarre. The case would never end. The case she should have never taken. But on the other hand, how would she have lived with herself if she'd capitulated to Angie? She'd given up her own power before and look where it had gotten her. Now she'd claimed it and look at the cost. The cost.

&

The office door opened. Celeste was saying something to Angie, and Angie said, "Yes, Mommy's here, Mommy's here. Her door's open so it's okay. Go get her. In there." Celeste shrieked "Mommy!"

"Hey, sweetheart! Come get a big hug." Then, to Angie, who followed, her pulling off her glasses and wiping them with her shirt, one Monica hadn't seen before.

"New shirt? Really pretty. Matches your eyes. I love that blue on you."

"Not intended to be used to wipe toddler prints from glasses," Angie said, rueful, "but apparently destined to be hopelessly stretched out and used for that. We thought we'd come by and see if you were free," she said. "I had her to the playground and she asked for you. Wouldn't have come in if the inner door was closed. You know…. Hope you don't mind."

"Mind? I'm delighted. Thank you." Monica jostled Celeste and twirled. "How's my sweet girl? Where'd you go?"

"Swing!" Celeste said.

"Oh! New word, huh?" Then, gesturing with her chin and speaking to Angie, "I swear her legs are longer."

"Lots of new words," Angie said, nodding.

"You're walking funny. Your back bothering you again?"

"Some. She's heavy. And I lost a damn filling."

"Oh no. Which one?"

Angie opened her mouth and pointed.

Monica peered. "No silver. He used the white stuff, huh? Good. I hope you used our dental insurance." The eye and dental insurance had been an add-on to the legal society's group insurance plan, but Monica had gotten it. Angie wore glasses, and her teeth weren't as sound as Monica's, her baby teeth not having been nourished or cared for the way Celeste's would be.

Angie nodded. "I did. Again. Thank you for that. Really."

Celeste wiggled. "Down?" Monica asked, turning her attention to the baby, who'd been playing with Monica's beads, hair, and right ear while Monica held her.

"Down!" The little girl was emphatic.

"You're right about the daycare. Her vocabulary is exploding, isn't it?" Monica nodded to Angie.

"Yeah. It's a quality place. She seems to love it. I checked out a lot of them. It wasn't just that this was the closest." Angie said and then gave a little laugh that sounded fake to Monica. "Actually, it's no way the closest."

"You're doing a good job. You always have taken really good care of her. I know that, Ang." Monica smiled. "You took good care of me, too. I hope I said thank you enough. For me and for Celeste." She stopped and then added. "I don't mean to say anything out of place. I didn't get to know her, I realize. But I think you must be a lot like Rose as a mother. And I know that's a good thing for Celeste."

Angie was quiet. The moment took on the weight of seriousness. It was how there was no smile at the mention of Rose, the small tremor in her voice as, shaking her head slightly, she said, "Thanks. But I can see she misses you. At night, she... well, especially at bath time. You know. And when I try to read her *Goodnight Moon*, she wants you. This is hard on our girl. I don't know what's worse. I mean what chance to take." Another hesitation, while she looked around as if to check on what the baby was getting into. "I could always trust you to be a good mother to her..."

Monica felt Angie working up nerve and wanted to put an arm around her. Angie, the fearless one, the tree that couldn't be uprooted. She knew what Angie would smell like, the faint green melon scent of her. "It's okay," Monica said. "I mean, she's okay." She meant that Celeste wasn't presently destroying anything in the office, only emptying the wastebasket, which Monica hadn't done in two weeks, bubbles of crumpled paper piling around her now. As she said it, she realized the other meaning and didn't clarify. Let Angie take it as a kindness.

Angie took in a breath. "Actually, I wanted to ask if you'd like to get together for dinner. Maybe Friday."

"The three of us?"

"Maybe just us."

"What about the baby?"

"We could get Samantha to babysit. I already checked if she's available. My place or...yours. Then she could just stay there."

Almost too surprised to come up with an answer, Monica hesitated and then made up for it with too much enthusiasm. "Absolutely! That would be great!"

"How about if I bring Celeste over at five thirty? Tell Samantha to be there at six thirty? Would that work? I mean, can you get home from work by then?"

"I'll do it." She'd cancel an appointment with the Queen of England to do that.

Now Celeste was pulling papers from her bottom drawer. Monica moved to stop the damage, moving her chair to block the baby's access. Celeste wailed a protest and Angie moved in to grab her up. "Oops. Should have seen that coming."

"Hey, Ang, thanks. I would really like…"

"Let's see, okay? I thought I could be sure, and I'm not. I'm scared that I can't be sure of anything. Whatever I do could turn out wrong. I'd give anything not to mess Celeste up." Angie turned a palm in the air and Monica couldn't tell if it meant resignation. Or maybe an offering.

"We always said we were…"

Angie shook her head. "What happens depends on how much people are willing to sacrifice, maybe. I don't know. Balance that against what we get." She shrugged and smiled. "We'll both see if it's enough. Gotta get this little one outta here before she destroys the place. Huh baby!" Celeste patted Angie's ear.

"Well, I'm grateful. Grateful." She kissed Celeste and waved. "Bye, bye, honey. Be good! See you Friday."

After they left, Monica sat back at her desk. She swung her chair around to face the window, lifted her face to the light. It could blind her with hope. It could blind her with fear.

52

ON I-76 TO PHILADELPHIA

The truck puzzle lay face up on the passenger side of the back seat. If Daniel glanced over his shoulder it almost looked like a map. A treasure map, Daniel thought once, then was overcome again with the impossibility of calling Susannah now, after screwing up. Again. But both his parents said the same thing at different times, in different words: apologize, try again. He'd been ashamed all his life, he supposed. The difference was that he knew it this time, and why. He was too disciplined a driver to use his cell phone while he was on the interstate heading south, but every time he stopped, no less than every two hours to stretch his legs and shoulders, trying to stay fresh enough to keep going, he looked at it, the number of unanswered calls from Susannah, the voice messages he'd not heard, the texts he'd not read. She'd never forgive him. Why should she?

The idea of just disappearing on Kyle, though—that was what got to him, not his own shame and embarrassment. He wasn't the little boy's father, of course not, but Kyle had been getting attached to him. Susannah had said so. Maybe he'd think he'd done something. Kids get all kind of weird ideas, bad ideas about themselves, no matter what the adults around them say.

What if he just sent Susannah his own message, didn't put himself through listening to hers. It was chickenshit, sure. This idea came to him at the third rest stop, with cardboard-tasting coffee from a vending machine. Jennie had packed ham and cheese sandwiches, carrots, baby tomatoes, and chocolate chip cookies in a small cooler with sealed plastic bags of ice. He wouldn't need to buy food until tomorrow. She was something, his mom. She'd asked him if ham and swiss with mustard and mayonnaise on rye, dill pickle slices between the ham and the cheese, was still his favorite sandwich. How would she have remembered that? "Some things you never forget, honey," she'd said, as if it were obvious. "You'll understand when you have kids. For heaven's sake, just look at what you've already glommed onto about Kyle."

"Me have kids? I doubt that's meant to be."

"Phooey," Jennie had blown him off. "That can most likely be up to you, my dear. These days we do know how to make it happen."

He had to admit what she'd said about Kyle was true. Not that he had the right, but he did know exactly where Kyle's ketchup had to be placed, on the separate plate so that it didn't risk touching his grilled cheese but was accessible to his fries—which also required a separate plate. Lord help the food that had come into contact with another food. It annoyed the crap out of Susannah, but

Daniel thought it was hysterical. "Good, then you do the extra dishes," she'd said.

He was sick of driving, tired already as the I-75 south freeway the length of Michigan got him all the way down to Dayton where he finally swung east, picked up I-76, on which he endured the whole width of Ohio. The scenery was boring; the news was depressing; no satellite radio meant he couldn't listen to the coffeehouse station he liked. Or anything that didn't run a thousand commercials an hour. How could he be so fed up with I-76 that once he crossed the Pennsylvania border and had only the width of that state to traverse he was exhausted by it? A week of not driving pretty much all day every day had been such a relief. Jennie got all bright and, ever the teacher, said maybe you'd want to get some more schooling. Brian had added, "We could help you with that." It would have been okay by them if he'd quit his job and stayed.

But he hadn't.

Now he was doing what he knew how to do. Stop in rest areas, sleep, two or three hours at a stretch. He could make it home overnight. Home, he thought. Now that was a ridiculous way to put it. He was a study in rootlessness, a damn gypsy for godsake. He guessed there was always Michigan, though. That was good, something to be grateful for.

Do it, damn it. Just do it, he told himself. Just think of Kyle he told himself, but Susannah and Kyle were the picture in his head, on the couch across her living room, Kyle bouncing up to insist he wasn't tired, just one more puzzle, just one more truck race with Daniel, one more drink of water.

It was crossing the Delaware river, heading into Philly, that finally made him do it, because he'd run out of time and road, of good and even crappy places to stop, the ones littered with cigarette butts, like so many burnt hopes. Daniel shrugged, refusing any optimism and started to text. Then disgusted with himself, cancelled that, went to Susannah's name, and pushed call on his phone.

She answered before the second ring. "Daniel? Oh my god. I thought...Are you all right?" Her voice high with anxiety, masking nothing.

"I'm sorry," he said. "I can't tell you how sorry I am. I went to see my parents—I'll tell you everything, and I promise, I won't ever do this again."

She'd answered.

His voice cracked as the pieces of himself came apart, to be saved and arranged like the puzzle in the backseat.

"Are you here?"

"Almost. I'm on the way. I'm so sorry."

"We'll work it out. Just come home."

"I will. I am. Already crossed the bridge."

&

ACKNOWLEDGMENTS

Authors get by with a lot of help from their friends. Stacy Testa of Writers House provided invaluable editorial input when this manuscript was in the draft stages, and the support and confidence she expressed in my work kept me going. I will always be grateful for her skill and kindness. Many thanks to my dear friend and former editor, Tara Gavin, who also read the manuscript more than once in various iterations and gave helpful input. Author Donna Everhart provided great help when she read the opening of the novel and gave specific feedback about pacing, which I so appreciate. And especially, enormous gratitude to another dear friend, the gifted novelist Randy Susan Meyers, who read the finished manuscript in full and provided invaluable feedback and suggestions for some final revisions.

Words are, of course, my stock in trade, but there are times they are inadequate. Thank you from my heart to the Amphorae Publishing team that first acquired this novel and since has worked so diligently on its publication. Special thanks to Lisa Miller, Editor, for her patience, sense of humor, and many many helpful corrections about military matters. Great gratitude also to Kristina Makansi, Designer, for the gorgeous cover and book design as well as to Jared Israel and Lisa Miller for their parts in arranging the audible book. Also, warm thanks to Laura Robinson, Marketing Director at Amphorae. Ann-Marie Nieves and the staff of GetRed PR do a brilliant and thorough job for which I am continually grateful.

Always, always, my special thanks and love to my husband, Alan deCourcy, for his steadfast care, both emotional and in the form of computer rescue, as well as patient, interested reading skills. Special thanks, too, to Jan, Brooke, and Ciera, as well as my sisters-in-law and extended family on both sides, who, along with dear friends, are a constant source of interest and support.

About the Author

Lynne Hugo is a National Endowment for the Arts Fellowship recipient who has also received repeat grants from the Ohio Arts Council and the Kentucky Foundation for Women. Mothers of Fate is her fifteenth book.

Lynne's memoir, *Where The Trail Grows Faint: A Year In the Life of a Therapy Dog Team* won the Riverteen Literary Nonfiction Book Prize. Another novel, *Swimming Lessons*, became a Lifetime Original Movie of the Month, and *The Testament of Harold's Wife* was a Buzz Books Fall/Winter selection. The 2014 edition of *A Matter of Mercy* won the 2015 Independent Publishers Silver Medal for Best North-East Fiction, and most recently, her widely-praised novel, *The Language of Kin*, was released in 2023.

Born and educated in New England, Lynne and her photographer husband live in Ohio. They are grateful parents and grandparents with a wonderful, rowdy family and extended families. Lifelong dog people, they now have a rescued beagle/Lab mix, the latest Terror of All Squirrels. Lynne loves family time, being out in nature, doing water aerobics, being at the ocean, and reading contemporary fiction. Learn more at www.LynneHugo.com.